Dragonflies

and

Matchsticks

BASED ON A TRUE STORY

Celestine O Agbo

Matador
9 Priory Business Park,
Wistow Road, Kibworth Beauchamp,
Leicestershire. LE8 0RX
Tel: 0116 279 2299
Email: books@troubador.co.uk
Web: www.troubador.co.uk/matador
Twitter: @matadorbooks

ISBN 978 1789016 109

British Library Cataloguing in Publication Data.
A catalogue record for this book is available from the British Library.

Printed and bound in Great Britain by 4edge Limited
Typeset in 12pt Minion Pro by Troubador Publishing Ltd, Leicester, UK

Matador is an imprint of Troubador Publishing Ltd

To the children who get trampled when adults fight,
This book is dedicated to you

Acknowledgements

It has been said that it takes a village to raise a child. This story is no exception.

For Boniface and Caroline Agbo, trailblazers of their time, like most, their journey was not a passage of ease. Thank you, Meg Johnson, for reintroducing me to my story via *The Biafra Story* and to Fredrick Forsyth for writing it. Thank you, Sam Nico, for helping me to find my pen. I'm grateful to Rose Lenihan, Mick Russell, Anjali Patel for the initial support and encouragement after the first draft of many. My gratitude to Victoria Bilotti for her everlasting support, you are truly awesome. My appreciation to Hazel Scotland Williamson, Onyedinma Ani, John O'Sullivan, Dr Vinod Bhandari, Cheryl Edwards, Dave Parnell, Richard Crosara, Richard Baptiste, Medhavi Patel, Tatjanya Keane, Alan McIntyre, Gail Dyos and Graham Satchwell; your love and faith in this endeavour has been grand. Decima and Arike, I would not be the man I am today without your love and protection as my 'big sisters' – love you always. My peaceful warriors Radhika and Anjalee, who chose me as their father, thank you. Anubhav Chakravarty for your constant reminder: "how is the book going uncle C?" and Anjali Chakravarty, my other mother. Aunty Huldah Agbo, Uncle Chris Onduka, Uncle and Chief Chris-Roberts Ozongwu; you have amazing memories of the past. For Ozo

Agbo, Dr Khagendra Nath Chakravarty, Mae Valencia Barton, Billy Webster, Micky Carney and Roger Gurr, you gave more than any role models could have.

In my attempt to maintain the integrity of this narrative I have endeavoured to retain the childhood spoken Ibo and Pidgin English of the time.

Bula
The Rani of my world

Foreword

In reference to childhood aspirations, the award-winning Nigerian writer Ben Okri is quoted as saying: "We plan our lives according to a dream that came to us in our childhood, and we find that life alters our plans..." The author Celestine Obiora Agbo survived three terrifying years on the run in numerous refugee camps during the Nigerian Civil War, also known as the Biafran War, of the late 1960s and early 1970s. As a young boy, nothing during that period of his life would have predicted his fate: to give a voice to the men, women and children who were victims of famine during the war when the Military Government set up a blockade severely affecting the lives of civilians in the Biafra region of southeast Nigeria.

An impassioned storyteller, Celestine compels his reader to identify with the daily lives of his characters portrayed in this well-crafted novel as they struggle for survival in the appalling conditions resulting from the terrible conflict. The author is careful not to allow political events to overwhelm the human story – the emotional truth – for, after all, this is a book about human beings.

Dragonflies and Matchsticks is a welcome addition to preceding literary works that have centred themselves on the Nigerian Civil War, and therefore sits well alongside such fictional material as Chimamanda Ngozi Adichie's award-winning novel

Half of a Yellow Sun (2006), convincing portrayals of the Biafra middle-class. In Chukwuemeka Ike's *Sunset at Dawn* (1976) and Flora Nwapa's *Never Again* (1975), and even emotion-moving memoirs such as *Surviving in Biafra* (2003) by Alfred Ibiora Uzokwe, and *Sunset in Biafra* (1973) by Elechi Amadi, which looks at the war from an anti-Biafran minority.

Celestine could be described as a 'renaissance man'. He has succeeded at so many things: be it piloting light aircraft; a chef, working in schools, social services, children and elderly services and charities. As a therapist he has worked within a variety of disciplines; not to mention winning numerous awards as a social entrepreneur. He dished out healthy food at his London trendy art gallery, vegetarian and vegan restaurant 'Pepperton's'. Celestine has featured in numerous TV, radio, and newspaper reports for his work and charitable involvements over the years. As if all this, and more, wasn't enough, Celestine completed a postgraduate programme for creative writing and now writes exceedingly good novels. Such an illustrious life certainly fulfils the quote by Ben Okri at the start of this foreword: "And yet, at the end, from a rare height, we also see that our dream was our fate. It's just that providence had other ideas as to how we would get there. Destiny plans a different route, or turns the dream around, as if it were a riddle, and fulfils the dream in ways we couldn't have expected." Celestine's stories have so far won him numerous awards. With *Dragonflies and Matchsticks* he looks set to win many more.

Donovan Lee McGrath
University of London School of
Oriental and African Studies.

...for I was then a deeply angry young man, and with cause. I had seen such misery, so much starvation and death, so much cruelty inflicted on small children; and I knew that behind it all were vain and cynical men, not a few in high office in London, who had closed their eyes, hearts and minds to the agony of those children rather than admit they might have made a mistake.

Biafra was a mistake; it should and need never have happened...

...the passage of time may mellow viewpoints, or expediency may change them. But nothing can or ever will minimise the injustice and brutality perpetrated on the Biafran people, nor diminish the shamefulness of a British Government's frantic, albeit indirect, participation...

Victors write history, and the Biafrans lost. Convenience changes opinions, and the memory of Biafra and what was done there remains inconvenient for many.

Frederick Forsyth.
The Biafra Story: The Making of an African Legend

On a country road a few miles away, relief workers held out bits of food to a group of hungry children. They ran, not knowing what to do with it. We are going to have to teach a generation of children how to eat again.

A Canadian nurse helping Biafran refugees.

1

Who will Love
my Children?

Caroline's life did not get better after marriage. She was not the type who believed that a husband was the path to salvation. With five adorable children, one for every year of her marriage, she was back to where she had begun her marital life: in the village compound of her in-laws. Life was not friendly even with two prized sons. Her previous unforgiving mouth had been tempered by encumbered motherhood and mindfulness. The bleak sleepless nights were incomparable to her overworked mind. Eyes once bright are heavy and sunken, face once full with youth is strained with fear and vulnerability. Her own mother had failed by not warning her of the consequences of parenthood.

The cement floor cools her aching thighs through the bamboo mat after another day of ferrying heavy loads on her head to the market and squatting for a child to climb her back. That was her job early in the morning before her other children woke up. Caroline was paid several *kobos* a day by her friend Millicent, who owned a food stall at the road on Ninth Mile. Night-time was when she could be at peace with her children.

They were asleep lined up on a mat with six-year-old Decima as a buffer between the wall and her five-year-old sister Arike, they lay face-to-face entwined like twins.

Caroline yawns and pushes out her arms to hook her fingers over her toes; she holds her feet for a relaxing pull. In the dark she oils and ties her hair for the night, wondering how best she could watch over her children and work at the same time.

Not the type of person who would leave things to chance, Caroline had already witnessed the harsh reality of living in someone else's compound, and now her choices were closing in on her. But how could she inspire her in-laws to have a change of heart towards her so that she and her family did not feel unwelcome? Her husband Benjamin had been away for a year and was not picking up the gold which everyone believed to litter the streets of England.

The venomous words from the villagers had not abated especially now that she was a mother. But when they were directed to bite her children, she had no hesitation in packing up their belongings to head back to her father's house in fury. The gossips and the relentless gnashing of teeth was darkening her mood and affecting her children, particularly her eldest daughters into invisibility, and she was no longer prepared to compromise their happiness for the sake of honour between the two families. On arriving home her children did not dare to run to greet their grandparents with the usual excitement of jumping up and down eager to be picked up.

At her father, Nnadi Nwangwu's house, her parents listened carefully to their daughter's predicament as Caroline explained why she had left the house of her in-laws. When he had heard enough he flicked his index finger at his driver to bring the car. Without uttering a single word, he got into the vehicle and told his driver to proceed with haste. Although he had been aware of his daughter's unkind treatment at her husband's compound, he knew better than to interfere uninvited. But that was until the problem made its way to his doorstep. His compound gathered to watch his car disappear towards that village.

Till this day, no one other than Ngwentah, Caroline's brother-in-law, knew the extent of the discussion between the two heads of their families, but following their meeting, Caroline returned to her husband's compound once more with her children.

The last thing villages wanted was unrest between neighbours. Caroline maintained an ever-increasing watchful eye over her children, particularly Obi, who was now two years old. Being a toddler, he posed a vulnerable target for the negative influences of spiteful women. It was not uncommon for someone who had a grudge or dislike towards another to use traditional medicine to take revenge. Caroline had four other children to watch over, and worried in silence about Obi. Especially after she found out from Lady Ani of the rumours in the village suggesting her son might be an *Ogbanje* child, children who are continually reincarnated, often to the same parents. *Ogbanjes* were also known as children who come and go, plagued by evil spirits that reclaimed them to death during their time of birth. Not that Caroline had dismissed that possibility herself; she was the first to notice that when her son, as a baby, slept, his movements were unlike that of her other children. Obi seemed more advanced for his age; his baby language was different from the Ibo dialect. He spoke words she did not recognise and could not ask anybody about, for fear of her son being called an *Ogbanje*. She knew her son's spirit travelled to other places that no one could see but hoped he would grow out of it as other children did.

"He is behaving as if he is playing with other children but there is no one here, it is the middle of the night – what am I to do?" Caroline asked her mother during one of her visits to see her grandchildren.

"*Biko*, please, leave him, let him be, can you not see that he is happy where he is? Early in the morning, we go to see the *dibia*, medicine man, beyond the river. What has he in his hand?"

Obi's grandmother thrust her chin towards her grandson's tiny clenched fist. His arms raised, though he was fast asleep, his gestures clearly suggested that he was touching something only he could see and feel. Occasionally, he let out a gentle laughter.

"See how happy the child is? My god."

Caroline leans over him, her eyes enlarged with disbelief. She pulls several thick golden strands out of her child's hand.

"Mama what is this?" she whispered.

"It is mane," she said on closer inspection.

"*Mane.* How can this be? We have no lions in our village; no animal will allow a child so close. I cannot believe my eyes."

"This mane is not from an ordinary animal. Take a look, hold it and see," her mother urged.

"Jesus Christ, this cannot be. It has vanished. It did not want me to touch it. What kind of power has this child?"

Caroline fell back against the bedroom wall; her kerosene lamp drops to the floor. The glass globe smashed and the shards dropped out of the metal frame.

"Do not be worried, my daughter. I will watch over him tonight. You must rest; you have been running up and down all day, sleep now. In the morning, we will take Obi to your father's village to see a woman there first before the *dibia*."

Dibias are highly regarded for their extensive knowledge and wisdom, they are doctors with generations of expertise in healing and treating people with herbs, root and natural remedies to save and preserve life. But *dibias* didn't only save lives; they knew how to take lives without being there if the correct amount of monies was exchanged.

"Sister Mercy, has she returned from her journey?" asked Caroline.

Her mother didn't answer her.

"Why does this compound not rest at night?" she said frustrated. "The atmosphere is different here to other villages I have seen. The night is filled with noise of mothers beating their daughters after discovering them with terrible men of the village." They laughed together.

"Only the other night, the whole compound was woken by the cry of another young man fleeing for his life." Caroline and her mother laughed and giggled into the early morning watching one another's happy faces. Breaking away from the moment her mother leans towards her and says, "Those fools do not know of your family and your people. I no know why you do not beat them; only then will they show you respect and let you be."

"We are all villagers mama, you forget, I no husband here, so no voice," Caroline replied. "Lady Ani advised the same of me in the beginning. She told me that, that was the only way their husbands made them understand anything."

Her mother was asleep before she had finished tying her hair for the night. Caroline oils her arms, massaging each finger with the other, then her arms and legs, ready for sleep. Turning down the wick of her broken lamp to a tiny smokeless flame she places it on the edge of her table before curling up at the foot of the door.

The village was very different from how she had perceived it before her marriage when she and Millicent spent happy times as children. Millicent had married and lived away in Port Harcourt with her new husband and family. None of the friends that Caroline went to school with lived in the village; they had all married and moved away with their husbands.

Caroline was pulled in numerous directions as letters from London played on her mind. She listened to others who thought her crazy for not already being in England with her husband. Should her children grow up without their mother and father? Should she travel to help Benjamin overseas, and abandon her children? She had no money and had confronted her mother about leaving cash in her room whenever she visited. Her mother offered to live with her to help with her grandchildren while Caroline worked in town, selling dresses she made from pictures in magazines.

News of her husband's hardships continued to worry her; she didn't know what to do for everyone's best. Benjamin's letters informed them of his difficulties; he shared his struggles, mostly highlighting his problems in finding appropriate employment in the land of many promises. He had read, talked and heard about the many career opportunities that awaited the educated within the Empire of the United Kingdom. Prior to leaving, he could not have imagined the extraordinary life-changing experience ahead of him. The opulent lifestyle, the affluent social circles in which he revelled – the tennis games, the latest cars and hand-tailored suits – would be a thing of the past. His new life would be the opposite in every respect as soon as his feet touched English soil.

In Benjamin's London, banking opportunities were replaced by new career challenges he had not expected. Sweeping, cleaning and labouring positions were the standard professions for 'well-educated' aspiring young men like Benjamin. Damp and mouldy slug-infested lodgings were the general accommodations accessible to most migrants like him. No matter where he went and how many evening schools he attended, his dreams tormented him. He lost his confidence. *I do not want to shame my family by returning to my country as a failure*, he often reminded himself when things became unbearable. His early letters to his wife filled her with concern. Obi's mother and grandmother argued over whether she should leave her children to join and support her struggling husband overseas.

"How can my husband be suffering so much in that place? What am I to do? I cannot take my children to join him. Am I to leave my baby and go?"

706 Bedford Hill.
Balham, London
SW18
14th November 1961

My Dear,

Life in the Promised Land is not as promising as we had all expected before I left. Having travelled with you in our own land, I now know that I have not journeyed until now. Here, I am living in a small town called Balham. It is said to be a cheap place to live and many people from Africa and the West Indies reside in this area. I live in a room I can scarcely afford on the second level of a big house with many rooms, each room with an African or Irish tenant. In this land, going up the stairs and having a home with two floors is less important than it is in our country. When it rains, the water finds its way into the room and it is known as 'damp'. All our clothes smell, and each morning the windows are clouded with mist as if a kettle has boiled. The bottom of every wall and window is black with mould and growth, similar to that of the trees in the forests back home. The cooking area is cold with moisture; as different creatures crawl around and share our living space.

Norton Udengu from Enugu is here at university. He is studying law and cleaning latrines by night. Norton reminded me that we used to have servants doing that for us, that which we now do for others. He seems to be enjoying his new life and making friends each day here. He is much younger and has no responsibilities other than to send money back to his village. He has become very popular with the English women who are all friendly with him. Because we share one bed, I am sleeping in the armchair. We have a television, and I have increased its crackling volume to avoid hearing him and his latest girlfriend. Norton introduced me to an Irish woman and her husband at a party we attended. The couple seem very good people and I think that only the Irish like Africans in this land. After Norton explained our living conditions, they said they would 'put in a good word' for me with the landlady of a house in Streatham. I have been to Streatham before to watch a film about the Zulus; the cinema is bigger than our compound.

I left you and my children alone to come here to make a better life for us but I have to say that each cold day I think that I have made the wrong choice. There are many people from the Caribbean here but they are even more unfriendly to us. I have tried to be optimistic, but cannot hold it for more than a few hours. Norton told me that maybe I should visit the doctor.

He and I take it in turns to cook. Yes! I am now cooking my own meals and visiting the markets. I have two good white shirts that I wash and press alternately. I try to maintain some of my previous standards by dressing smartly with a tie and clean shirt. It has not made any difference to finding a good position in a bank. Each Saturday, I go to the market in Brixton. It sells bitter leaves, okra and plenty of other back-home foodstuffs. Petticoat Lane is another good market for cheap and good clothing. I bought a top coat from there.

It will soon be one full year I have been looking for a position in the bank. Even after opening an account with them, I have not managed to see the manager. One of the clerks told me to go to the main head office to enquire about an opening. He told me that they may give me a paper test, and, if I am lucky, I could be offered a junior clerk's position, or alternatively one in the bank's canteen as a teller, taking food money.

My dear, it would seem that the education in our country becomes useless once out of our country and that my banking days are now over. So I must fix my mind on working any job and returning to you, my children and my people, because the gold that littered the streets has all eluded me. Believe me; I have looked hard and fast for it.

I have been managing well the money I took to come here, but the payment for the room is eating it. Some help may come after I move to the room in Streatham. You must not worry. As God is my witness, we will be a family again. I hope Obi is being a good son. Give my kind regards to Ozo and our children.

Benjamin.

280 Leigham Vale.
Streatham, London
SW16
21st November 1961

Dear Caro,

Each day that I am in this cold country, I think that I may have made the worst choice in thinking that an African bank manager can come to this country and hope to find suitable employment in his trained profession. I travel everywhere to look for the employment I am qualified to do, but instead I am offered cleaning work. I have declined those jobs, but know that it is only a matter of time before I will have no other alternative but to accept one. Cleaning floors and latrines cannot be what I spent years in education for. I know that once that happens it will be difficult to change and come out of that line of work again.

Norton is now living with a white woman in her house in Golders Green. Just the other day he told me that her family has cast her out, so he and she will marry. I now attend evening classes so that I can improve my chances of finding a more suitable employment. As you can see, I have moved to Streatham which is an easy journey from the place I work as cleaner. It is only a few stops to where I disembark at Cats Whiskers to walk along Leigham Court Road. Walking is good because I am not cold when I step in the house; if you were to join me to work here, then maybe we can find a better place to live, and later bring our children to join us and attend good schools.

In this country, I am no longer an Ibo man but a coloured man who people cross the road to avoid.

My dear, *Biko*, pass my regards to our children, my
dear brother and others in the village.
Your husband,
Benjamin.

Benjamin's letters pained his wife, his anguish increased her
dilemma of whether to leave her young family to support her
husband or not. Caroline knew the time had arrived when she
could no longer delay making a choice in her life: only that her
choice would this time affect her children in ways she could not
imagine. To abandon her children to her widowed mother.

"A wife must be by the side of her husband," advised her
mother.

"I cannot leave my children just because a man cannot find
the post he likes," Caroline replied angrily. "Here everyone
becomes foolish around the white man: 'Yes Sir, yes Sir', the fools
run around them like begging dogs. Now in their own country,
all we are good for is sweeping their floors. No! I will not go
there."

"He is your husband, my daughter, do not be angry with
him, give him a chance. Help him to find his way there – you can
return to your children after."

Her mother held Caroline's hand, wiping tears she had not
seen since childhood.

"What if you are not there?" Caroline asked. "Decima is
too small for such responsibilities as watching over her sisters
and brothers, and Arike will fight anyone who troubles her
family. I may not return if I go. I may not even see you again,
my mother. Have you known anybody to return from that
place alive?" Caroline mops her tears with the hem of her
wrapper.

"I will stay here and help my children to find their way." She
snapped out of her grief.

"He should return. The idiot! Still think he is better than everybody here. He only writes his hopeless letters in English when he knows that I will struggle to read and understand them." Caroline stares at a letter on her table.

"How will I manage there, and how will they understand what I am saying? Obi has been unwell as a baby; what if anything happens to my children?" Caroline looks for other reasons to add to her resistance.

"I will look after the children. My daughter, it is your place to travel, to be close to your husband, to help him build for your future." Her mother continued in a hushed voice.

"Men become very lonely when they are in limbo. You have married him, so you must go to him when he calls."

"*No*, I will not go. It is my place to be with my children before any man, even my husband." Caroline is furious that her own mother should suggest such a thing. "What if you, or any of them, became sick? Who will care for you? I cannot go. What if they turn on you like they did me? You are of another compound, and my father is no longer here to help you. These people already suggest that Obi be an *Ogbanje*. How will they look on him when I am not here?"

"Obi has a good face for a boy, but that is not a good reason for anyone to think he is *Ogbanje*," said her mother in a whisper. "Other than his gift of travel in sleep, your son does not behave like *Ogbanje*."

According to traditional beliefs, mothers protected their suspected *Ogbanje* children and kept them out of sight. Many *Ogbanje* children did not mix well with their peers. Some were sullen, with pale complexions, coming out mainly during the evening after the busy village was dim and quiet. They would sit close to their mother's kitchen alone and away from other children, where their mothers kept a watchful eye on them. Although the days when *Ogbanje* babies were tossed alive into the woods had gone, most mothers of an *Ogbanje* felt cursed by the stigma of burying their child after the spirits came for them. Often *dibia* protection was passed on by the tips of razor blades: cuts to the child rendered them no longer beautiful or attractive to the attention of evil entities, some believed. *Ogbanjes* were the spirit of the deceased that drifted between the two worlds. With beautiful faces they could be recognised by the scars and birthmarks from their previous lives. Obi had heard it said that those who squandered, and had little value for their lives, lived an *Ogbanje* existence.

"Obi's face should be dulled and not smooth. It would shield and protect him from the danger of being taken back to the spirit world before his time," discreetly her mother suggested.

"It would involve an expensive ceremony, which will be conducted only by the most senior and powerful *dibia* of the region. Your father's people would organise everything. The cuts will be made to Obi's temple and shoulders; it would help him when he becomes a man. The *dibia* will rub strong medicine into the cuts. When the medicine is applied, it will give him protection for all his life. The child-snatching spirits will no longer take an interest in him. He will forget the pain within two days. The spirits, on seeing that he is damaged by cuts, will leave him to live out a full life."

"Mama, I know this well, but how can I allow my son such pain?"

"But what of the greater pain? My daughter, do you think he did not feel pain when he came into this world? Life is pain."

After discussing her situation through with her mother, Caroline agreed that it would be best if she travelled to England. She accepted her mother's offer to look after her children in her absence.

13

Caroline had never taken up the opportunity to develop her English, even though her parents had encouraged her, she remained indifferent to anything foreign, unlike other wealthy folk. Had she imagined a future in England, then maybe she would have endeavoured to learn the language.

2

Enugu, 1954
Twigs and Footprints

Caroline seemed snared by different traps. Amongst her peers she had remained the last eligible teenager without a husband. Her strength and determination easily rivalled that of any man, physically and emotionally. She gave as she took, her self-confidence did not render her arrogant and she brought no shame to her family's door. *What is left for me to do?* She thought. *If I don't marry Benjamin, even my own people will think I will forever remain a spinster in my father's house. I will accept his hand in marriage.*

Caroline was the first girl born to a long line of boys within her father's compound; she knew some villagers believed this was the basis for her audaciousness. Her father's position within the coal corporation brought its own challenges to her and her family. She openly opposed and argued with her father for his part in helping the white men to exploit their land and wealth in order to build their empire. This was a difficult period for her, she felt alone and isolated within the village while her contemporaries headed for universities and city lives. A sense of gloom befell her, causing her to retreat into herself. In reflections, she thought that she might have dishonoured her parents by not attending university. People of her village did not understand why she would not join in the celebrations and prospects of being accepted by *oyibo,* 'white people'. When her father hosted the white men's hunting parties, Caroline refused to take part or eat any of the sweets they brought to her village. She stayed out of sight, unlike the many that followed like sheep, singing and clapping hands in the rhythmic tradition of worship.

They will give you the rubbish they no longer want, and you tell them thank you. They will render you weak when they tell you that you are kind. That is when your life will finish as you do everything to be a likeable person. They have many ways of distributing their poison; Caroline was heard telling one of the *adas,* 'young women', once.

The *adas* laughed, mocked and called her foolish, but surprisingly Caroline did not fight them. Something happened. A change she did not understand nor had control over, separating herself from most of the village and the few she considered friends.

At eighteen, Caroline's first blessing arrived nine months after her marriage to the aspiring banker Benjamin. It was a marriage between two influential families from a long line of Ibo descendants. Caroline's father, Neugwunwa Ozodue, was head of the colonial Coal Corporation Company, a position his daughter did not care for. She did not forgive him for accepting an award for his services to the Crown and the British Empire. Ozodue accepted the award bestowed upon him by the Queen of England during her visit in the 1950s.

Benjamin's family were traditional farmers who supplied yams and cassava to the local regions of Igboland. His brothers, like himself, were white-collar, government workers. Benjamin was the youngest of five brothers and an older sister.

"This child has the spirit of an ox, do not expect her spirit to be bound by anyone, or that she will be servant to any man as a wife," Lady Ani warned the compound of elders before Caroline's marriage was agreed.

Caroline did not want to dishonour her family by leaving the house of her father without a husband. She knew time was closing in on her and that she had to accept one of the offers of marriages from a line of hopefuls. Her father received proposals for his daughter's hand regularly from other leaders of various villages. It was not that Caroline was used to getting her own way all the time. She was not willing to subjugate her life and desires, even though she was not sure what exactly they were aged seventeen.

"I am not cattle. I will not belong to a man – the property of a husband in becoming a housewife," she protested when the subject was raised.

*

The marriage ceremony was the biggest event in the village; their wedding guests arrived days before the ceremony from all corners of the neighbouring villages, towns and cities.

Ten frightened cows pinned down, their necks stretched and bound by ropes. Gaunt faces with saddened onyx eyes the shade of a darkened universe glazed with fear stood shoulder to shoulder, each with their own bucket next to their necks. The buckets beside them would not be sufficient to collect all the blood. Shiny blades from the butcher's daggers, machetes and axes caught the morning sunshine and reflected the humongous dark soot-laden cooking pots. The mothers had wailed all night, fearing their imminent death at sunrise, when their throats would be slit, drowned by the cheers of joyful children. Their cries echoed around the village throughout the night and could not be drowned by the all-night celebration of live bands.

A day prior to the wedding, more guests arrived with goats, yams and baskets of fowl laid out on the ground, covering every inch of the joint compounds. Gifts of colourful bundles of cloth piled up outside like reinforcements against a dam, ready to be accounted in the village recording book for which Mr Uwani set out his desk for the ceremonial accounting of the gifts.

"If the audit is not accurately recorded in the book, it will cause difficulty in the future ceremonies that will follow. If you do not know who gave, and what was given, you will not know what to give when it is their turn to receive," Mr Uwani announced in his official spoken English, to the children who watched his every move with awe.

Bishops and priests arrived from most of the eastern states; they pretended not to notice the other guests who queued in long winding lines to bow and curtsy before them as they ceremoniously occupied specially allocated seats in the open fronted marquees made of draped fabrics for dignitaries. Everyone was accommodated in the celebrations: the senior village women, the *adas*, the in-laws, the mothers, the mothers' families, the musicians from the various towns and villages. Four men were on guard duty to make sure the contents of the two trucks carrying stout and mineral drinks did not go astray. The trucks were parked outside the village centre because the village had run out of space. Women cooked non-stop for two days, just as they would for the funeral of an important elder. When the stock of firewood diminished during the night, the women sent strong men into the forest to cut down dying trees. Oluama School had the nearest open grounds, which were adequate to host and accommodate a wedding of such epic proportions.

All ceremonies and celebrations were too important a tradition for the Ibos to not be done well. After burial ceremonies, marriages came next as the most expensive of events.

Armed guards escorted Caroline's special delivery to her father's house: white silk and lace gown, gloves and veil. News had spread that the gold, silver and pearl encrusted dress took two months to make by the hands of the finest English tailors. Benjamin's black silk suit and fedora came tailored from London's Savile Row. His shoes shone like polished marble.

Only Caroline's beauty prevented the guests from constantly gazing over at the white people, who were seated in their elevated marquee. Even the bishops were fascinated by being seen at the same place as the *oyibo*. Eight of the most popular bands circled the school field, as guests danced and celebrated into the night.

After three daughters in succession – Decima, Arike and Onyi – people in the villages continued to talk behind Caroline's back.

"There is after all, something she cannot manage."

"Where is the boy child? The bank manager's wife is only good at bearing girls. If she does not bear him soon a son, he will have to take another wife who can."

"We are not *oyibo*, we are Africa. The obligation of a married life is not complete until a son is born into that union."

"His senior brother has six wives. No say he has no money." The jibes persisted.

Caroline longed to have a son and knew it would be the only way to stop the wagging tongues. The miracle she longed for was not within her grasp. She could not put her hands anywhere but together for a son. She prayed silently in the dark and to the spirits of her ancestors, but nothing changed. Caroline finally decided to consult with the most powerful of *dibias* to beget her a boy child.

"Why can I not have a son? Is this my punishment for not having time for men in the past? Dear God. Why can I not have a boy child now?" Caroline's anguish grew by the day and the hurtful taunts continued, no longer just behind her back.

"When a seed falls, it shall grow. Be patient; do not give your ears to idle gossip," her mother reminded her. "The privileged position of being a mother of sons who will grow to become strong men and providers for their people has not escaped you. You are still young, God is there. *Biko,* please my daughter, no shed tear."

She searched her soul for the reason of her failure and asked herself the same questions time and again. As a child her father had never shown or led her to believe women were of a lesser standing than men. Caroline felt the same way with her daughters and was never going to raise them to be subordinate.

She left her children with her mother when she ventured deep into the forests alone in search of new *dibias*. From each journey she returned with a calabash of the *dibia's* root medicine. Behind closed doors in the silence of her mother's home she continued her prayers and drank from the calabash, and vomited violently to the reaction of the root medicine.

She was now a wife who had to broaden her horizon and factor in everything that came with marriage; her life was changing at a rate she did not always understand. In Minna, Northern Nigeria, the dutiful wife and mother did her best to make a new home during their earlier postings.

Four years after their marriage, God answered her prayers; blessing her with a son she named Obiora, heart of the people. During the first week of the new year Obi arrived healthy and effortlessly into the world. Caroline's joy and laughter echoed throughout the maternity ward. She thanked God for the mercy and grace; she held baby Obi to her chest and fell asleep smiling.

New mothers appreciated the revitalised maternity ward, no longer with cobwebbed ceilings. The ward soon filled with visitors, the likes the hospital had not before known; a welcome normally reserved for government ministers' children. News had travelled that Benjamin's son had finally arrived. Unfortunately for Benjamin, after a day of pacing the corridors, he had to go back to work so missed the birth of his son. The news of his baby came from his driver, who had been busy ferrying freshly-cooked foods to his expectant wife each day. Benjamin's darkened sleepless eyes were visible through his black-rimmed spectacles. Before he arrived at the hospital to see his wife and welcome his son, he asked the driver to stop at his tennis club in order to share the good news. Returning later to 'wet the baby's head' which indeed was the case as he took over the entire bar of the well-known hotel for the day. Free drinks were served for all who entered the establishment.

When Benjamin set eyes on his son, Obi was fast asleep on Caroline's chest. Caroline had never seen tears in her husband's eyes before, until she woke and saw him slumped in a chair next to her bed.

"My husband," she smiled at him. "You have a son."

"God is the all mighty," Benjamin smiled, gently scooping his son from Caroline's chest to his. On Benjamin's departure from the ward, he handed bundles of cash to the ever-increasing members of the hospital staff, as is expected from a man of his standing. Doctors invited him into their offices like traders beckoning customers, each stating his expertise as they held open their hands for the bank manager's cash. Benjamin was known for his wealth and generosity. Hospital staff arrived early for their duties and left late, so that they could take the opportunity to hold Obi and see his generous father. As the staff took a special interest in the newborn, it wasn't long before rumours spread that people had to wash their hands before touching their precious newborn.

With Ike Chukwu's arrival a year later, Caroline's life seemed more fulfilled and promising than ever. She regained her sense of joy. But this feeling was short-lived when her husband announced his imminent departure for England. He told his wife how the North no longer welcomed Ibos, and that London held greater promise. Benjamin was surprised at first that his wife did not challenge him, although Caroline was not happy that she had not been consulted beforehand. It was all too soon, everything had happened very quickly, and now he was abandoning them.

"Where will we live Benjamin? Where will I find money to feed our five children when you in Britain!?"

"My brother will give you a room." Benjamin could not look into Caroline's red eyes.

"Ha! A room now. What of our belongings? Six of us in one village room, look, am I not still feeding your baby my milk? Oh, I must also abandon them to look food? Forgive me dear husband, you is crazy!"

The following day before his departure, he arrived with his car full of provisions to ask for Caroline's forgiveness.

Before Benjamin left, Caroline organised for a photographer to take some family portraits which she sent with him for company.

"This way you will not forget that you have a family at home," she reminded him.

Benjamin thanked his wife with an embrace.

"The photographer has truly captured you and the children. Why is it that only you and Obi are smiling?" he said.

"Your son is too small to know he may never see his father again," Caroline told her departing husband. "They return from that cold place in a casket."

"I will buy a top coat first thing when I arrive in Britain," he assured her. Benjamin was pleasantly taken by his wife's new-found composure and acceptance. He could see how contented she had become although he was to disrupt it. It was said that although men longed for sons, they do not realise that the son would replace them, especially as the mother pours all her love on her son.

Shortly after Benjamin's departure, Caroline left Minna to return to her husband's village in Enugu to live with Ngwunta, her husband's senior brother and his six wives. This was a time before he was honoured as an Ozo, 'chief'. Upon her and her children's arrival, the entire village came to welcome them home, as was the Ibo tradition. The crowd descended, dancing, clapping and embracing. The children snatched in different directions and her baby from her hold and out of sight. Dragged away by her peers in the opposite direction Caroline didn't want to ruin the welcome celebrations but could no longer bear the ceremonial traditions, knowing it would not bode well on her, she wanted her children back.

As head of the family, Ngwunta welcomed Caroline and her five children. He gave them a room in the main house. She recalled the times when she pleaded with Benjamin to build a house for them in the village. Being beholden on others was not the life she wanted for her and her young family. Benjamin did not want to live anywhere other than in his brother's compound when he was in the village and Caroline could not tell any man not to be with their brother.

Motherhood seemed to have taken its toll on Caroline, making her more vulnerable to what other wives in the village said and did. Without her husband and five children to look after, Caroline had to bite her tongue for a peaceful life.

"Things are no longer the same now. We will teach her a lesson! You watch and see how she will not cope with those children. She is now a mother." The spitefulness continued behind her back.

Village life was exciting for the children. It was a novelty that they would live like villagers. Every morning Caroline sang to her children and praised God as she washed and dressed them.

She was delighted that her children were going to have the opportunities and the experience of village life.

Obi was an eager and inquisitive child; he toddled around the compound exploring his new surroundings, often finding himself in the kitchens of his uncle's wives. He visited the goats in their enclosure and disturbed the hens roosting under trees and bushes. With a fondness for bright colours, baby Obi pulled and ate his way through the heads of marigolds in their garden. Calls from the compound women fell short of Obi's ears as they ran out towards him, and his mother would apologise.

"Obiora! Leave my garden be. *Biko* go find your *moda*," the wives would shout, as they lifted and turned him around like the clockwork toys he played with. In the opposite direction, on hands and knees, Obi crawled away, often with twigs in his mouth as he mimicked the goats, following them about the compound.

Caroline sang and hummed her favourite tunes as she went about her duties in the compound, much to the annoyance of most of the wives. The family of six lived crammed in the small room in the main house. Every night Caroline lay with her back next to the door, arms stretched protectively over them as they all slept on the floor. Despite the hardship, Caroline was appreciative of the hospitality. Her daughters had friends, and Obi could walk and play with other children of the compound.

She and her cousin Millicent were best of friends and met regularly. Caroline listened as Millicent talked of her business plans with her, while they watched and laughed at Obi who chased chickens around Millicent's home. Their joy echoed around the compound and drifted into the village centre, reminding them of their own childhood.

Millicent shared how well her catering business was going and pleaded for her 'sister' to work with her, so they could expand outside of Ogbete Market. Both had astute business heads, but Caroline looked at baby Ike in her arms and declined. Although she was happy to work with her best friend, she reminded Millicent that she had five children to look after. Even though her husband had left no money to maintain them, she could not leave her children.

She explained: "I would have to leave them at three in the morning to cook and carry food to sell at the roadside by 5am. How can I do that? It's impossible."

At three years old, village life suited Obi who loved the carefree living as he ventured further out of the compound each day. Once, when he accidentally broke a pot that belonged to one of his uncle's wives, the devil descended. Caroline apologised to her sister-in-law and offered to pay for the damage. The woman refused her offer.

"The child must pay! The child must pay!" the woman raged and jabbed her stubby finger towards Obi, who was crying inconsolably into his mother's blouse.

Beads of sweat ran down Caroline's contorted face. She didn't know how to placate the hell-bent threat aimed at her son.

Wives and mothers watched from their doorways, eager for Caroline's demise. Suspended in silence, the compound held its breath until Lady Ani's door slammed behind her, and she marched from her house towards the women around the mango tree.

"Ha! Shut up your foolish latrine mouth. Do you think Caroline is without a family, that you should behave like hens bickering over one worm? Heed my warning: value your tongues!" Had it not been for the intervention of Lady Ani silencing the mother, who knows what the outcome would have been?

"That child must pay. That boy will pay," the mother repeated as she headed out towards the woods. Lady Ani took Obi from Caroline, uncurling his arms from around her neck; he looked at his mother collecting the broken pot as Lady Ani carried him into her house.

The vicious tongues of the village wives were a blessing to Caroline instead of a hindrance. It confirmed to her that she must leave the compound to ensure the safety for herself and her children. Every now and again news arrived that a child had mysteriously dropped dead in front of their mother, and no one dared to mention why. Village wastelands were scattered with discarded bundles of unkind medicine made by resentful individuals seeking to harm others. Although Caroline did not truly believe such evil could affect the strong-minded, she didn't want to take any chances in case it found its way to her doorstep. This unforgiving and irrational way of life was not how she wanted her children raised. She knew that no matter how much she had conformed to fit in, kindness and love would never be forthcoming as far as she and her family were concerned. Caroline understood the village mentality and knew that the woman actually wanted her child to pay the money directly out of his own packet, otherwise the child must be punished by a beating. Enraged, she recollected other occasions when her children received harsh treatment that was intended for her. She swallowed her pride, which by then came with a bitter taste, as she thought of how best she could protect them in the future.

The worst incident was with Ngwunta, her brother-in-law. Decima was five at the time; she and the other children were helping to shift building sand in the compound. The children sang as they followed one another carrying buckets of sand on their head, stepping into the same sandy footprints as the one before. Decima mistakenly emptied her unbalanced bucket short of the designated spot when her uncle, who was watching from his armchair in the front veranda, instantly shouted out, pointing and waving his arms at Decima. His fury continued as he rammed his chair against the wall and stormed towards the child. He towered over the five year old who trembled at his rage. The compound had fallen silent as the sound of breaking bark saw Decima slammed to the ground from a slap from her uncle's massive hand.

Caroline lowered baby Ike on the floor the second she heard Arike's scream, she ran towards the front of the main house where her girls were. The stillness of a busy compound was usually not a good sign. Caroline picked up a burning log from underneath a boiling pot of rain water and charged towards her brother-in-law, who was stunned and motionless on seeing her. Lady Ani dashed out of her kitchen and stood in front of Caroline and shouted for her to stop. Like a lightning bolt she whisked the smouldering log from Caroline's grip, as Ngwunta approached her.

"*Biko*, Sir, *biko*, my brother, no beat my child. She is your junior brother's child. You are her father now. I beg you, no lay hand on my children again. My daughter did not intend to drop your sand. I beg you, no beat my daughter. I will pick up every grain from the ground, sorry, *biko*. No beat my child!" Caroline cried at her brother-in-law's feet as she picked Decima up from the ground.

Ngwunta's fury continued into an almighty blow upon Caroline's head. He slapped and beat her repeatedly on the head and face as Caroline cradled Decima's face against her chest absorbing the onslaught. Ngwunta sprayed a mouthful of saliva at the ground beside her and her daughter before he kicked the log towards the pot of water with his bare foot and marched back to his house.

Ngwunta re-emerged moments later with Caroline's suitcase and threw it at her feet. She was still trembling; her child clung sobbing into her blouse. Hidden behind her daughters embrace, tears gushed down Caroline's swollen face like an overflowing water tank during monsoon.

My children will not grow up in fear of anyone, Caroline believed. She knew Ngwunta was not a bad man; she took his anger as a warning and reminder for her to do something with her life. Ngwunta had always encouraged her to visit her sister Millicent more often. Caroline thought of her parents, and her people. Her father had never lifted an angry finger towards her. Yet she knew she had to endure her predicament for the time being, and that her children's lives were turning out so different to hers. It would bring shame to her husband's people if her parents knew of their daughter's experiences in the compound of her in-laws; that would not be her intention, therefore returning to her father's house with her children was not an option.

To struggle is to be part of the living. We must all suffer in life for what is good. Lucifer's work is easy.

The discussions with her mother before her marriage to Benjamin echoed in her head, she understood that marriage involved many sacrifices, though her letters to Benjamin reassured him that all was well.

"Because of her father, she has a bank manager for a husband. My idiot husband go walk two hours each day for work," a young woman grumbled to another, using Caroline to vent her marital frustrations.

"Moneyed children do not have dirty fingers," the wives spoke aloud, knowing that Caroline could hear them.

"She can try all she likes; she will never be a part of this place."

"My dear, she must now live in a village. No *moto* car come carry them away after they have eaten!"

The taunts continued as the women casually ambled past the compound.

Caroline's reputation for being a no-nonsense upright person preceded her, but it did not serve her well among the latest edition of wives; they feared her presence and the impact it could have on them. They were warned by the female elders that their idleness and reckless engaging with men other than their husbands would have to stop upon Caroline's return.

Lady Ani scolds the women on hearing their venomous attacks. "I have seen how much that woman works, she alone puts shame upon the women of this compound. Do you not remember when you were new to this village, now you want her to turn bitter like you? Foolish idiots! You call yourself women? You do not know the meaning of the word. I pray that when you beg her one day, she will not show you the mercy you have refused to show her today. Do you think you will be the last wives to enter this compound?" Lady Ani pushes her way past the women, her hand raised sharp like a sword, just short of their faces. She turned to look at them with revulsion, sending a jet of saliva scattering from her mouth. She wiped clean the remnants of dribble from her chin.

"No make me slap you," she warned the women.

"*Biko*, Auntie, *biko*, we no mean any of what we say about Caroline; *biko,* no speak of us to her," they pleaded as Lady Ani turned to walk away in disgust.

"Caroline has not been brought up by her parents to think that women are less than men. Just you watch, you will all see how useless you have allowed your lives to become. That is why you fear her even before you get to know her." Lady Ani pushes her palm in their direction as an insult to them and heads to the village centre. "Nothing she does will ever be good enough for you. See how hard she works! Shame on you, instead of following her example, you gossip about her, too afraid to look into her eye and see that she is your sister."

Lady Ani gathers her wrapper, tucking it into her waist, cursing the women so they could still hear her. Dumbstruck they watch until she looks back from a market stall at them and they look down to the ground ashamed.

3

October in the Rain

Caroline arrived to a gloomy October London. When her jet touched down in Heathrow she watched what the other passengers were doing before she unbuckled herself to stand. With an uncomfortable neck she waited for someone to let her pass. She emerged after everyone had filed past before she tugged at her bag which almost sent her to the narrow floor with its weight. Towards the exit she'd seen the two air hostesses walking away after they had said goodbye to the passengers before her.

"I go to join my husband," she told the stern-faced immigration officer before he nods and stamps her passport.

"Thank you, Sir." She looked around before following the direction of the masses.

Fascinated by the carousel and the amount of heavy luggage of various descriptions, Caroline barged her way towards her bag fearing she'd lose it as other passengers collected theirs. The vast arrivals hall dazzled her eyes; she didn't know where to look, all the welcoming eyes seemed to be on her through the walkway gallery. It could not have been a regular sight to see a woman carrying heavy luggage on her head in a 1962 London airport.

"Caro!" Benjamin called from the crowd of people awaiting their guests after he had pushed his way to the front. Caroline looked about into the masses, certain that she had heard her husband's voice. She turned to see Benjamin's arm waving at her before he squatted and squeezed under the barrier and ran to her. She struggled with her heavy bags, she stopped to greet Benjamin and Norton. Onlookers watched as new arrivals dispersed around them like an unearthed ants' nest.

"*Dayja* sister *dayja*. Welcome," Norton said and struggled at the clearing to carry Caroline's bag for her.

Although their lights were yellow, Benjamin could not hail a taxi outside the terminal until Norton stood in front of an empty cab before the driver could slip away.

"I know we should also have lights in our overcoats in winter," he joked with the driver who only responded with: "Go on then, jump in."

"I go sit before he drive away now o," said Caroline.

Benjamin slammed the door shut after he had shifted the case in before him.

"Royal Windsor?" suggested the driver shaking his head.

"Streatham," Benjamin replied as the taxi pulled away.

"One of them chiefs are you then? Wish I could afford to live in Streatham."

No one responded to the driver.

Caroline appreciated the smooth motorway and how every car had working lights.

"Please take the Hammersmith route, Earls Court will be hell this time of the evening."

"You drive do yah?" the driver enquired, looking at them from his rear-view.

"*Ha Chineke m o.* Oh my god," Norton tells his friends. "Well, seeing you're ever so intrigued with my life. I actually drive an E-type. Here is my key as I'm sure you would want proof." Norton jangles them behind the driver making sure the key ring badge was visible.

"Because our queens never travel light, and the boot is small in comparison, we are in this marvellous taxi."

"Ha. A house with step. You have done well my husband," said Caroline as they entered the tall hallway of the Victorian house, making their way to the long flight of stairs to the first floor.

"Sister Caro, welcome to London where the streets are paved in gold. I will see you at the party tomorrow. Enjoy this night. He has waited too long for his wife." Norton slaps Benjamin's back and shuts the door behind him.

The bedsit was airless with rolled up newspaper wedged between the sash windows. Two thin floral curtains sagged on a line of plastic-covered coiled wire, nailed to either side of the window frame with flaking paint. It seemed an ill-fitting end to her long journey, not to mention the curled up wallpaper ends hanging from the ceiling. Caroline burnt her hand when she tried to move a stumpy cylindrical object from the centre of the room out of the way so she could drag her luggage through.

"What kind of machine is this?"

"It is a paraffin heater." Benjamin lifted it away from the centre by its handle.

"You will feel the heat more from there. By the morning everywhere outside will be covered in snow." Benjamin suggested that she should sit in the armchair next to the coal fire that glowed from the wall. "We will go to buy you warm clothes and boots tomorrow," he said.

"How long do you plan for me to be here my husband? I no need to waste money on clothes."

"You are always a clear-thinking individual Caro. Leaving our children, even for a short time, to help me in getting on with my profession in England is more than any husband can ask of his wife. *Biko*, we must buy you warm clothes otherwise you will soon fall sick in this weather."

"Okay my husband. I thank you. You have done well."

"Ha. Caro, I cannot believe you are here."

The coal fire that Benjamin had built before going to meet his wife at Heathrow burnt slowly through the night. The small rented room was cosy and warm when they awoke in the morning.

Caroline was upset for a second when her husband brought her breakfast in bed. It was not customary for a husband to cook and serve his wife food in the village. "Do you no longer think I am your wife, or have you already taken another? I should have risen and cooked your food."

"Welcome, my wife. *Dayja dayja*. You have done well to follow me."

"When will you go work?" she enquired tucking into her eggs and fried bread from her lap.

"I don't work today. When you have rested, we will go to market and do some shopping."

"Ha! The bank manager *na* have plenty of money o," Caroline laughed as she slurped a hot cup of milky tea and looked around their room. "This tea is good."

"What kind paint on this wall, my husband?"

Benjamin let out a hearty laughter. "Wallpaper – it covers every wall in this country."

"What of paint?"

"Paint is there." He pointed to the ceiling, window and skirting.

"I have put on the geyser; the water will soon be hot for a good bath."

"Thank you my husband." Caroline leaves the bed to look out of the frosted window. She is completely fascinated by the garden. "What is the time now in Africa, how is my mother and our children managing in your village?"

Benjamin's smile fades. "I check the bath."

Caroline continues to look out of the window into the garden below as she dresses.

"You have land here," she joked. "We can build on it," said Caroline, proud of his efforts. The room overlooked the fenceless back gardens of the neighbouring houses. "It is high here." She tried to look up from the closed window. "Do people fall from opening the window?"

Benjamin smiled from the door eager to show her the other parts of the house before they leave for shopping.

"The bathroom, kitchen and garden are shared by everyone who lives here," he said taking her hand. Caroline laughed when she saw all the tins and colourful packets and boxes of various breakfast cereals which Benjamin had stocked up on the day before.

"Why are you laughing?" he asked with an anxious face.

"So you no eat back-home food in the UK, bank manager?" his wife laughed.

"Here I no bank manager, I am a nobody," he replied with a lump in his throat.

"How did you find this good room, is it a hotel? Did you not say that all the houses have warnings against dogs and people like us?"

"No. The hotels here are like you have not imagined. We are renting the room for the time being. I have found a small job at the nearby transport garage which will pay me enough for this rent," Benjamin explained as they walk back from a tour of the communal parts of their home.

"I will go there with you to ask for work," said Caroline promptly with an air of excitement.

Caroline loved her new coat from Petticoat Lane, it was the warmest clothing she had ever worn; just like the ones she'd seen in magazines in Lagos and never imagined owning one herself. Out of bed she is wrapped in her coat, lost in the comfort of soft animal-like fur against her neck until Benjamin's snore distracts her attention and she turns to watch him still fast asleep.

She looks at her suitcase on the floor before she gets dressed and takes her husband's keys from the table and leaves the room without waking him. At the front gate she said hello to a woman walking her dog past the house. She noticed that the woman had looked down ignoring her good manners. Caroline looks right before she turns left down the road of her new neighbourhood in her warm overcoat.

Further along the street she sees the same woman with the dog greeting a man with familiar openness. Her husband? Caroline wonders.

She didn't know why the people she smiled at looked down or crossed over to the other side of the road, she remembers Benjamin telling her the very same scenario in his letter. Turning left up Stockfield Road, she hoped she wouldn't get lost if she kept turning left at every corner, she didn't want to miss any of the perfectly placed slabs of the tidy, lit pavement streets. It was a delight for her to walk on a level surface, unlike the roads and paths of her motherland. The elegant concrete lampposts were perfectly located to light the way; the immaculate painted red letter-posting towers all seemed beyond the imaginations of any villager of Iboland.

Windows of so many different kinds of houses lined the streets as Caroline appreciated how neatly they are kept by their owners. She touched large trees and appreciated the young saplings ringed by wire netting propped by a grey column, wooden stake. Although she couldn't see the stars for the streetlights that lit her way back home, she recognised the parade of shops and pondered looking into the darkened, windows. Except for one, she saw the owner, a kind looking Indian gentleman named Ashok. He waved at her beckoning her in.

"Welcome. You are the wife of Benjamin?" Ashok asked shaking his head.

"Thank you, Sir, I am Caroline, Benjamin is my husband. I arrive last night in Britain."

Caroline looked about the shop fascinated. "You have fridge?"

"Yes, he has been expecting you. Please come and buy your food here, I give your people good price."

"How much good price?" Caroline asked.

"The more you buy, less I charge you," replied Ashok from his counter where he rubbed his palms before putting something between his cheek and gums. Caroline saw the redness of his teeth and mouth.

"I don't smoke, this my tobacco," said Ashok. "It is called Pan."

Benjamin woke from his nap when Caroline closed the door on her return, she told him of her experience in the streets.

"Britain is not like anything you have witnessed before, my dear. You have not been here a day and already you are seeing for yourself the circumstances I told you about in my letters."

Later that night they took the underground from Brixton to North London to attend a welcoming evening arranged for Caroline by some Ibo friends. Caroline preferred the bus journey than the underground; the fact that a bus could have steps to another floor amazed her.

"*Oyibo* people are clever o," she whispered to Benjamin from the top deck. "Obi would enjoy the buses here."

Monday morning and Caroline was up before her husband. He'd agreed that she could accompany him to ask about a job at the bus garage. The suitcase on the floor was open and Caroline was in a blue floral dress which her best friend Millicent had ordered for her going away gift. Carefully she cooked her husband a breakfast of omelette, fried yam with onions and tomato without staining it. Although her shoes were not properly suited to October weather, the white straps matched her dress and hand bag.

"My husband, what is problem?" Benjamin's eyes were as wide as his opened mouth on seeing his wife dressed up.

"You look wonderful, Caro."

Embarrassed, his wife looked down to the floor, bashful as was the norm of most young women back home.

Pulling the heavy front door shut they left for a day of opportunities as Benjamin handed her a set of her own keys which he had cut the week before. When they walked past Dunraven, the local secondary school Benjamin pointed out that this is where the evening classes took place.

"It is very close to our home. Decima and Arike will enjoy English education," Caroline suggested.

Benjamin continued in silence, crossing the road while Caroline was still admiring the school.

The walk to Benjamin's workplace at the bus garage took twenty minutes. When they arrived everything stopped and men whistled and called Benjamin 'a dodgy bastard'. Caroline was furious on hearing them speak to her husband in that manner but, knowing his wife, Benjamin quickly reassured her that they meant no harm and were actually complimenting them both.

Caroline smiled and walked into the manager's office; pleased with herself she re-emerged with a cleaning job for which she was delighted. Re-tracing their journey she walked past the secondary school, changing her mind she decided to turn around and head towards the entrance.

"We are not the evening institute," the woman in the office told her. "Do you live far?" she continued.

"No, my home in Britain is only behind this school," Caroline replied. After her enquiries about English classes Caroline asked the secretary if she had any jobs at the school.

Mrs O'Patrick was the school's secretary and had taken an instant liking to Caroline.

"My name is Marian, what is your name?"

"Caroline Agbo."

"Come with me Caroline," she said, walking around her desk to lead the way across the small hall towards the headmaster's office. Caroline tried to keep up with the bundle of energy that was the petite Irish woman, Marian O'Patrick. She tucked the stray strands of hair which had fallen across her face behind her right ear. She wriggled and tugged her well-fitted purple skirt down before she knocked and entered without an invitation.

"Ronald. That vacancy for the cleaning lady we are about to post, don't. It has just been filled. Meet Caroline. She starts tomorrow morning. Caroline, this is Ron, he hates being called that but he's stuck with it now. Even the kids call him Ron. See you later, Ron. Oh, by the way, Caroline has children old enough for us. Make sure places are reserved ready for them for when they arrive. Oh, thanks."

She backed out of the office and Caroline saw Ron's embarrassed red face before the door closed. Caroline thanked Mrs O'Patrick with a handshake.

"If I can call you by your own name chosen by your mother, then you must call me by mine. Marian."

Two good jobs in one hour, Caroline was very pleased with herself. "I will soon begin, send money back home," she told herself.

As the weeks passed Caroline thought of broaching the subject of bringing their children to England. She knew it would be a struggle for them in the one room but at least they both had jobs.

Undeterred by her language barrier Caroline mixed well with the staff team especially with Marian, who looked out for her and put others in their place if they stepped out of line. Break time was a struggle for Caroline, seeing the children of similar ages to hers was almost unbearable.

Now that she was settled at work Caroline wanted to make better use of her evenings. She attended a class on Monday nights for English, but there were six more evenings available to fill with work. Caroline was amazed that she had earned £40 within six weeks of being in England and that Benjamin had agreed for them to open a joint account. She loved the opportunity of making money by working hard in England, but the grey days got to her and made her homesick. She missed the African sun, the intensity of its light and the boldness of village colours; yet she was in England to do a job to help her husband and her family. Her purpose was defined when she left her children behind to join Benjamin. It wasn't just the weather that got her down, the thought that she had abandoned her children was unforgivable as far as she was concerned.

"How could our people live in this land, they still think we are from the bush?" she complained to Benjamin. In Africa they welcomed and entertained English visitors to their land and their homes as part of the Nigerian upper-class elites. Never could anyone back then have imagined the reception that awaited them in England. *How could this be so? In our country, white men are treated like kings and their women like queens,* Caroline often questioned herself.

As the months wore on, the heavy burden of leaving her children behind began to weigh on Caroline's heart. News was beginning to trickle in about a war between the Northerners and the Ibos. They bought a second-hand television from an electronics shop in the high street to keep in touch with the political developments in Nigeria, but they got more news from their network of Ibos.

Whenever Caroline recalled the complaints their friends made during their weekend visits regarding work, she added that it wasn't the same for her in her school job. However, the garage workplace was a different story altogether during her night shift cleaning the canteen.

"How much do we need to buy our own house Benjamin?" the subject often came up after they had paid the rent.

"Are you planning to stay in this country all your life Caroline?"

"Why must you always say the same thing Benjamin, why?" Caroline looks at him for more. "We can sell when we return home." She wants to beg him to buy a house so they can bring their children to England but knows that they would end up fighting. She wants to control her temper but can't help getting upset and angry because her husband will not say why he doesn't want to bring his family to England.

"*Biko*, my husband. We can also rent some of the rooms."

"Oh, now you want to be landlady?"

"I want our children here before the war breaks out. *Biko, biko*, Benjamin I'm begging you."

Caroline shares her concerns with her friend on the communal telephone on the first floor landing, she spots that the Yoruba tenant on the floor above is eavesdropping. Looking up at the man she covers the mouthpiece with her palm.

"Yes! Mind your own business!"

She sees him retreat back into his room before continuing with her conversation.

Marian did not look up when Caroline emerged from the headmaster's office. Caroline had told her earlier that morning about her plan to leave her job at the school for a better paid one at the factory. There she could work as many hours as she wanted in the meter factory which was only a short bus ride away in a neighbouring town called Mitcham. On her last day at the school, Ron and his staff lined up to say their goodbyes with wrapped up boxed gifts. Mr Ronald made a speech for her in the staffroom and Marian joked that he only liked being the head because he loved the sound of his own voice.

Caroline worked at her jobs and began to support her husband, who was able to return to education. She started to put more money aside towards a house and imagined a second house even before the first.

"You are illiterate. That is all you can do, sweep and push heavy barrels in a factory."

"My dear, I am happy that God has blessed me with strength."

"We are not staying here, so why waste money buying a house here? *Mek* us finish and return to where we belong. All people do here is work for nothing," said Benjamin, when the subject of owning their own house came up.

"Working is good. Not everyone can work with a pen. Only when you have sweated in hard labour can you know you have done good work. I am an African woman, an Ibo woman. I must work, I have children. Working is one of the things we must do." Caroline looked Benjamin in the eye, fed up with having to keep explaining why it was good for them to own their own home in London. The factory work was demanding but she was able to earn the same pay as the male workers who admired her for her work ethics. She even agreed to accompany them to the local pub on Friday nights after work for a pint of Guinness.

4

Nigeria, 1967
Mr Emanuel's Daughter

War did not come early to Obi's village. It probably began its destructive journey in a faraway land called England, and from a meeting chaired by men without children. One of the misconceptions about war is that most people think it begins when the first bomb is dropped. The fact is, only the few want war and those few would often not suffer the effects.

Seven-year-old Obi and his sisters Decima and Arike lived in their uncle's compound, in a village smaller than a grain of sand from space, and yet war headed towards it. He didn't know what war was and nor did he know there was a war going on in his country.

In the compound, Obi was worried because his aunties would be home soon and his sisters, Decima aged eleven and Arike ten, had not finished their chores around the compound. He didn't want them to get in trouble, especially because Lady Ani wasn't at home to look out for them. He'd linger around his sisters while they swept the grounds and washed up the various utensils left in front of the aunties' kitchens.

"*Biko*, Obi, put that down," they often told him when he'd pick up the broom to sweep for them. "You must try and read your English book," Decima would remind him before Obi started to complain that he wanted to read his book with them.

"Decima," Obi whispered unsure if they would hear him.

"Yes, what is it Obi?" Decima answered.

"Did you dream of our mother?" Obi enquired hoping that she had had one of her prophetic dreams.

Most mornings before school Obi ventured out on his favourite journey to the main roadside, in the hope of seeing a real-life monkey at work with its driver. The length of the journeys depended on the kinds of distractions he encountered. But often he stopped to look at the flat-pressed shirts with huge floral or cubed patterns at Mr Emanuel's tailor shop. He imagined owning one of them as his best church-going outfit. The clothes hung on buckled wire hangers on a slack clothes line across the front porch of his shop and home.

Mr Emanuel's daughter is a year older than Obi; she sweeps around the Udara tree in her compound before first light. Retreating a few steps back on spotting her, Obi watches the girl work. Her small hands barely managed to grip the bunched bundle of fine sticks of her broom head with which she created delicate patterns on the earth as she swept. Obi thought they looked like fine racing tracks made by ants, and concentrated to count them.

"Be careful near that road, Obi," Mr Emanuel's daughter mumbles, head down, still sweeping. Her name is Uzoamaka. *How does she know I am standing here? She has not even looked up,* Obi puzzled over it for a second and continued on his way.

His eyes drift to the next stall in front of him. The collection of dead insects behind the smudged glass of the bread cabinet had multiplied from the previous day. He spots a new poster of city people drinking stout in front of a car. Leant across the car is a slim woman in a white sleeveless dress, they seem to be smiling at Obi. He glances back at them, returning the smile, continuing his journey. *"How can the men's white trousers not be dirty?"* His thoughts a whisper.

After school, Obi's friends and cousins play games from which he is excluded; games such as 'go find your mother, go find your father'. Behind an old avocado tree next to his goat-pen, Obi stands but not invisible from anyone entering the compound. The tree is one of his favourite places from where he can also watch the various events in the village. Often he hides behind it to avoid being caught staring at the mothers and their children's joyful reunion. His feet shuffle under him, toes scoop at the dry earth around its base, making a trench. Pulling at the holes of his tattered T-shirt unaware of his own anxiety, he taps his forehead on the trunk again, and his hands become chalky from brushing against dried bird droppings. The compound around him is neat with similar swept lines from Decima's broom. Behind him by the well, Arike's hands are black with soot from the pot-bellied utensils she was washing.

"Obiora! It will soon be dark, come inside," Decima called from the doorway of their uncle's house. Her face no longer attracted pleasant comments; instead she carries a mother's burden long before her time. Decima used to like when strangers thought she and Arike were twins, they used to spend time combing and tying each other's hair and taking turns to read from their favourite books. Arike's slim build made her seem a lot taller than her older sister, but in fact it was only by two inches. Arike had always seemed more headstrong of the two; however, Decima was the more reticent and cautious. While Arike would look anybody straight in the eyes, Decima always made do with a quick glance, which was all she needed to gauge the energy of others.

They had become more distinguishable after Caroline left for England. Decima and her sister could no longer spend hours huddled in a corner reading the same pages. Obi had not seen them fight until Decima refused to cut Arike's hair and tried to hide the scissors from her. Decima's hair mostly stayed in braids unlike Arike's, who decided to get her hair cut by a friend in the village. Arike liked her new short boy style.

African marigolds, big as China teacups, dance in the compound and around Lady Ani's house. She is his favourite auntie. Her house is tucked inside the lush foliage of oranges, whites and yellows, within a garden that neither goat nor child entered. Darkened bumblebees the size of thumbs basked in the delicious scent of velvet blossoms.

It was that particular time of the day when everything changed for Obi. He watches his friends and cousins abandon play to join the other pot-bellied children racing naked towards the procession of colourful traders returning home. Mothers, who had toiled under the dry heat all day, came home to their children as the big orange sun started to set beyond Uboji village. Close by are the magnificent heights of the Milliken Hill. Picturesque it might be, but when the rain came down, 'big news' often followed – that vehicles had crashed and tumbled over the hillside. Not lately though, no recent disasters.

Obi peers from behind the tree, feet still shuffling uncontrollably beneath him. His fingers locked around the trunk, knuckles pale from the pressure of his grip. Pressing his body tighter against the tree, curling his arms around its girth, he watches the children hug and touch their mothers. The old avocado tree becomes his anchor; it stops him from joining the other children or begging for affection. His mind slips away to a place only he knows, desperately trying to piece together fragmented memories of his own mother. But she would never be among the traders returning home. After five years, he no longer remembers his mother and he didn't want to be smacked for crying for her.

Glued to his spot Obi remembers once when he ran with the other children, before his cousin Vasco stopped him; jeering "orphan boy, orphan boy! Why do you always run with us? It is not your *moda* coming home!" Vasco's eyes were angry, his lips pinched. Obi stood rigid to his spot upon the hot earth, he couldn't swallow enough saliva to ease the burning in his throat. He looked down at the ground, teeth clenched and toes curled into the hot earth that refused to swallow him up.

Anxious that the mothers might hear and scold him for stuttering, he made himself invisible behind the tree; lips involuntarily miming the songs the children were singing.

"*M-m mama anata oyoyo*, mother's home yeah, yeah, yeah."

Obi tried to take comfort in Lady Ani's words. She once told him that his stutter would stop when he saw his mother again. Before sunset the women traders made sure that unsold goods were bartered or exchanged in business, after which they started their journey home. Dexterously balanced upon their heads were yams, *gari* and cassava which they bought for their kitchen larders along with other delights for their children.

"What kind of sense is this? Trading with one hand, spending the money with the other," one of them exclaimed.

"Some for you and some for me my sister, all our children must eat." The banter would continue throughout their journey home.

The aunties walked slow and steadily, the miles of sweltering dry African heat left them drenched. Securely bound babies slept like they were not yet born, except their heads rocked with the motion of their mother's sway. Even when the women paused to re-tie their wrappers, or when a passer-by begged them to show what they had left to sell, they slept on. Often when one hummed a tune, a hymn or folk song, the others burst into a chorus. Rhythmically in single file the procession arrived back through the narrow pathways to their compounds. The women politely re-greeted the same neighbours who had bid them a safe journey when they left early that morning.

Ceremonial greetings were a big part of Ibo social etiquette and respect. Everyone observed them, unless of course during a falling out. Watching the women with their babes in wrappers, Obi wondered if he was ever cradled like that on his mother's back. His mind was blank, no experience recalled.

It was a hot humid evening; proud elders looked on at the women, calling from shaded verandas and under cool leafy trees praising them for their hard work. Old women chuckle and remembered their youthful days when they could carry the world above their heads.

"*Dayja mama dayja!* Welcome mama welcome!"

The children greet their mothers, hugging their clammy bodies. They clap and dance around their mother's legs, jumping up at the baskets of treats still too far to reach. The women lower the brimful of goods from their heads; inside are sweetbreads, condensed milk, 'Man power' popped corn, peanuts in glass bottles, yellow cashew fruit, mangoes and guavas. Obi watches the children rub their naked bellies and smack their lips with glee. He wiggles his tongue, trying to imagine the different tastes in his mouth. He licks his upper arm like he did the time he ate a succulent yellow cashew fruit and its juice ran down his arm, staining his top. But all he could taste was his own sun-baked, salty skin. A hunger pang reminds him that the small chunk of bread with condensed milk he'd eaten that morning was well and truly digested.

"Orphan boy," Vasco calls, appearing from the back of his mother's hut where he'd hidden to eat a whole mango by himself.

Vasco's chin and cheeks look like a baby that had fallen asleep in their food. His red top, drenched with fruit juice clinging to him like he'd been splashed with water. He held out his hand offering a mango from his mother's basket. Obi smiles and reaches out to accept the gift, but in his excitement he had forgotten his cousin's cruel ways. Too late, Vasco snatched the fruit back, smirking as he held the ripened mango under his chin and continued to tease and mock his cousin. Yet again, Obi had been caught out by Vasco and didn't know what to do except to look down at his curled up toes in the dirt, his ears hot. Pearls of sweat burst across his forehead, he grinds his teeth and his throat seared with pain, again.

"Obiora, run quick and fetch me my pot," shouted Lady Ani from her kitchen window. Startled and relieved by her familiar voice, he runs towards his auntie's veranda.

"The moon will shine in the darkest corners, my dear. Never mind them, they will be as foolish as their fathers," she said, in a voice that showed she did not care if others overheard.

Curled up like prodded millipedes, Obi looks at the pair of scabby compound dogs, awake with closed eyes. They raise their heads and snarl at the noisy children, who had earlier lamented under the Mother Tree about being abandoned.

> "Mama no there - o - o - mama, Papa no there - o - o
> - papa, sister no there - o - o - sister, brother no there -
> o - o - brother, Mama no there -o - o - mama, Papa no
> there - o - o - papa."

Obi stares at the emaciated dogs; they tremble from starvation while sniffing at the sand around the children eating their biscuits. Anticipated treats did not fall to the ground; the children caught every crumb in their cupped hands. Disappointed, the dogs circle one another and sniff the empty ground once more before they lay back down, still hungry.

Disgusted, he watches the pitiful dogs snapping at flies that buzz around their heads and crawl about their weeping eyes; aiming a stone, Obi remembers Lady Ani's words. *There is nothing to gain in wickedness* – not to mention his friends that use them as target practice, aiming at their tails. Obi throws his stone to the side instead of at the dogs.

"Obiora! Stop troubling those dogs before they trouble you," Lady Ani warns him from her kitchen window. Distracted, Obi remembers where he was supposed to be and sets off towards her door.

"They have no mother," he whispers before knocking at his aunt's door.

Within the compound, Obi knew his uncle was an important elder, an Ozo, the highest title an Ibo community could bestow upon an elder. His role as head of the family and village community meant that he would be the first port of call in matters of the village and its people. Other leaders never openly questioned his wisdom, not even the Christian elders. Known to be a thoughtful person, Ozo took time to deliberate before decisions were made; he considered how it would affect the person and the wider community. He was accepted as the wise one; once a resolution was made he stood by it, even if it meant he stood alone. He knew well that ten different people would want ten different outcomes to any one problem, so that it suited their own personal interests.

Obi and the rest of his peers didn't know the first names of Ozo's wives, not that it mattered, however, it saved them from being smacked. It was considered disrespectful for anyone junior, especially children, to address their elders by their names. In the case of mothers, they were called by the names of their children, but with a *Mama* in front followed by her child's name. All of Ozo's wives were of similar ages to him; he did not take any more new wives after his sixth. It seemed a miracle that all six were happy and contented with how and where they were placed within the household ranks. Women on the whole were dominant forces within the village; they were grafters who did not shirk their responsibility unlike their college counterparts.

Younger men of the village had just one wife, not that it made life any more manageable for them; they struggled to provide for their household with an honest day's work, and fought, often in public.

"Generations of our men who cannot even manage one woman; how are they to cope with two?" Chief Ikenji always commented within direct earshot of those that needed to hear. He often wandered about the place inspecting nothing in particular. Village life was transient, with people coming and going without being accounted for or anyone noticing.

"Before the savages arrived on our land, our men knew how to be men. They defended our territory and villages; they hunted and bore scars on their bodies to show their worth. Now they sit waiting for the ways of the 'white man' to be given work in their own land."

Obi was proud of his uncle and saw why the village respected him so much. To Obi's surprise his uncle even reprimanded adults if they shouted at Obi, even when his goat ate his way through their flower beds. A man of honour, Ozo cared for people, not just his family. He was broad-shouldered, fair and resolute in his conduct. Squabbling traders often found their way to his door to resolve their disputes. Ozo's presence seemed to have a peaceful effect within the village. On official matters Ozo used a ceremonial staff; poised and erect, he carried himself with confidence, head tilted ever so slightly to his left, like a cautious animal on the watch for predators. Obi liked seeing his uncle's favoured yellows, dark greens and red circled traditional attire; with his elegant white horsehair swatter he carried in one hand.

At times when Ozo didn't want to be burdened with carrying his drinking horn and sitting stool, he asked Obi to carry them for him. With bated breath Obi would wait on the veranda outside his uncle's room in the hope that he would be asked to assist. He didn't miss any chances of spending time with his uncle. The Ozo meetings where he watched the elders flick about the long swatters over their shoulders to shoo away mosquitoes and midges, while they sat around the bonfire. Obi wondered; *how come the insects are attracted, when they will be killed?* He had not seen such irritation amongst the elders; they argued with each other before the meeting started and he noticed that there had been several absentees over the past few weeks when he had assisted his uncle.

It wasn't difficult to see and understand why Ozo could not overlook his nephew, Obi's thirst for every kind of questioning for knowledge and keenness to learn was endearing. Obi often wondered if his uncle missed his eldest son who preferred to live outside the village. He felt ten feet tall whenever he was able to help or spend time with his uncle, even his fear of the dark evaporated when they walked back home from his late-night meetings.

Although Ozo had six wives, none of them ever accompanied him to the important meetings. They had other pressing matters to concern themselves with, such as planting crops, running the household, settling the financial takings of the day's trade, making sure their larders are full, and of course, advising new wives about how best to deal with their husband. The senior wives were wiser and appreciated a peaceful life, unlike the younger ones who squabbled unashamedly at any opportunity in and about the marketplaces.

Obi could ask for nothing better; how peaceful life was when they played all day until it was time for him to wander to the road's edge before the happy chanting began. Happiness for Obi included when he was left alone to spread his wings and be at one in the wilderness. He could talk to the trees, animals and himself without the fear of being told off, enjoying conversations he felt too shy to have with others until someone unwittingly takes a shortcut through the forest and overhears.

"*Biko osisi.* Please tree, is it okay? I come up, I climb you," Obi would ask before starting his climb.

"Have you ever known a tree to talk, my dear boy?" A woman looks up from the ground below, squinting to avoid the sunrays inbetween the branches of the tree where Obi rested. The village women knew him well and teased him for being the only child to ask a tree's permission before he climbed it.

"You will fall and break a leg if you sleep in those trees, just like that monkey that fell last week."

"Do you think a fall from the tree to the ground will be any softer for your head?"

The women's laughter drifted up like a cacophony of crows from below.

"Then you will not only have one bump on your forehead, you will own two!"

"My dear, it is no laughing matter that boy's love for the trees and the animals. One day he will turn into one of them."

"Then he would become one of the fireside stories at night-time."

"Look at him; he does not know anybody is here."

Obi pretends to be asleep; his forearms as pillow, his legs dangle either side of a narrow branch. It made him feel like a panther he had seen in the pages of a book. He knew his trees well, for instance some were better for sleeping and others were more suited as watchtowers. When his friends stopped by to call for him at his compound, and didn't find him, they would head out into the woods to search for him. But Obi heard them long before they arrived.

The tendon-like branches provided perfect lodgings for his slim body: he stretched his arms to squeeze tightly into the groove and his head turned away so they could not see the shine of his eyes. At one with the tree, he was near invisible from the ground. He could remain incognito all day and his friends would be none the wiser, although he could see them from the corner of his eye. Obi was always on the alert and spotted them first, they did not have the same kind of deft animal instincts that he had acquired. Their footsteps were noisy and voices loud, similar to a pack of ranting schoolchildren.

The story of the bump on his forehead came about when he fell asleep on the veranda wall. It was one of those hot, still afternoons. The entire village silent, people and animals retreated into their corners other than the crickets who continued their chatter. Ozo had returned early from checking his traps in the woods.

"The ground is like hot pepper in open wound," he said.

Obi had not heard his uncle complain about the sun before, therefore it must have been bad. The melting point of the midday heat was getting to Obi too; he resisted falling off to sleep during the day in case it meant laying awake alone all night in the dark, which sent shudders through his body. He thought that his uncle was in his room, polishing his rifle, so he tried to stay awake for when he was called to hang out the small polishing cloth. After quite some time, Obi was fed up of waiting so he decided to check in on his uncle; he pushed the door open to find him flat on his back fast asleep, on the bed. Obi pulled the door to a gentle close and went back to where he had been perched. He hopped onto the wall and surrendered under the veranda roof and the midday sun. Sleep was sweet, maybe even a bit like after palm wine. Comforted by the heat and lulled into a false sense of security, he rolled over, forgetting he wasn't in his bed, splat, on his forehead against the concrete floor. For a time, everyone who saw him laughed at the bump on his head.

"Now, dear boy, try sleep only in your bed."

"You have been named well, my dear: Obiora, the heart of everybody," the mothers laughed.

"Obiora, see how happy you make us old people. When I next meet your *moda*, I will shake her hand," an old man laughed leaving the compound.

Obi ran after the man, catching up with him before he disappeared out of the compound.

"*Biko*, uncle, have you news from overseas?" he begs.

The man could not stop laughing at him.

"*Biko, uncle*," Obi follows the man until he hears Lady Ani's call for him to come back. He could no longer remember what it was like to have a mother of his own, nor the concept of a complete family. The elders of the compound and the village were his surrogate parents and he had accepted that without question. Obi knew he had two other sisters who he had never seen because they were born in England, and of course the sad time when another sister and brother were taken away by their Uncle Harry when he came in his Volkswagen. Obi often overheard conversations of his parents, although he had no memory of them. He was happy when he finally decided he no longer had to fight the children who teased him that he had forgotten his own mother. Obi had also developed a habit, where he used to randomly stare and wave at mothers and their children, but that soon came to a stop when Lady Ani asked him, "Why?"

Obi knew that he and his sisters were not orphans. He had heard many stories about his parents, who were far away in a country called, 'London'. He couldn't remember what they looked like, but knew their names are Caroline and Benjamin, and that his father was a bank manager, although he still wasn't sure what a bank was. It became an ongoing mission for Obi, whenever the chance happened, to find out about the lost memories of his absent parents.

The orange sun fell into a faraway horizon after another exhausting day of baking all who dared to be out. Obi jumps from Lady Ani's veranda with a mango in hand. He runs to find his sisters to share the fruit. Decima and Arike had finished washing and oiling themselves after the chores around the compound. As children, no one would disagree that they should not work to help the mothers out.

They plucked chicken, pounded yam, peeled and washed vegetables, and finally watered the vegetable patches with water that was saved after they scrubbed clean the blackened pots, pans and dishes. Obi was always fast on his feet, ready to escape having to take his bath, so when he tried to make a dash out of the door his sisters held his arm and gave him the soap and his towel.

"Sister, can I go to the roadside with Goliath? I will wash when I return."

"Come back before dark," Decima replied in a quiet voice but Arike shook her head while braiding her sister's hair. Head down, Decima's lining up threads on her lap; she tries to catch sight of her brother without disturbing her sister's flow. Obi likes her round face smiling at him, as he admires her long, oiled hair, loosely tied in black thread.

"It looks like the pig's tail," Obi comments before turning and running off.

Obi often remembers how his pet goat Goliath came to be in his life. But that story should not really be told without first mentioning a bit about Mama Toni. Her slight build did not stop others calling on her if they needed help to move or lift things around their home or compound. With strength to rival all but the strongest men in the village, her face was pleasant without drawing charcoal on her eyebrows. She rose before the morning cockerel crowed, after her bath she set out to collect firewood from the forest. On her return, she cooked and packed her wares inside her large metal bowl, ready for the market. Reliable in whatever was required of her, she even cleaned out the toilet enclosure when it was full without being told to do so by Ozo. She preferred her own company which was probably why she always left early with her food basket to catch the hungry overnight truck drivers before they arrived in town. She didn't like it when women asked her to predict their future. It was rumoured that the origin of her gift of sight came from a distant line of warriors who could kill just by looking and cursing death on their enemy. Her younger brother is a wealthy rain-stopper in another village. When she first arrived in the compound, the gossip was that her father came from a pygmy tribe.

It had been a time of excitement in the compound for the children. Encircling Mama Toni while she supervised the birth of Goliath, the goat; the children gasp and look away. Obi had not expected for the moment of birth to be the moment of death. The midwife picked up a rock, intending to club the stunted newborn to death. It is cursed by the devil, she said, and was having no such trick played on her. Greeted with a rock to the head from the midwife, Goliath tried to stumble away on his knees, sending Mama Toni running for her life and screaming that the stunted newborn was cursed.

The children, having listened to Mama Toni's abhorrence, spat, kicking sand and twigs at baby Goliath, who was trying to crawl away. Obi watched from behind the crowd as the kid's efforts to escape weakened almost to a surrender. He didn't dare cross Vasco who led the onslaught. Vasco was older and Obi would not stand a chance of winning any kind of fight against him. It would not be much of a fight because Obi was known for running away from confrontations. But when they picked up stones and started to strike, Obi rushed from behind the crowd to grab the deformed and motionless kid. The smell of blood on sand was unpleasant. Obi ran, with the slippery creature clutched in his arms. Repulsed by the bloody bundle, the children parted and gave way, as Obi ran through them. It felt like the story of the Red Sea when the waters parted, but not without spitting and throwing more stones at them.

He pleaded with his uncle to keep the animal, even though the villagers regarded it a bad omen.

"Keep the animal if it survives, Obi. Do not let it go into any of your aunties' kitchens," Ozo agreed. "You must find wood and branches to make it home. I will assist you."

"Thank you my uncle. I will look after Goliath."

"Goliath. You are calling it a giant name?" Ozo's laughter followed him out of his compound. Two years since Goliath's birth and no curse had befallen the compound.

Like a favourite food, he likes the sound of the name and how it vibrates in his throat when sounded slowly. "Go-li-ath. Come – let us go!" Obi commands his stubby-legged, brown and white goat from its pen. He had barely lifted the tatty bamboo gate when Goliath pushes past him, sending him on to his bottom. "Wait!" Obi props the gate back closed before running after Goliath. The goat obviously has plans of his own, charging towards his auntie's vegetable patch. "No!" Obi lunges forward, pulling the animal's head back until it retreats, but not without a mouthful of long onion leaves.

"My n-name is Obiora." He said aloud to himself walking along the path with his goat. "Many p-people call me Obi. I do not mind that. I like my name, even when it has been sh-shortened. When the elders tell me off, they always use all of my name." Distracted by birds in the tall trees, he loses balance looking up and falls to the ground. Picking himself up as fast as he fell, he checks to see if anyone saw him. Obi continues his journey to the roadside with somersaults and long jumps. "I think we will see the truck monkey today, Goliath."

Startled by an unexpected voice he doesn't know or recognise from the bushes, he is alert.

"Practising English for your *moda*, Obi?" the voice interrupts him. "You will make friends after your *moda* return, and take you and your sisters back to England."

It was morning when the woods are busy with people doing their morning ablutions. "Thanks, Sir," he acknowledges, quickening his pace. "Why do people talk when they do toilet? The smell gets in the mouth." Breaking into a run, the stench follows with the tail breeze behind him. Goliath remains at the same spot, head butting the hedge for no particular reason. Only when Obi was far from the smell does he stop to take a breath before he calls his goat, and Goliath takes his time, nibbling as he goes.

Village life means living close to nature. Obi knows the variety of sights and smells integral to his community. His stomach knots every time, ready to puke at the smell of excrement during his morning adventures. By noon the smell was less intense after the dogs had polished them off. Obi went to great lengths to avoid walking past houses with newborn babies in case a mother calls him over to dispose of a bundle of pooh in the bushes.

He continues with his walk, practising English and keeping an eye on Goliath and entertaining himself, firing incessant volleys of stones into the air from his catapult. The clanging noise of the stones hitting the tin rooftops of the big houses did not deter him. Not until an irate voice from the direction of the house approaches him.

"Idiot! *Mek*, Make I beat you well *o*. Obiora! Go trouble your uncle's roof."

Obi stuffs his catapult into his pocket. He could hear the voice but could not see anyone. The sound of rapid chopping and parting of tall grass accompanies the exasperated voice drawing closer by the second, making Obi looks around for a tree to make a quick getaway. But there were none, not with low hanging branches within easy reach. Being a quick thinker, Obi pushes Goliath forward, away from himself. The goat runs on ahead. Obi holds his breath, tiptoeing out of sight behind one of the larger trees. He watches the man walk past him in Goliath's direction, waving his stick.

"Obiora stay there! Do not move until I have reached you! I already have a good stick to cane you." Obi can see the man hunched over his stick, out of breath. If only he knew he was following a goat. Obi giggles cupping his mouth with both hands, trying not to give his position away.

Heading back, Obi leads the way with Goliath leaving scattered hoof prints along the red earth behind them.

Turning to Goliath to hurry him up Obi picks up pace. They take the short cut into the heart of the village. Instantly Obi is in the midst of it all, the familiar smells of boiling yams and tomato stew stops him in his tracks, he wonders which of his aunties' kitchens the delicious food is in. He watches younger children playing different games; some run about in circles and jump in the sand. In his head he counts in the start of a clacking stick game in English. As fast as they can, the children count to five: *Otu, abuo, ato, ano, ise*; before the laughter and screams of joy spill out. Obi is drawn to a corner where boys are swapping various pets: grasshoppers, birds and lizards, midriffs tied with strings. The animals are barely able to move due to shock, exhaustion and hunger from being held captive; more so, there was little chance of survival, once caught by the children.

"Sing!" a child shouts, tapping a frightened canary on its head, unable to understand why it will not sing or eat from his hand. On seeing the string tethered to the scrawny leg that had stripped the skin raw, Obi said in a dazed whisper, "It is afraid." He rustles around his pocket for something to offer in exchange for the ailing bird with limp wings sprawled on the ground.

On his way home Obi passes another group of boys, he heard them plotting and scheming how they could sneak into a mother's kitchen to steal dry fish and smoked beef to snack on during their adventures. Not wanting to attract their attention, he surreptitiously hides the canary under his top. He didn't mind that he'd swapped his catapult; he will make a new one.

On entering his compound Obi is more at ease, he sees that the scabby dogs had not moved from the same spot. He rushes towards the house and into his sisters' room, and Goliath voluntarily enters his pen.

He wants to make his bird a nest under the bed before the sun sets. It's an exciting time when the fathers come home, and hunters return with honeycomb wrapped in banana leaf and the day's catch of otter, bush rats, pigeon, on their shoulders, as children watch the limp swaying heads. Men cleared new pathways through the undergrowth with their machetes. Each man held his tool with pride: razor sharp blades and handles that have moulded with wear to fit their grip after years of work on the land. Their machetes serve many purposes: gliding effortlessly through ferns and shrubs, raking the ground, cutting grass, and trees, splitting timber for firewood. Obi would, on occasions, watch the men return if he wasn't at the roadside, however, he had more important matter to deal with; his canary's life was in his care, so he goes to look for nesting.

Usually Obi would be the first to hear his uncle's whistling on his approach to the compound. However, observing the remaining white clouds dotted under an immaculate blue sky, he became conflicted between running to be the first to greet his uncle or watching the racing clouds. Cheering when his chosen cloud drifted ahead of the others, Obi runs to Ozo who pats his head.

"Welcome uncle!"

Ozo was seldom seen leaving the compound with his spear, departing even before Mama Toni. Obi was too scared to stay up all night, just to see Ozo leave the house so early.

"You have the rest of your life to get up before dawn," his uncle once told him patting his knotted hair on his return from checking his traps. Obi remembered the variety of catches he would bring: wild birds, otter, freshwater fish, and the all essential firewood. Obi gauges his uncle's load before offering his help; he hadn't forgotten the time he tried to help; dragging, pulling and pushing the large spiky collection of firewood his uncle had thrown onto the ground from his head. Never mind how much effort was put in, he just could not budge it, the jagged ends lodged themselves into the ground. Eventually, he abandoned the firewood and asked his uncle for his help.

Obi wished that his uncle would one day bring back a live animal for him to keep as a pet instead of food, especially a monkey or a talking parrot.

Among the dead creatures his uncle brought home, none was as exciting as the snake.

The biggest snake Obi and his friends had ever seen. Its skin shone and flickered like shattered mirror glass which caught the sun's reflection through the leaves of the trees. The once awesome creature was transformed, limp and lifeless. When Ozo arrived with the dead snake draped around his neck, children gathered from around the village into the compound.

"Only in my compound does the whole village know what my evening meal will be," Ozo said to one of his wives as she collected the paraphernalia to clean the beast.

"They have not seen a snake like this before," she replied.

"Even in death the limp beast still commands fear among the children," he said undraping it from around his shoulders.

The excited children gather to watch Mama Toni preparing to clean the long snake. She chops its head from the body, smells the blood before tossing it into her aluminium bowl. The crowd sit hushed on the ground under the sun and anyone would be forgiven for thinking it was Lady Ani's hair day.

Like attentive school children they watched the snake being dissected. From the top, where the snake's head had been severed, Mama Toni inserted the tip of her knife into the throat and held up the snake with her left arm. She glided the tip of her narrow blade from the snake's throat down towards its tail, slicing the soft underbelly in one swift motion. When the knife glides out from the tail with a final tug; those closest to her swerve to avoid the limp, blood sodden flesh swinging at them. Extending her arms, Mama Toni rips apart the entrails, tearing at the flesh like a tailor ripping cloth, separating the dead beast from its internal organs.

She throws the entrails to the scrawny dogs who fight one another, biting at the jumble of stringy innards. The children were shocked at the level of noise that came from the warring dogs, each wanting the bigger piece, almost devouring each other's noses in their haste.

The boys didn't mind not having the snake entrails to roast and eat, like they normally would with chickens, instead they watched the dogs who continued to fight and snap at each other, even when there was nothing left to fight over, until eventually they were shooed away with a bowl of dirty dishwater. The excitement had come to an end as Mama Toni washed and chopped the meat into small chunks for cooking the evening meal.

"You can all return to your *moda*, no more thing to see," Mama Toni said looking up and turning from the crowd. She mumbled under her breath; "I have my own mouths to feed." She heads off to her kitchen.

Toni nudges Obi to look at the raw, red tail end of the chopped snake.

"It looks like the male dog's part," he said under his breath, being careful not to be overheard, especially by his mother.

When the meal was ready, Obi and his cousins sat themselves down, ready to eat after washing their hands. Closer to the food bowls, Toni, Obi, Suzanna, Chidi, and Sam are ready to tuck into the delicious-smelling food. They were already drooling, their small hands hovered over their food as grace was said, blessing it with thanks. After the quick and collective "amen", they begin eating. Swift hands move from soup bowl to mouth, heads occasionally turning and tilting away from the circle, tiny pin-like bones are spat to the ground. Between each mouthful, they licked each slippery finger clean of soup, so that when they next helped themselves to the *fufu* they did so with clean fingers. Eating from a communal plate was a fine art they had to master early, nobody liked to share food with a messy eater.

The children's attention did not drift from their enjoyment of the feast. Other than the sound of sucked fingers, the children eat in silence. Taking great care in separating the *fufu* and soup inside their mouths before swallowing, mindful of the needle like bones. Obi watched his cousins, completely fascinated by the speed and accuracy with which they ate. Not being a fast eater meant that he would usually be hungry again before bedtime.

"Obi, do not forget you are also trying to eat," an adult would remind him.

"That is why you are too thin, and people think you are a girl from behind!" Lady Ani would tease him.

The story of when Obi and Toni spoiled their uncle's *fufu* soup still haunts them.

What happened was that they had all eaten their meal and were full. They never understood why Mama Toni's cooking tasted so good. Delicious, even though she smelled like pencil-sharpening and mothballs. They loved her cooking and returned to sneak some more from her pot. There was no refrigeration anywhere within the village so the fish and meats were smoked and dried for storage. Mama Toni was not in her kitchen but had left the pot of meat soup on the floor. It was covered with a plastic plate loaded with her husband's freshly-pounded *fufu*, and covered with a cast-iron domed lid for warmth. After they crept into her kitchen, the boys lifted the plate of *fufu* and dipped their hands into the chicken soup. When Mama Toni returned to serve her husband's food, it had gone off.

"My soup has spoiled! My soup has spoiled!" she cried, before shouting for Obi and her son. "You boys have killed your uncle's food. Did I not feed you enough? You go put your dirty hands into my pot. Come now, I know you hear me. You cannot remain outside all night. When you return I will beat you well." All the wives came out to console her and cuss the thieves.

"Ha! Bad children, do you think you can run and hide from your punishment? I beg you think again," Lady Ani said. She was looking down on the wanted boys. "They are hiding inside the bush closest to the house. Mama, come! Those naughty children are here, I have them. I am looking at them and they are looking back at me like two trapped otters. Shall I beat them for you or do you want to beat them first?" she called at the top of her voice.

"*Biko,* my sister beat them for me. Beat them well well. I am too angry. I may not stop if I start. I am again cooking a new *egusi* soup with mushrooms and bush meat for their uncle's meal," replied Mama Toni, knowing that this was the boy's favourite soup.

"When they return for this soup, I will trap them," she tells herself, banging her wooden spoon against the rim of her pot.

Obi could not divert his attention from what seemed imminent. Lady Ani's punishment was different from the smacks and whipping of others: she did not beat the children; instead she made them sit and look at pictureless pages from her collection of books. The boys preferred to look at the pretty magazine covers of white women in elegant flowing dresses accompanied by white men standing beside them with upturned faces; they knew they had better learn a good reason to appeal to Lady Ani with.

"I see that you have already selected your beating sticks. I will not dirty my hands or spoil my newly painted nails on your bottoms. You will make two trips to read to me tomorrow instead. I know that you have no school, so I will expect you at my *kitchen* door first thing in the morning. Do you understand? Outside, not inside the *kitchen*," emphasising kitchen, to shame them even more. "Chicken stealers! Now go. Go wash."

"Yes Ma." Obi and Toni answered like twins.

"Off you go," she sent them running.

Ashamed of what they had done, the boys sat under a tree, out of sight. They were too afraid to face Mama Toni to say sorry. Instead, they rehearsed what they had learnt from school that day in the hope that it would impress Lady Ani so she would not make them read from the books with no pictures, which would be far too difficult.

5

Innocence

During midday, when the sun cooked everything in sight, people rested under the shade of trees and open veranda roofs. Women elders in their wisdom used the time to clean and separate grit from rice, ready for the evening meal. On large trays they sloshed, teasing out grit and finer husks, blowing them away with powerful breaths. Children stopped their play to watch the skilful elders with awe, gasping when they threw the contents into the air, catching every grain back on the tray like iron filings to a magnet.

The relentless sun had crystallised the moisture on Obi's face into dusty grey salt trails. His sisters were not about to tell him to wash his face, and Lady Ani was asleep in the chair on her veranda with a book upon her lap. In their room, Obi is immersed fixing a new piece of rubber to his catapult as he thinks of his day at school. From the bedroom he listens to his quiet compound but his keen ears can hear the goings on in his neighbour's house. In Lovlin's mother's home something was happening. She was an obsessive and intense woman, and the children revelled in her antics. That day she was in a hysterical state, she chased her neighbour's goat around her house and finally out of her kitchen, for what seemed like the hundredth time. It maddened her to see the large clusters of droppings that resembled a string of black beaded necklace strewed across her kitchen floor. As the careless goat sauntered out she saw the bunch of dried bitter leaves hang from its mouth, the same ingredient she had intended for the evening's *fufu* soup.

"Foolish goat, it no longer feels my heavy pot upon its dirty backside," she cursed the animal as it continued to stroll out of her kitchen unfazed, to resume its tour of the neighbourhood. Lovlin's mother kicked the bottom of her foot into the sand outside her kitchen in an attempt to remove the sticky, moist pellets.

"That idiot of an animal! One day it will understand the meaning of the saying – you will eat and I will eat. That is when your meat will be equally divided. Eating from my kitchen and leaving me your droppings to walk on." She sweeps frantically, fully aware that the goat did not care for her words or feelings.

"*Ijekwerri oyi?* Did you go well?" she enquired of her neighbour who returned from the market; her legs astride, loosening her wrapper from around her waist to re-tie it while prolonging her rant. Obi listens smiling at what was going on outside.

"Those smelly animals think they own this place. One day when it is in my pot, we will know who is in charge. Christmas is soon coming and your belly is getting bigger for our feast, for Jesus." She continued with her obscenities, even after the goat had long gone. "You are no good for babies; all you can do is feed dirty flies from your dry nipples! Next time, I will not be waiting until Christmas; you will feed my children for a month if I find you again in my kitchen." She securely bolts her kitchen door and storms off towards the market to buy more bitter leaves.

*

Ever since his parents left, Obi's memories of them had all but vanished from his young mind, but he has not forgotten the times when he, his brother and all his three sisters lived together. They were better times, when he felt more part of a family, until the day their Uncle Harry arrived in his Volkswagen and took his younger brother and sister to live far away with Auntie Josephine.

Saddened and shocked, he cried, not knowing why they had to go away since nobody gave him an explanation. People gathered around the compound to watch, as they usually did whenever anything out of the ordinary happened in the village. Obi did not chase after the car with the other children waving their arms; he stood between Decima and Arike and watched the dome-shaped car meander away until it disappeared.

He had many cousins that lived in the nearby villages and town, and some much further away. Most he'd never met, but he could remember all their names: Cosmos, JD, Vasco, Peter, John, Nana, Julie, Prayer, Chinwa, Benjamin, Maximillan, Chizoba, Ikechukwu, Chiwa, Ibe, Mimi, Suzanna, Thank God Jesus, Nice Baby and Margaret. Occasionally when his cousins from town came to visit, they moaned and complained about everything. They fussed that nothing exciting ever happened in the village, and that life there was too difficult. They were snooty and refused to play with their village cousins, until of course they got a scolding from their parents, who merely pretended to mind when they bossed their cousins. There is no running water, they whinged. You people have to walk a long way to fetch water, you go to toilet in the bushes, they complained. The girls grumbled about the insect bites and scratches, and that they loathed it when the village children touched their dresses 'with dirty village hands'. We have servants who do our duties for us, and we can call them at any time from their servants' quarters when we do toilet on newspaper in our room at night. They come carry it away.

6

Dragonflies and Matchsticks

I t is Friday afternoon when most of the village *adas* returned from school. Obi thought it best to have warned his cousin, Mimi, that it is Lady Ani's hair-fashioning day.

He's seen more of Lady Ani's hair-braiding days than any other child in his village; he'd carried his auntie's chair to the shade of her tree far too many times.

"Obiora! Bring me my chair!" she shouted through the cool afternoon breeze. She knew he could be trusted to do a good job.

"I will call the children to sit and listen to the stories, I will also listen," Obi suggested before he ran off to find his friends and tell them that it was his auntie's hair-plaiting day. His friends laughed and made fun of him for being her 'baby.'

"My stories of events from the past, when I was a young lady, much younger than I am now, are important, and they are a part of our history." She points and wags a long slender finger at him. Obi drew lines in the ground with his toes, often something he did when he was told off, put on the spot or felt shy.

"Will you have new stories, Auntie?" he asked.

The children had heard her stories countless times, but still gathered to listen to how she used to reach the mangos on the tree without having to stand on top of a wooden box, unlike the men, or how she would outrun any young man of her village into town. Known to be an athletic woman with sharp wit and humour, she laughed and teased the men when she overtook them at the one-mile mark, especially when they had a head start.

"Strong men but only in looks and without stamina," she'd say. "They are too foolish to take the time to do things well. Always rushing, and never arriving anywhere." Often, Lady Ani continued her conversations alone in her kitchen, even after the person she was talking to had left. Everything about Lady Ani was elongated: her smile stretched across her long face, and her narrow nose was unlike the short, broad noses of most in the village. Her green eyes with long black eyebrows that stretched across her forehead to her temples set off her pale smooth skin, which gave her importance and higher status within the village. She was a trendsetter. Her immaculate hair was always the talk of the village and copied by the young women; they admired her elegance and called her *oyibo*.

Whenever she sent Obi to fetch something from her room, he liked to linger, charmed by the multi-coloured array of cosmetics on her dressing table, sparkling and free of dust. The shiny burgundy-coloured lipstick capsules stood like little soldiers on parade; the collection of small colourful bottles of emerald green, amber and reds called out to him. He loitered around the table a while before picking up the emerald green container; Obi held it to the light and watched the rays dance when he rotated it around his hand. It reminded him of dew-laden leaves catching sunlight in the wind.

The lotions, with their foil lids and screw-on covers, oval powder compacts stacked on top of one another looked fascinating, but he hastened not to send them tumbling with his touch, reluctantly he stayed away from them. Memories returned of the time when he could not get the smell of rose musk out of his hands and everyone in the village knew what he'd been up to. Obi liked the feel of the memorial cloth of independence draped over Lady Ani's mahogany table. At the end of his bedroom tour he perched on a stool having found a double-faced oval mirror on the dressing table; he spun it round like a globe, watching his reflection: big face, small face, big face, small face. Photographs of Lady Ani in long Western dresses, leaning against different cars were lined up in a neat curve. He looked at her poses, and it reminded him of the ones from the *oyibo* magazines from England. He saw a strand of long hair on the end of his T-shirt, it reminded him that he must get back. "Nowadays she wears only wrappers and white blouses," Obi whispered to himself in Ibo.

Most women with long hair wore it with pride, but kept it covered under colourful head scarves as they went about their work. Trading under trees and gathering firewood, they were prone to bats' and bird droppings. Townswomen worried about dusty, fume-filled roads that polluted their hair, which even Lux soap could not wash off.

"Go call those idle children," Lady Ani said to Obi. "Tell them they must come sit and take English tuition." Lady Ani shifts around on her chair for a more comfortable position. "My dear, what can I do?" she exhaled a long breath and tuts, shaking her head. "They are ignorant, like their parents."

At the end of every week, when Lady Ani's hair parlour spilled out into her courtyard, the entire village came to know of the activities. The clever *adas* made themselves scarce, disappearing into their homes with heavy text books tucked under their arms. Knowing how much the community values education, they felt assured that they would not be disturbed from 'reading their books'. Obi felt sorry for the four *adas* who often became victims to hair duty as they were the ones who couldn't read.

Culturally, it was forbidden to say no or refuse the requests of an elder, so the unfortunate *adas* took turns to braid Lady

Ani's hair with yarns of black thread from Ogbete market. The younger girls sat themselves on the ground by her feet to watch her hair being oiled. The older ones carried their siblings on their hips with legs dangling, almost touching the ground. They settle in front of Lady Ani's veranda from where they will witness the four-hour ordeal.

"Anti. My *moda* say I too small to plait anybody hair," whispers a frightened four-year-old from where she was sitting on the ground with the others.

"If your mother does not allow you to touch her own hair, you are already a fool at four years of age to think that you can touch my head."

The child did not understand and turned to look at Obi.

"Why are you looking at Obi? It is you I am addressing."

The little girl continued to look at Obi, until he acknowledged her with a smile. The sweet scent of Lady Ani's hair pomade drifts past their noses diverting their attention. Lady Ani encourages more questions from the girls with a beckoning hand. Although she liked having her hair done, she detested it at the same time.

"Make sure you girls have cleaned your hands well before you touch this hair."

"Yes ma," the *adas* reply in melancholy voices.

"Yes ma, no ma. Please make sure you do this hair well today!" Lady Ani commands.

"Anti, can I have the tin when it finish?" a bemused child asked, nudged by the girl next to her.

"*May* I. Not *can* I, and finishes! Come now, learn how to speak; every day you girls trouble me with your inattentive selves. I have to sit here the whole day, absolutely still." She kisses her teeth and crosses herself, looking to Obi for sympathy.

"Anti, Obi touch the belongings on your table," a boy piped up.

"My dear, what can I do? Very little, other than shift my bottom around on this hard chair," was Lady Ani's response as she unwinds black thread from its coil.

"Any woman who has hair as long as mine will know exactly what it is like to maintain. Beauty comes with its own price you know."

Although she pretended not to, Lady Ani liked it when the children came to listen to her talk in English. They learned to put up their hands if they had a question; plump little palms with straightened fingers point towards the sky when she invited questions about her past life in the city. The *adas* knew most of her stories well, looking at one another in silence, daring each other to speak unnoticed above her head.

"Do it have lice?" the same child enquires, with Obi fidgeting in the background.

"*Does* it have lice? Not a poor question, considering that most of you children are made to wear skin-short hair, shaved with a naked razor blade. When you stop thinking that you are like the dirty boys, and respect that you are a female, only then will you have long hair and Cutex-painted fingernails similar to this. It does not have lice, unlike your *moda's* hair!" She flashed her painted nails towards the open-mouthed audience, staring at the four-year-old. "Look at your bald heads. You have more cuts and scabs than those dogs." The children turn in unison to look at the dogs, as did Obi.

"What of the tin?" Lady Ani interrupted herself and asked the little four-year-old who had requested it.

"I want put vaseline," the girl said in a whisper, looking away from her.

"I want *to* put vaseline *in it*," Lady Ani corrected the child. She did not stop at that, she scolds the children some more. Most would think she was talking to a new village wife. Lady Ani told the girls that she saw them, locking heads and fighting with the dirty boys with head lice. She glanced over to see if Obi was still there and winked at him. Obi blushed with embarrassment when the older girls turned and stared at him. He looked down and pushed the sand around with his feet and moved closer to where Lady Ani was seated.

"Your hair is good, Auntie. It is very long, the longest in the whole village," said Obi almost in a whisper continuing to look into the ground.

Lady Ani smiles, pushing him away from her side. "Go, rascal boy, even at your age you can put a smile upon a woman's face." She grins and straightens the line of threads on her lap.

"If the boy know how to fight, nobody will trouble him," Mama Toni commented from her kitchen from where she overhears the conversation as Obi set off out of the compound.

"Idiots know only one way to fight. Obi will know many," Lady Ani replies.

Turning back to the children Lady Ani engages them, "How many of you have seen a woman rolling on the ground, wrestling with men?" Lady Ani asked, uncoiling and laying long strands of black waxed threads on her lap after she had knotted the ends to stop them from slipping when the girls use it to wind around her hair.

"After a woman has taken her morning bath, she should keep herself clean. What should she do?"

"Keep herself clean," the sombre audience responded.

"That is correct." She points a finger to the ground. "Move!" Before the children could get out of the way, she jets a line of saliva from the diastema of her front teeth, which was regarded as a sign of beauty by the Ibos. The spray of wet spittle fans out like a serpent's venom on the parched ground beside her feet; absorbed into the hot thirsty earth leaving tiny beads of saliva in its place. The children lean back, aghast, watching as it disappears like the first droplets of summer rain. The *adas* looked at each other and quickened their pace, their gaze fixed steadfast upon Lady Ani's hair. After all, it was only a matter of time before her sharp tongue would turn on them.

"And you girls should not be angry when you are working," she said. The *adas* hasten in silence, eager to finish, but the braids were long and numerous. As the day wore on, most of the children had fallen sleep against each other like dominos.

The hair salon attracted the attention of passers-by. Men in particular nodded and bowed their heads; they lifted the flat of their machetes to their forehead as a mark of respect to Lady Ani. The *adas* worked, exchanging swift glances and miming words to each other in secret, away from Lady Ani. The long, exhaustive, boring hours eventually made them indifferent to Lady Ani's sharp tongue, and they cared less of what she thought. They dared to give each other that look of disdain, regarding Lady Ani; the type a woman did not like to receive. The burning question being: could any of those men once have been Lady Ani's secret lover? Their shoulders juddered with giggles as their fingers move like fast knitting needles in and out of her hair. They hasten to finish their chore. Lady Ani grins and straightens the line of threads on her lap.

"Anybody who gossips to you about others will gossip to others about you," she said to the *adas*.

The teenagers looked down, ashamed; they continued to work in silence because she could hear their every whisper.

The sound and smell of frying onions and hot chillies wafts over the compound.

"*Biko*, finish and return to your homes before dark, the young men of this village will soon be on the prowl," Lady Ani warns.

"Yes Anti. Thanks, Ma,"

"We soon finish Anti." The *adas* replied in English.

"Ha, now you have English. Tomorrow I go tell your father to find money for university." Lady Ani jokes with them.

The *adas* work in harmony, styling the hair into what resembled a mangrove.

Obi sees his cousin Peter making his way towards the compound and runs to meet him and find out what he has missed while he'd been busy with girls' matters. They crash into each other, and grapple in a pretend fight.

"Lady Ani, she praise you to my *moda* when she visit her stall for *gari*. She say you is good boy," Peter teases, nudging and bumping him as they walk. Obi nudges him back before they run to play under the Mother Tree. Once there, Obi quizzes his cousin to tell him more.

"She say your *moda* will proud you when she see you," said Peter and Obi's ears prick up.

"H-ha-have you any news of my mother and father? Wh-when will I see them?" Obi pesters Peter for more. Unable to contain himself, he runs back to Lady Ani breathless with excitement he manages a word. "Aunty."

"Rascal boy, you return for more. Ha! What kind of man will you be?"

Obi forgot about his shyness of the others and asked Lady Ani. "Aunty, did you get news of?"

"My dear, you and your sisters will be the first people I will give any news of your parents to, that is if I have any. I too pray to hear from them soon, my dear." She tries to reassure him, also struggling to look into his searching eyes. "Who will be the first to hear from my mouth when I get news from overseas?"

"Obi will, Auntie!" The children reply to everyone's surprise. Obi jumps and spins in mid-air before he set off again.

It was almost evening when Lady Ani's hair was done and all the children had gone home for supper. She gives the *adas* a *kobo* for their efforts.

*

Education has been an important part of Ibo life for as long as Obi can remember, even in the absence of his parent's he was reminded to pay attention in school by his elders. He recalled Mr Uwani lecturing them about the tribes of Judah and their exile from their kingdom in 586BC and that is when some of them travelled to Igboland and settled here. "You are descendents from the tribes of Judah," said Mr Uwani.

As important as education was, it rendered poor families victims to the whims and ridicule of the wealthy. For the sake of their children, the poor begged and borrowed from those with plenty, often resulting in them being permanently indebted and beholden for generations; servants with few options other than to clean and tend to every demand of their masters. That is Peter's situation. He and his family lived in a small room where his father had grown up and served as a child. Obi was grateful that he did not have to clean lavatory buckets each morning before school; he often wondered how Peter managed to put up with it.

The children lived out their days after school playing and exploring deep into the woods, caves and in and around the ancient trees of their village. As well as everything else, what they must be careful of was not touching the fluffy white cuckoo spit dotted on leaves. This made Obi squirm. The slippery slimy stuff was difficult to shake off and if they touched or prodded it by mistake, tiny nymphs with eyes and legs would look out from their bubbly spittle blanket. But they didn't know that the tiny creature could grow into sprightly frog hoppers, which could have entertained them for hours. They swam in an enclosure of water, which the boys imagined to be the Nile, and wrestled boisterously with one another on the warm sands of their village before running home with exfoliated bodies covered in red sand.

Later in the evening, after their mothers' return, everyone knew what was going on when the cries echoed from compounds and verandas around the village when their sand-caked hair was being combed.

Obi loved to play with his steel wheel on his uncle's front veranda, especially because of the smooth concrete floor. Uncle Ozo's house was at the centre of the compound, flanked by his wives huts, with Lady Ani's furthest away; she is Ozo's sister-in-law who only fools would dare to challenge.

The humming of Obi's wheel drifts across the compound like a tuning fork when it bounces off the cement floor, the sound of which Lady Ani loves.

"Ha! Obiora, are you now too big to sit and look through my magazine as I read it?" she calls out on hearing his movement beyond the avocado tree. "Are you trying to do a disappearing trick? Was I not hearing the noise of your wheel?"

"No, Aunty. Yes, Aunty," he said running to embrace her with an apology.

"How are your marigolds looking in this dry heat? Have they not all died?" She nudges her chin in the direction of Obi's small plot.

"I was just going to look at them now, Aunty, before you called me. Every day I give them water first thing when I wake up."

"I know you do, dear boy. I see you sharing the water when you wash your face in the morning." She smiles at him.

"I will bring you some for your table, Aunty," Obi replied.

"I know how much you love those bushes, my dear, but the bush belongs in the bush, not on my table. My dressing table is already full, is it not?" She smiles hugging his waist. Obi looks into her eyes; he wraps his arms around her neck and returns her love.

"Go into my kitchen. You will see the used matchsticks I have saved for you, the ones to replace the creatures' tails with when you catch them. They are on the kitchen table." Her expression changed. "Do you and those boys think the insects feel no pain?" Her face was stern. "I like to see those green-winged dragonflies resting on my umbrella when I walk back from mass on Sundays."

"I did not know you still used the river route, Auntie." Obi said.

"You are a rascal. You are lucky I have not told your uncle that you still play in that river." She whispers so the younger children could not overhear. "I too, as a child, used to pull out the long tails of the dragonflies and replace them with sticks and watch them fly."

"Thank you Aunty. But we don't hurt them like that anymore. We let them keep their own tails."

"Go and play with your friends and do not mind the likes of Vasco; there will always be other Vascos in this world, those foolish children. They will all be road hawkers, just like their mothers."

*

After school Obi spots the back of Lady Ani's red umbrella in the wooded area near his school. Without thought he jumps down the few concrete steps of his school building to chase after her. Before he arrives to be by her side she offers her hand and Obi grasps it with all his might. They walk without words, only the sound of Obi's rushed breath and his tired footsteps is evidence of life in the secretive wood. Obi says nothing when they pass an ancient tree, massive like the Mother Tree. He tries not to look up at his auntie in case she finds out about his secret place in the tree. But it's too late, their eyes meet and he couldn't look away in time before she asks him questions.

"Do not get lost or sleep too deep inside that old tree, Obi."
He feels his heart beat and blood rush chaotically around his
body. She knows everything.

"You think it is your secret that only you alone know of?" his
auntie warns. "I know where it is, your secret place. I see when
you enter that old hollow every day."

"I am sorry, Aunty," Obi said, not that he was being told off.

"Sorry for what? I was there long before you, when I was a
little girl. I too saw the vanishing creatures through the same
blue, golden lake that you can now see." Obi doesn't speak; he
wipes his forehead, still holding Lady Ani's hand not knowing
he was squeezing it.

"All the birds and animals that live there are smaller than my
hand. My dear, how I miss seeing what you see. But make sure
to return in time for your supper, everyone will worry. You are
fortunate that your uncle does not beat you when he has to send
a search party to look for you before the light fades and your
evening meal is ready." They arrive back and Lady Ani refastens
her wrapper before heading to her garden and into her house.
Obi stands looking at her with tears in his eyes but he doesn't
know why he's crying.

"Obiora! Why are you standing there? Come here now, now."

Obi runs to her veranda and through her door, where she
hands him a packet of biscuits to share with the other children.
Obi hugs her waist before he ran out looking at the biscuit packet.

"I will not return late for my meal," he assures Lady Ani
before running in to hide the biscuits, then setting off to find the
other boys under the Mother Tree. *My uncle does not beat me*,
he thought to himself. His footprints in the sand fill up as fast as
his heels leave the ground.

Lady Ani and Obi would talk about his family when they were
together. Often she told him stories of his mother's struggle for

a son. Obi liked the idea that he was wanted before he was born, but it saddened him to know of his mother's sufferings.

"When your mother had no meat in the kitchen, that's when you wanted it the most. You would run to your senior uncle who sent someone to buy you meat from the market. What a spoilt boy." Obi enjoyed stories of when he was a baby and the times he spent with his mother before she went to England. It reassured him that he had parents and it kept alive his desire of being reunited with them again.

"You must never think you don't have a mother," Lady Ani reminded him time and again. "Come what may, a time will come when all your family will be together again." She told him this whenever he felt sad, or alone, especially after he and his friends quarrelled. "When you cease to be upset, that stammer will also cease, my dear. It is good that you are beginning to stay on the ground instead of always hiding in a tree where no one can find you. The branches of old trees are weary." Lady Ani watches him heading towards his goat's pen.

"If God wanted you to be a miserable boy, he would not have given you such a big heart and smile!" she said, loud enough for him to hear.

The sisters had spent the entire day reading the same book on their bed. The book had lost its cover with age and use, but had their teacher's name etched in bold green letters along its spine, Suzanna. Obi was nowhere to be found when Decima told Arike to look for their brother.

"Aunty. It is getting dark and we can't find Obi," the sisters told Lady Ani.

"Wait, I will come with you." Lady Ani emerged with her headscarf. "Ok let us go." Towards the woods, looking up at the trees, they called for him. After he had cried himself to sleep tucked up inbetween the branches of a tree, he remained. Wiping the dribble from his mouth; he woke at the sound of his sisters' voices. They watch him climb down, his feet hugging the slender trunk like a cricket on a strand of grass, his hands gripping branches either side, twisting and manoeuvring his body around the tree.

"Aunty, I think he has been crying for our mother," Arike said, looking up at Lady Ani.

She embraces Arike in acknowledgement as they watch Obi's descent, meeting him at the base.

"My son will send money soon, plenty of dollars and we will go to Ogbete where I will buy you many things." Lady Ani hugs him, wiping tear trails from his cheeks with her handkerchief as they make their way back. The sisters rush to pick mushrooms from a clearing in the shaded moist undergrowth.

"N-not a big car wh-which w-will sit and gather d-dust under a tree, Aunty," Obi suggests, not taking his eyes away from his sisters. "I am too small to drive, Auntie." Obi lets go of Lady Ani's hand and runs after his sisters who cradle in the hems of their dresses bundles of mushrooms. Squeezing between them he forces them to hold his hands.

7

Onugbu
Bitter Leaf

The chatter of birds and crickets, once synonymous with village life, had all but gone. No one seemed to have noticed the eerie silence, and, if they had, perhaps they preferred to ignore it. Obi and his friends found themselves exploring deeper into the woods, searching for stones for their catapults and chasing retreating prey. Birds and animals had left in droves, unnoticed. In front of their doorways, the traders laugh while counting the day's takings of worn-out notes. Meanwhile, most elders chose the comfort of their homes rather than to come out to greet passers-by like before.

Apathy swept over the village, hidden, lying heavy like a cannonball at the bottom of an ocean. Uboji Village was becoming unrecognisable. Market squares where elders once laughed mindlessly with the young or with neighbours without doors had all but vanished. Like a sealed chamber, former life in the open seemed diminished of oxygen. Children ran home from school instead of to the Mother Tree where they once played and frolicked. The unspoken was on its way, dragging with it a time that will see the undulating red earth and velvet green landscape of Iboland transform in the wake of a terrifying future.

The warnings were subtle but palpable, and came from a time when the ground was dense with giant ancient trees with root tendons that sprawled taller than the men who rested amongst their smooth groves. The counsel of *dibias* had become lost in the fabric of folk tales from yesteryears and in the make-believe superstitions of a time past.

Life continued, the villagers grew envious of the prosperity of city dwellers, in place of the traditional ways that had served them well in the past. The village became a place for mothers, elders and children. New traders, unconcerned with tradition, moved in. Roadside hawkers from other communities set up shops dotted around the old village, bringing with them inevitable changes, which were noticed by the elders; the younger members of the community were less courteous, and strangers no longer greeted each other in and around the village. The *dibias* had warned every village in the region of the misery that awaited them in times to come, after which the traditional healers and rain stoppers retreated deeper into the forests to preserve and safeguard the ancient practices and customs of the Ibos.

At dawn, when the first birds ate the strongest worms, Obi was awakened by a sound outside his window. The strange noise hummed, unnoticed by those who slept. He lay pensive and silent huddled between his sisters on their bed, in two minds of whether or not to investigate the sound. *What if it was a spirit? What if it was a giant flying beetle?* It was too late; curiosity captivated him before he crept out of bed. Yawning, he rubbed dried sleep from the corners of his eyes and wiped it on his shorts.

Obi picked up his chewing stick from the windowsill, blowing off the tiny insects before popping it into his mouth.

He rubbed and scraped the soft pulpy mop up and down his teeth, and continued to do so as he left the room. He checked that his catapult and the stones he had picked up the day before were in the pockets of his khaki shorts. This was not a morning for sweetbread and powdered milk; it was the school holidays, so he knew his sisters would not be waking up early to make his breakfast. Obi finished cleaning his teeth, spitting the creamy white saliva into the bush on his way out of his compound towards the main road. He hears the cockerels wake-up calls in the distance behind him. He looks down observing his footprints in the wet sand after the night's downpour, pleased to be the first person out of the village that morning. Uzoamaka wasn't out sweeping her compound as he passed their shop, and nor was her father, Mr Emanuel, sitting with his feet up on his veranda. He quite missed them.

An old woman wanders alone foraging. She collects sleeping crickets too damp to fly before the sun had a chance to dry their wings from the morning dew.

Obi wipes his eyes on the back of his wrists, unaware that he is walking parallel to the old woman towards the road's edge. Separated by palm trees and long-bladed grass, he ambles along pulling long stems of grass, nibbling at the soft tips before he draws his arm back to throw the long stem up towards the sky like a spear. With a smile he sends the green stem of grass high into the undisturbed air. He skips along the quiet path scooping damp sand with his feet leaving long trails behind him. Obi doubles back on spotting the old woman when the bushes came to a clearing. His heart misses several beats before he ducks behind the grass borders to watch. He wonders if she had been watching him all along. Taking care not to think aloud, like he so often did, Obi remembers that he had seen her before at exactly the same spot.

Turning away from the old woman he bends forward to look

at her upside-down through his parted legs. The village children knew that one of the ways to tell whether a person was a ghost or not was to bend over and look at their feet to check if they hovered above the ground. Obi peers hard to see her feet, but his view is obscured by grass, nor could he see her face, although he could hear her mumbling to herself. He wonders if she is talking to him, and what if she turned to face him; he imagined her to be faceless with withered skin like parched earth, no eyes, mouth or nose.

Her skin was wrinkled like crunched-up paper, with three kidney bean holes for her eyes and nose, and a hollow slit for a mouth. Obi hid behind a tree, hardly daring to breathe; he watched her closely, trying to memorise everything so he would be believed when telling his story in the village. Obi did not take his eyes from the hunched, wizened old woman who ambled alone looking for *onugbu*, bitter leaf, with which she could cook her evening meal. Obi saw that she was the same height as her knobbly walking stick which was resting against a tree close to her. Squinting to see through dry eyes, Obi watches her every move. Her face intrigued and scared him simultaneously; an unwanted fruit, black and shrivelled by an angry sun. The skin on her arms is tight against her bones, and Obi imagined her feet were grey and cracked. Her toes spread apart like fingers resembling the village women who had no closed shoes, and her toenails black shrivelled and shrunken back like bits of broken twigs.

"Only God knows what will be. Nobody listens to anybody anymore," she said aloud as if she was talking to someone. "The way their mamas and papas raise them as children."

Slowly she lowers herself trying to sit upon a fallen log, but she remained frozen as her bottom hovered above the trunk. Obi is mesmerised by her, and wondered of the pain and discomfort she must be feeling, not being able to rest her bottom. He imagined what her name could be and if she knew or remembered his mother.

"Even the plentiful bitter leaves are all dead. What curse is this?"

The once-abundant vegetable that grew everywhere had curled up with disease. Tufts of moist grass and withered plants were strewn around the open ground. Pointed towers of sandy termite palaces stand erect and unfazed by the seasonal torrents of night rain.

Both hands upon her knees she squats over the log unable to sit or get up, her wrapper slips and gathers loosely by her thighs, she looks at her headscarf, which had fallen to the ground. Gripping her knees, her bottom suspended in mid air and she falls back on the log. Her frail, hunched figure hovers above the same spot after several failed attempts to stand. Obi wants to laugh and cry. Her feet sink further into the soft earth like a coconut dent on a sandy riverbank. The deluge from the previous night had left the thirsty earth quenched and docile. She looked at her stick; it lay just out of reach.

"Let me die from this life where I cannot find bitter leaf to cook my food. My dear, what have the men of this village done to kill everything? Money, money, that is all they know. They will sell their children's souls for money. My dear, let me just die," she grumbles to herself. She looks again at her headscarf on the ground, like a conjurer willing an object to move. It did not budge. Obi was about to run and help her when she began talking again.

"The hands of your own kind will destroy all that has been good. Your lives will never be the same. Replaced by churches, crucifix, stout and whisky instead of palm wine," she complained.

Obi didn't know what was happening to him when his body was saturated with sweat and his hairs all stood on end. He felt his head swell and his legs unable to hold him, a seminal moment of realisation that the distant humming he thought was a giant beetle or bumble bee outside his window was in fact the wrinkly old woman.

All of a sudden, the frail woman springs to her feet like a child pulled from danger. Terrified; Obi's legs collapse beneath him, his knees scrape along the dirt track on all fours as he scrambles to find his feet before running home to his sisters. He could not escape his fear no matter how fast he sprinted. He resisted the temptation to look back in case the woman was a ghost about to fly at him and turn him into a child ghost. He ran over his own footprints back tracking, and not noticing that Mr Emanuel was standing and cleaning his mouth outside his compound.

"Good morning! Dear boy, you are moving as if you have seen a ghost," said Mr Emanuel.

The other traders were opening up their stalls when Obi darted past. They laughed at him.

"Obi, Obi, the boy with arms like tentacles!"

Obi bolts into the main doorway of his uncle's house. Ozo was not in; he was out checking his traps in the woods. Slamming the door open when his body fell against it, he dives onto the bed scrambling between his sisters and hiding under the sheet. He hoped that they would be awakened by his desperate scramble over the mattress. But they had better ideas about how they wanted to spend their morning. Obi wasn't sure if he wanted to share what he had just seen with his sisters because that would mean validating he had actually seen a ghost. Unable to calm his racing heartbeat he got up and hurried back out into the compound and towards Lady Ani's house. The smell of fried plantain welcomed him on entering the familiar kitchen before his heart settled.

"Ah, Obi, come. What brings you here so early in the morning? Did you have a bad dream, or was the lure of my cooking to blame?"

Obi stands with his arms wrapped around her waist, his words stuck in his throat. "Oh my god what has happened?" Lady Ani picks him up and looks into his face, but Obi hides from her gaze, wrapping his arms around her neck. Lady Ani pulled a stool from under her dining table and Obi slides onto it in an instant as she serves him a plate of plantain before sitting herself opposite him.

"Thank you, Auntie."

Obi tucks into the sweet breakfast and tells his story of the old woman near the roadside. The security of his auntie and the taste of happiness in his mouth enabled his words. Looking up he sees the bewilderment on her face. Her raised eyebrows and enquiring eyes confused him. Obi did not know whether the look was because of what he had told her or because he was eating too quickly and noisily.

"*Chineke* no," Lady Ani exclaimed finally. She went to the open window and called out.

"Mama Toni! Come now, now! Come and listen. Oh my god!"

She crossed herself as Mama Toni arrived; followed by other women of the compound who gathered outside on the veranda to witness what was going on.

"Obi, tell Toni mother what you just told me."

He spots his sisters standing outside towards the back of the crowd when he begins to tell his story again. In his hand are two slices of plantain, resembling tongues, he saved for them. Obi likes the attention at first until Mama Toni screamed and beat her head in disbelief.

"The boy see Madam Magdalene, who is not yet buried, and she has already returned to where she die."

Obi stutters losing his confidence, his worst nightmare has been realised. He had seen a ghost.

Holding his sisters' hands they walk back to their room together.

"Where have you gone in your head now?" Arike asked.

"Remember?"

"Remember what?"

"First time we went to fetch water with the others, all the way to the water-pool. Remember? We left early in the morning and did not get back until late at night because I got lost; it became dark, didn't it, my sister? One of our aunties told me not to wander off. But I found a baby parrot in the tree. It was tiny. It could not fly properly and I wanted to keep it. I chased it, but it kept hopping from one branch to the other. When I turned around to show you the parrot, I could not see you or Decima. I turned to look at the parrot and it had gone too. That bird must be; must be."

"Obi. You must speak properly!" Arike said.

"Maybe that was a ghost too. Ghosts do not only come out at night," Obi continued. "I was afraid. I cried because I remembered the stories of the butterflies that led children away. I cried because I thought I would never see you and our mother again. Do you remember now? I was also crying because it was dark when the women found me. They came calling, "Obi, Obi!" They brought big, blazing fire sticks in their hands. I saw them waving them above their heads in the dark. I thought they were fire-breathing demons."

"That is why you should sleep and not be too quick to be out before first light," Arike advised her brother.

"Let him be, Arike. You know he is not like the other boys," said Decima.

"Why am I not like the others, my sister?" Obi enquires.

"Because things affect you emotionally more than they do other children Obi. It is called being sensitive. There is nothing wrong with that and that is normal too." Arike explains.

*

Madam Magdalene's wake lasted a week and for those seven days Obi's nightmares continued. He asked his sisters if they could all sleep in Lady Ani's house or with Ozo. The whole neighbourhood came out in mourning and sang funeral songs every day. For the entire week, most of the shops were closed. A queue of women and men lined the paths to Mr Emanuel's tailoring shop, each of them with bundles of cloth and style patterns in their hands.

The burial uniform had been announced four days before. Uzoamaka had to set up her own sewing table close to her father's bench, and the orders continued to pile up over her head. The festivities of singing and dancing lasted all day and night; Obi lingered around the adults as much as he could. He would nod off, perched at the end of a bench, his eyes flickered when the tempo changed, unnerving him further. The women played their musical instruments throughout the night. His sisters banged and clanged the hollow instruments as Obi shook and shivered with trepidation unable to cling to them unlike during their grandmother's funeral a few years ago.

"The boy must be a man, just because his mother is not there, you cover your brother like a baby," an unknown woman commented to them. Obi had abandoned his activities for that awful week, he didn't hunt with the boys, nor would he return to the road's edge. Knowing that spirits came out to enjoy music of the night, especially during mourning, he decided it was far safer to follow his sisters around like a shadow.

After the wake keeping, a sea of colours enveloped the village, ready for Madam Magdalene's burial. Hundreds of people gathered from all over the village and beyond, dressed up in their best wrappers and head dresses to attend mass. Obi tries to block out the funeral songs, but sticking fingers in his ears did not help to overcome his inner fear of ghosts and death. Lady Ani was busy with all the organisation of the ceremony so he couldn't be hanging around her. Thinking about seeing his mother didn't give him the physical security he needed, nor could he run or hide away from the sombre death songs all over the village. It was everywhere. Finally, he stood behind the safety of the door to watch the colourful crowd, relieved that children were not allowed to attend burials, even though it might have meant a new outfit from Mr Emanuel's shop.

Obi had heard that the dead attended their own funerals; even as the events came to a close he continued to linger around the grownups. His sisters had fallen asleep after doing their hair, too terrified to sleep, he snuck out to listen to the fireside stories. He'd always loved the evening story times by the fire in his compound.

Wedged between elders, Obi felt safe listening to their account of how the state government never did what they had promised. He was relieved that no one was talking about how well the funeral ceremony had gone. He was not particularly interested in matters of the government although the elders always quarrelled whenever they talked about the subjects of the leaders. Obi catches himself when an elder stands up to chuck a lump of wood into the fire.

"I no untruth you," the elder said, sitting back down without considering that Obi had toppled over his seat.

"Boy move," the man said and tilts Obi's limp body back against the other man. The calm night was unlike the usual vibrant fireside experience of laughter and reflections, there was no criticising of the funeral. Ozo sat in his usual armchair observing his compound.

"Obiora, *je jinaya*, go to bed," one of the mothers reminded him as Obi was fast asleep with his arms crossed between his chest and knees.

"By tomorrow evening, the entire village will again be out searching for you and you will be fast asleep in the bush with that goat." Obi didn't move. "Look, the boy is nearly falling to the ground, but his bottom remains fastened to his seat." An elder said before Joseph scooped him up in one sweep towards Ozo's house to tuck Obi up inbetween his sisters. Ozo smiled at Joseph, reaching out from his chair in the veranda. Joseph bows in acknowledgement and whispers; "Good night Uncle," accepting a fruit from Ozo before making his way home through the dark woods.

8

Ekelere m Chukwu
I thank God

The school day was all about Ibo history, a subject close to the teacher, Mr Uwani's, heart, a subject he knew well and insisted others should share the same interest. However, Mr Uwani lacked the nuances of a good storyteller.

"Today! I will teach you about who you are," said the teacher. "You are Ibos, do you understand?"

One by one the children began to look up from their writing boards. With a tatty book in hand he continued to lecture the class like a Sunday preacher.

"Ibos live in Iboland! There is no other kind of people like the Ibos! Where do we live?"

"Iboland!" Obi and his class echoed.

"None of your fathers will know that before the *oyibo,* white men, came our country used to be known as Geebuu. People of strong values; go ask your elders to tell you about your people when you reach home from here today. We have maintained our traditional and spiritual way of life."

Obi listened as Mr Uwani read from his big book and

continued to learn new facts about the Ibo people. He did not know that there are Ibos living outside Enugu.

"Originally, Ibos had an animist belief system. Although most Ibos now follow Christianity, we used to have our own gods and held our children in the highest regard, next only to *Chukwu*, God. You children were the most valued and gifted blessings to your parents and village."

Obi looks around the room, he is confused about words he had not heard before and wondered how he would remember and practise them out of class. His classmates did not appear to be listening; their eyes were barely able to stay open after running around in the sun during play followed by the midday Angelus, a devotional prayer. Obi loved to hear others read and longed to be able to read when he is older.

"Ibos believe there is a king in every man and that every adult within a village has responsibility for the children of his brothers and sisters," the teacher continued.

"We are a 'do unto others as you would have others do unto you' people. The Ibo way is that, no matter which mother give you life, or which father fathered you, every adult must care. Who knows what responsibility means!? He interrupts his speech to look at Obi who fidgets while most of the school are asleep with their heads resting on the long table. Mr Uwani seems to not have noticed that he has already lost his class, apart from Obi.

In the village, misbehaviour always resulted in immediate chastisement. There was no waiting until a father returned home. If children were naughty outside, they were swiftly dealt with by any senior who was at arm's reach, much like Mr Uwani's teaching.

Most children in the village feared words much more as punishment, than the stick used on them. The impact of words and the way they made people feel often lasted longer than any physical pain, and Obi was no exception. Many unkind words upset and hurt their recipients, even 'bastard' was a standard address from a parent to their offspring.

Obi became aware of the power of the spoken word when he sat in on the folk stories, shared around the fireside. He'd listen to each and every word, carefully, wondering what else the words could mean. He imagined himself inside the different stories. Immersed in them, he took in every word he heard, particularly from his elders.

"Boy, bring me my stick, fool, idiot!" An angry father scolds his son, unaware of the hurt he caused. Gone are the days when parents valued their children as gods

*

Of the many routes out of the village, walking through a wooded path was the one which could invite unexpected encounters. Obi loved it for the choice of small game that he could catch within its quiet seclusion but mindful that he wanted a pet to take home and not a dead limp animal. However, the woods were not without the added anxiety of encountering evil medicine, snakes and animal attacks. Walking along the roadside was another favourite; the anticipation of maybe today he will see a truck monkey was a dream that made him smile.

It served him that he wasn't one of the noisy children who would be easily noticed if absent from the village or compound. Like most of the boys, one of Obi's greatest desires is to own a pet monkey or a talking parrot. So whenever he had the chance he set off to the roadside in the hope of catching sight of a working truck monkey.

Obi shudders on remembering a story of a pet parrot killed by one of his uncle's wives when it spoke an Ibo word. She ran, terrified that an animal could talk, returning with boiling hot water to throw over the bird, killing it instantly while cussing the devil.

Obi felt like an intrepid adventurer during his morning jaunts, keeping a keen ear out for sounds of rustlings nearby, he prays it's not a snake, the sheer thought pounds in his tiny chest. His senses sharpen; his grip tightens around his stick at the ready, fearing the brunt of a startled creature. Attentive to every sound and movement around him, Obi recalls a story of how wolves synchronise themselves to the pulse of their prey; he moves with stealth and caution. Obi listens to the silence; he engages a pebble into his catapult, snakes are masters of camouflage and he wasn't taking any chances.

Regretting wasting his best stones on trees and tin roofs, he wades through the dense grass that close in behind him with the haste of a thief in the market place. The hunter didn't mind when his stick was snatched from his grip by the dense shrubs, like an angry mother taking a knife from her child. Obi's ears prick up at the commotion of hungry flies that he unwittingly disturbed. He holds his breath, knowing what will follow. The stench of fresh excrement engulfs his nostrils. Gasping for clean air, he jumps out from the hedge onto the soft path, spitting and wiping his face with frenzy and sweaty palms, he wiggles his toes into the friendly red earth. Brushing away the cobwebs from his face and hair, Obi continues his journey to the roadside.

"Thirty days in September,
April, June and November.
February is twenty-eight alone,
And all the rest are thirty-one."

Singing and quickening his pace into a run on hearing the vehicles on the main road, hopeful that he will catch sight of a working truck monkey as they sped past towards town. Seeing his old footprints from the day before, Obi selected a vantage point to observe traffic. His excitement that he might glimpse a monkey in the cabin of a truck erased all his anguish.

Obi's sole mission was to catch sight of a working monkey; he jumps up and down, and shuffles and fidgets around on top of the dirt mound each time a truck passed by. Waving like a frantic man stranded on the moon, he continues to jump on the same spot, like a child enjoying a tantrum. His feet move against the sloping ditch, trying to gain higher ground in the hope that a truck monkey will see and wave back to him. But that never happens, although occasionally he imagined it did.

The bright letterings on the stubby-nosed trucks attract him; battered vehicles of all shapes and sizes make him hold his breath until the last minute. All the buses and trucks had names and slogans emblazoned across them and Obi imagined sitting in the cabin of the *Bata Ekpere*, welcome prayer, an enormous white truck without a windscreen. Obi practises his English during his lookout for the *Ekelere m Chukwu*, his favourite truck with a working monkey. It was covered in maxims and paintings of Christ, depicting various parables.

The entire vehicle is adorned with stylised images of the nativity, slogans and psalms. Obi waves at the trucks until they vanish towards the busy marketplace of Enugu. He memorised the tune and hummed along to 'You're too young for me', one of his favourite songs, which he and his friends danced to in the village.

Meanwhile, hawkers dodge inbetween the enormous wheels and overheated engines, losing their slippers hurrying. The temptation to run towards the congestion of colourful vehicles merging with each other like puppies trying to feed at the same nipple, he averts his gaze towards the colossal upturned trucks that had all met the same fate over the steep drop at the edge of the uneven road on the bend. The abandoned rusty shells are sprawled like dead carcasses with vegetation that grew out of the skeletal remains. Obi and his friends often wondered if those were giant dead creatures, when they spied upon them from the invisible boundary line that their aunties and mothers drilled into them not to venture beyond, especially Mama Toni, who was always cautious.

"I tell you, do not go beyond Uncle Augustus's house, and those trees, if you want to return home safe for your meal!"

Silent from up in a tree, Obi watches and giggles at frightened men trying to navigate the busy road. They cross themselves quickly in the name of Jesus, before negotiating the safest gap between the oncoming vehicles. Holding hands, their feet step on and off with hesitation across the road. Their embarrassment does not diminish when they spot Obi watching them behaving like wary old women at the road's edge.

"Obi, Obi. In your own world again!" The men try to discard the awkwardness with laughter. "Boy; be careful o - the ground is far from that branch you are sleeping."

Pretending to be asleep, Obi said nothing when usually he would say thanks Sir. Like men they walk towards the village, no longer hand in hand. Obi could still hear their conversation, "Does that boy not have friends?" when they pass under him with long bundles of firewood balanced upon their heads.

With wrinkled brow, Obi's eyes drill through the back of their heads. "I have friends," he tells himself. His grip tightens around the branches and he imagines the dry bundles of wood catching fire above their heads. When he remembers the men holding hands and running across the road, his face turns to a smiling laugher. He remembers Lady Ani's words, from the time when he hurt himself with his steel wheel.

Cry if you are crying, Obi. Why do you smile and say all is OK when it is not? Your smile is for joy and not for hiding your pain.

Recalling his observations from the day's events, Obi wonders why people spoke to objects that did not and could not reply. Like a man at the roadside who begged a damaged wheelbarrow: "*Biko,* just get my goods back to my house." Another man begged the sun and sky: "*Biko,* bring us rain." A driver asked his car: "*Biko* o, why do you stop here? Take me to my destination!" Obi spent a few hours up in branches of the tree and remembered that his sisters will be expecting him back for supper. He hurried home, hoping to reach it before dusk; otherwise he'd have to run singing 'You're too young for me', at the top of his voice to ward off any spirit that might think he was alone.

"You're too young for me, you're too young for me, you're too young for me, I'm too old for you. I'm too old for you, I'm too old for you, I'm too old for you, pam – pam – pam – pam – pam."

*

Obi remembered when Decima was explaining to him that their grandmother had passed away, she didn't want to frighten him by saying that she had died.

He sat on the veranda steps squeezed between his sisters and watched the courtyard of the family compound fill with near and distant relatives, consoling one another with words and hugs of comfort at the passing of their grandmother. They could hear, "*The poor children must be afraid. Abandoned by everybody who has ever cared for them. First, their fada travel to the UK. Then their moda leave them, and now their moda's moda die and leave them also,"* people said feeling sorry for them.

"Sorry, sorry, I know your mother, she will return, she will never abandon her children," said Lady Ani stepping up to the veranda and Obi involuntarily reaches out. He was petrified, he had not been so close to a dead person before and now she is in the same house. His face buried into Lady Ani's white blouse, his crying turned into hiccups and she patted his back gently. Her long arms embraced all three as she reassured them again that she will look after them until their mother returns. The smell of Rose Musk from Lady Ani's blouse overwhelmed and uplifted them momentarily.

"Until your mother come back, the compound will watch over you all, it is tradition. We will care for all of you like our own. Your mother and me have been good friends from our childhood. Our mother come from the same village." She repeated the same words as she patted the sisters on their head and turned to walk into her kitchen.

"The village is your family now, you will never be alone, do not worry, do not worry," she continued from behind her closed door before she reappeared with pieces of dried coconut for Obi and his sisters, hoping to soothe them.

*

At school Obi led the run to greet his teacher first. He liked the idea of sharing the new English words he had picked up over the weekend or evening. On seeing his teacher, Obi's eyes focus on the cradle of the front pocket of his teacher's shirt which was threadbare from rigorous washing to get rid of the ink from the tips of his biros. Mr Uwani did not indulge Obi's questions regarding knowing anything of his parents and would send him away.

"Go and find your friends. I think they are all playing football."

The teacher pats Obi's head with a chalky hand, waving him off towards the group of boys that are chasing a tightly bound ball of rags around the parched school field.

"Yes Sir!" He obeys, running off towards the far end of the ground to join his peers it seems.

Mr Uwani watches him sprinting as he carries on past the football pitch towards the school boundary before he calls out.

"Obiora!" His teacher's voice silences the entire school ground, as dust clouds scatter around Obi's heels in the direction of his compound.

"He go see if his *moda* has returned for him!" someone shouts out before laughter echoed around the playground.

*

Palm wine season saw the jubilant village market close early, in time to taste their first pot of the year. Obi runs with other boys towards the palm trees and strapping younger men wrestle one another in tournaments. Other men limber their muscles for climbing. Poised with daggers clenched between their teeth, seasoned elders that could still negotiate their way up the vertical palm trees re-tie their loin cloths. Packs of children jostle their way to the front for a better look.

Offor is the senior wine tapper and the oldest man in the village. He walks around his tree inspecting it. "If my knife fall," he warns without looking away from his tree, "it will cut off all your heads. Move! Go back; let me climb this tree in peace," he mumbles. Obi drops back, hoping that the other boys did not notice and call him 'coward who does what Offor says'. He is further back amongst the girls who shuffle back and forth as Offor is about to ascend. "It is a man's duty to climb and tap for wine. Why are you girls here? There is nothing for you to learn, go to your homes." He spoke in a loud tone of voice before the girls run back to their mothers' kitchens, and Obi eases away towards the hedge.

"Soon even this will be taken by them; we have few traditions left that are sacred to men," he declares to the male spectators; his eyes meet Obi's by mistake which freezes Obi on the spot.

Offor grunts at him, his machete firmly between his white teeth, he bites hold of the blade, which glistens in the sunlight at the onlookers with their backs against the setting sun. The boys watch and record his every move when he begins: his bony toes grasp the trunk, his wiry legs clinch the tree and his torso collides with the swing of his harness on his ascent. Offor continues with each toss of his thick rope around the girth of the palm tree, moving upwards in rhythm, like a frog, Obi thought as he studies his every move. Pausing midway he looks down at Obi and shakes his head. When he reaches the top, he rests in the safety of the cradle of his rope. His hands are free to swap the pot of wine which had filled overnight with an empty one that's strapped to his waist.

"Will your wine from that tree be sweet for my mouth, like that from Udi palm?" a woman's voice rang out in a mocking tone on their way home, startling Obi from behind.

"Only time will tell. You can find out when I come down from this forever tree!" Offor snaps back, irritated with having to remove the knife from his mouth in order to oblige a response.

Obi remembers when Offor used to lower the pots of wine from the tree with a long rope, but he put a stop to that after a group of naughty boys from a different village ran off with all his hard work and Obi got the scolding for not stopping them. Obi kept out of Offor's way from then onwards. The children looked on with excitement, laughing at Offor's testicles which dangled like fatigued bats on display for the whole village to see. Obi didn't join in.

9

Prelude

During the night Obi fidgets between his sisters who are asleep. It wasn't only the heat that irritated and kept him up all night; he was thinking about all the 'what ifs', and 'have you', questions he had been asking of strangers lately. He'd been considering over the past few weeks that it was perhaps time he became a bit more helpful to his sisters instead of spending most of his time at the roadside and up in trees.

"Mosquito," he said mindfully, slapping his face in the dark. His sisters did not stir.

Obi stretches up to touch the drooping mosquito net above their bed, but snatches his hand back with a jolt when Decima told him to go to sleep.

"What is that?" he asked, looking into the darkness around them. "Sister, I hear something outside."

Decima was too tired to respond to her brother who was sitting up next to them. "*Biko*, Obi, sleep." Decima's arm flops over her brother's stomach. He was sure he heard a truck approaching their compound. It was not one of the usual night-time sounds of crickets, dogs barking or adults exchanging breaths. From his daily roadside escapades Obi was well-versed with trucks and their engine sounds. Obi shuffles to the end of the bed onto the cool floor without a sound. He blinks, and blinks some more to adjust his sight to the darkness. Looking back at his sisters, the noise gets closer, and traces of migrant lights penetrate the plantation shutters of their bedroom. He wants to shake Decima to wake but gives up for the growing noise outside. *Only bad news arrives at night*, he remembers someone say once. On hearing his uncle's door open, Obi runs to his doorway to take a peek across the parlour to his uncle's room. He can hear some of the women that had made their way out, but his attention is on his uncle. The whispers from the women started to intensify from every angle of the compound.

Obi watches his uncle leave his room, heading out towards the courtyard, he had the same look when he had an important elders' meeting to attend.

"Go back to your houses; you look for what you do not want to know," Obi heard him tell everyone before he headed back to his room.

The elders had been meeting every evening for the past few weeks, Obi picked up snippets of conversation from women in the market of something heading their way, but no one said what that something was.

People gathered under the Mother Tree in Ukwuachi the following morning. They hoped for news of the gossips of war in the north. The gigantic tree is said to have stood at the centre of their village for centuries and had witnessed many events which had become folktales over the years.

Children laugh and giggle, they run around the tree while others played jax and hopscotch in the sand beneath her shade. One of their favourite activities is to gather around the Mother Tree to measure their growth by her waist. A four-year-old would find seven friends of similar height to link fingers together in a chain, embracing the old tree. A five-year-old joined up with six friends of similar height and so on. Eyes closed and pressing their ears against her, humming, hugging and longing to hear the old tree's vibration.

Obi and his friends were curious to know what the top of the Mother Tree looked like, because close up it was a dense insurmountable forest mountain. Frequent attempts to run as far as they could to the edge of their village from where they could stand upon a vantage point and look back but it always failed; only on their way back home at the end of the day they realised that again they have been distracted by their games and pranks, and had forgotten to look for the top of the tree. One of the prophecies of the old Mother Tree was that if ever she fell or died, it would signal the end of all that was good in the village.

The Mother Tree is like an ark, she teamed with countless species; no one actually knew how many. One of Obi's favourite tales was about the giraffe, an elephant, a hippopotamus and a big black hog that had trekked across land and water to seek shelter under her leafy shade. Undisturbed, they would sleep and rest until they were well enough to continue their onward journey. People of the village did not stop to question why or how so many of God's creatures knew to make their way from different corners of Africa to their village. Another story about a time when white men with rifles came to look at the old tree: The men did not ask the tree's permission before they sunk tall rods into the ground around her roots; huge white canvas sheets were draped around it to set up a marquee, which meant that children could no longer play there. The men had also shot a crocodile, which was said to have journeyed for many days to rest under her. The Mother Tree shivered with sorrow, shaking her branches vigorously until the entire camp collapsed under her weighty branches, and the leaves buried the men for five days before their bodies could be recovered for burial. That was the last time anything was killed in the market place. Meat traders moved to other locations, away from the tree. 'No blood can be spilled here' became a way of life around the tree.

When children hurt themselves under the tree, they simply picked themselves up without crying for attention; the pain dissolved faster than it had arrived. Vibrant *Ogbanje* children even sang and danced in words of happy gibberish, which no one other than themselves could understand.

By day, the Mother Tree shielded shoppers and traders, by night the spirits traded under her shelter. The village folk had gradually forsaken their tradition of welcoming the evening swarm of homing bats back into the Mother Tree. Every villager had grown up waving the bats home, flapping their hands in the air and singing *shkolocobangosha* as they returned to hang upside down among the dark shades of the tree. They had not noticed when the bats changed direction in search for different trees; confused by the distorted sound waves in the evening sky which warped their senses. The sound of war approached, as traders counted the day's takings.

A ghostly silence descended like sudden dark clouds on harvesting day and the lively noise of people haggling, laughing and quarrelling in the village continued. The trees echoed an eerie stillness of a breezeless night. Birdsongs became voiceless, nervous crickets cling to each other with a blade of grass between them. Not until the trees shook and leaves rained upon their heads, did anyone take notice. Stunned and bewildered, the traders rush out of their shops to gawk at one another with dilated pupils, disbelieving the inevitable. They beat their shoulders with folded arms and watch the heavy branches crack and split to the ground. The table tops loaded with yams and sweet potatoes crash upon the earth, becoming part of the debris, and the ever hungry dogs run off with dried fish inbetween their jaws. Rusted tins of tomato puree, stacked in pyramids, scatter upon neat piles of *gari*, rice, *egusi* and peppers. There was no mercy when the larger branches crushed the last of the traders' huts.

The region was not known for earthquakes, yet the ground wobbled like the belly of a rich man. The tremble sent traders helter-skelter for clear ground frightened for their lives, others look on with frozen fear, terrified. One unfamiliar noise followed another. The same children that played under the tree run to their mothers, crying with their tiny hands over their ears.

"This is heavy artillery, the war has arrived!" a trader shouts, trying to salvage what he can of his scattered goods, his trousers drenched with urine.

"It is only heavy storms, do not be foolish," a man retorted from a neighbouring stall. "You hear that? Thunder – that is all!"

Bulbs flicker and explode. Hurricane lanterns smash, causing shoppers and traders to collide with each other in the darkened village centre.

"The old tree is weeping for what she is feeling within her roots, which touch the centre of this world!" cried a woman bystander.

"Devil is arrived!" She pounds her chest. "How did we ruin what we have? *Biko, biko Chuku*, save us from whatever evil is approaching." Mama Toni waves her arms and slaps her head, harder than if lice had bitten her.

"Shut up your mouth! Do you not know that we have suffered enough?" replied an angry trader, tilting his table back into place.

"Suffered!? You have not seen suffering. This devil will affect our land, long after new generations have come and go. Even if you no stop shouting at me." Mama Toni continued her prophecy of doom from under the Mother Tree.

"It is going to be hell!" she convulsed like a woman possessed. Some traders held up their oil lamps and dragged her out of the path of a falling branch. She could be heard ranting as she is led away to her hut by two of her relatives. "This mayhem is not natural."

People stood about shaking their heads in disbelief, they remember the calamity that Mama Toni had foreseen earlier in her dreams, about death's arrival at night.

Lady Ani appears with Decima and Arike in each hand. She marches over spilt food, unconcerned that her feet might touch them.

"Where is Obi? I have been looking for him since all this started," Lady Ani shouts at the traders. Their eyes dart here and there over the upturned market place. "No worry, I know where he is." They hurry towards the wooded area on the outskirts; hand in hand both sisters trot beside Lady Ani.

10

The Night of Change

Meandering along the main undulating dirt road towards the village is an invisible truck, its labouring engine reverberates through the many compounds. The arrival of an uninvited monster of the night which will change everything, forces its way towards Obi's home. Headlamp cutting through the night, it squeezes its way into the sleeping silence, leaving a trail of choking clouds of exhaust fumes. The rounded steel nose and gnashing sabre grill spew clouds of scorching steam, killing fireflies in mid-flight.

Obi and his sisters were asleep. Hours of running around had worn him out otherwise he would have been the first to know of the truck's arrival. His feet were still grey and dusty from the previous night, when he'd escaped bath time. He woke when he heard the truck's arrival. Like a child pulled from drowning, Obi jumped out of bed, he could never defeat his curiosity.

Taking his usual place at the window, transfixed by what was unfolding out in the compound so late at night. Through the cracks of the wooden shutters he watches, his eyes dart around to gauge what's going on. He strains to see the heavy metal door that had screeched open and watches a huge silhouetted figure of the driver emerge and proceed towards their house.

Remembering what Lady Ani once said that 'no one brought good news at night'. Obi held his breath; as the man walks towards the house, a quick glance at his sleeping sisters, he runs towards his uncle's room. In the dark parlour, Obi collides with Ozo, who was heading out with his hurricane lamp to meet the stranger at his door.

"Stay in the house, go to your sisters," Ozo said, waving his lamp towards Obi's bedroom.

Confused about what is going on, Obi steps back behind the front door. He peers out from inbetween the frame, pleased that his uncle had the lamp. He too could see what was going on in the darkened compound.

Obi's heart jumps on seeing the driver; he imagines him to be his friend, Joseph, who he had not seen for a long time. It was only wishful thinking, he was much too old. Obi startled himself again on hearing the sudden hissing splutters gushing from the bonnet, letting out steam clouds that evaporated on rising. His attention distracted away from the driver. In the dim light he watched a pool of hot water form on the sand from the constant dribble of the radiator before it hissed into a final rest.

Ozo stood before the man, who asked for some water for his radiator. Obi had never seen a military vehicle before, not even by the main roadside. He wanted a closer look but was afraid. Even the open cinema truck that visited to show moving pictures at the village centre was not as big.

A distant thunder of boom, boom, boom sounded nearer.

"My name is Eze, I am from the Biafran Army. Lieutenant Colonel Ojukwu send me to evacuate this compound," the stranger said to Ozo. Obi presses his ear closer to the door frame. "Owerri may soon be out of Ibo hands."

On tiptoes, Obi runs back to his bedroom. He wants his sisters to wake up but resists shaking them. From their window he watches.

Eze continues his pacing, waiting for his engine to cool. Obi's view is obscured when Eze stands in front of the one working headlamp and Obi presses his ear harder against the rickety window.

"Enugu will be next to fall. They will wipe everybody. They make fathers look when they kill their children first. After they rape women and girls they, oh my Jesus." Obi could see the rapid movement of the driver's lips. Not understanding all the words he could hear but Obi knew they were not good, he sensed the fear and wanted to hide between his sisters.

"Over one million Ibo people have died in the north. Butchered like market cattle. My duty is to evacuate this compound before the Federal Forces arrive." He mops sweat from around his face and inside the collar of his saturated shirt before pushing the handkerchief into his back pocket. "Get me water, I want drink water."

On hearing his request from where Obi was standing behind the window, he runs out with his white enamelled cup, full of water. Eze accepts it without looking, nor did he say thank you. Obi watches as water spills from the corners of his mouth onto his beating chest, dissolving into his sweat sodden shirt. The driver mindlessly discards Obi's cup upon the parched ground before Obi retrieves it, and lingers outside, mindful of staying out of Ozo's way.

"How can our people be so hated that they should be destroyed like diseased animals?" Eze asks himself rummaging for something under his vehicle. "I have seen villagers who choose to remain in their homes; I would not want to tell you of their fate at the hands of the Federal Forces."

Bewildered, the rest of the compound begins to empty out from their homes.

"To stay and protect our homes from being ruined is foolish," Mama Toni announced, restless on her feet while maintaining a distance from the driver. Her voice was soft, yet loud enough for both men to hear. "That cannot be God's will, to face the soldiers," said an elderly neighbour on arrival. "Soldiers! They are not soldiers! Those *anu ofia*, bush animals, will vanish everyone when they step out of their armoured vehicles!" Eze reiterates, realising that the men are thinking of staying and taking their chances. "They have mop-up animals that will nail you to your door before they pepper your body with British bullets."

The elderly neighbour, a former Nsukka University lecturer replies, "Enugu Radio say Biafran troops are outnumbered one hundred to one, and are without bullets, boots and ammunition. They say that Europe is sending the Federal Army more weapons to crush and slaughter the Ibos." The old man shakes his head in dismay before he continues. "How can Ojukwu agree to a surrender to end all Ibo people? *Never!* We will all die first. I am too old to worry about what happens to me. The old have already lived their lives, so we are not in rush for more."

"Idiot! What good is you? We must protect the young to carry on," an old man interjected from a small gathering of elders. Obi is surprised, he's never heard the elders being unkind to one another. They suck their teeth almost at the same time and shuffle their feet, cussing *tufia*, they spit on the ground in utter disgust.

"Joseph?" Obi whispers to himself, entranced by the stranger until his eyes start to water, forcing him to blink. "No!" Obi gasped, forgetting for a moment that his sisters are still asleep. His mouth ajar, the muscular man is unlike anyone from his village, and his eyes refuse to move from the enormous visitor with arms as big as logs and a chest wide like a wall.

Obi remembered a story he'd heard around the evening fire in the compound, of the night during a mighty storm when a stranger fell from the heavens. It was a time during the wet season, when the rain was at its heaviest. People came from their homes to witness the event when the stranger asked them to light a fire under the heavy rain with the saturated logs. When the smoke rose towards the skies the visitor stepped into it and vanished.

Men arrive with their families from surrounding neighbourhoods; news of the truck's arrival had spread. People huddle together like penguins, awaiting word from Ozo; a continuous line of uninvited guests file past him into his compound which becomes a melee. It seemed the entire village descended, crowding out the courtyard and every given space. Obi is engulfed by the mass; he no longer recognises his home ground and pushes through trying to reach his sisters.

"I want every woman and child to board this truck! You are to be evacuated this night!" Ozo's voice cuts through the troubled night. "The rest will follow on foot."

Hearing his uncle's words sends more panic as he feels the strength draining from his body trying to get through to his sisters in the house.

"What if the enemy arrives before the truck has left!?" a mother enquires, cussing and kissing her teeth at the night; her weary children follow in tow to the open truck. She starts to load her children like luggage on a moving bus.

Ozo nods in agreement on seeing Lady Ani hurrying towards his house. Obi catches up with her at the door as she slams it open, shouting for Decima. His sisters jump out of bed, Obi crashes into the room with Lady Ani way ahead.

"Quick, quick Decima," said Lady Ani. "Take this," she hands her a cloth bag. "I will be back soon. Take your sister and brother into that truck, now, now."

Lady Ani leaves for her house.

Obi jumps when Mama Toni opens their window from outside, her feet shuffle and jitter on the ground; she has one of her flame torches above her head. Although she was known for her erratic reactions, Obi has never seen her so petrified.

"My children! Take clothes. Take food. We must leave. It is very bad; it is going to be hell in our land o."

It was past midnight when Obi and his sisters were told that they must leave in the truck with the others.

Unable to contain his fear any longer, Obi starts to scream with the madness in his home, tears soak his T-shirt.

"War has broken out in our country," repeating what he had heard.

Obi sees his sisters pull dresses over their heads on top of what they are already wearing. He is alone with his tears.

"Decima come!" Lady Ani calls from the compound. Arike goes for the few bits of food items in their room, she picks up the small container of salt and a bundle of *eguise* seeds wrapped in old newspaper, tied with white thread. Her sister helps by reaching for the *gari*, which was kept in an old Cow and Gate milk powder tin, and then collects the few family photographs. Obi watches helpless, his busy sisters moving from one corner of their room to the other without collision. They grab Obi's hand and pull him towards the door.

Obi can hear his uncle's movement from the room behind them. Ozo unlocks the tall metal cupboard in his room and snatches his twin-barrelled rifle. Obi's mind is with him in the room and he recognises every sound. Ozo snaps his rifle apart and peers down the long, polished barrels; Obi had seen him do this many lazy afternoons when he'd clean it under the shade of his veranda.

In Ozo's cupboard is a box of cartridges with shiny gold tips. Ozo loads the rifle and snaps it shut before walking out with it tucked under his arm pointing downwards.

"Decima, be quick, take your brother and sister and be in that truck now!" Ozo commands from the veranda. In a file, they squeeze into the crowd of people towards the truck. Obi smelt the naphthalene balls from his uncle's wrapper as they passed him.

In the compound Lady Ani is directing people.

"Obiora!" Lady Ani shouts from the crowd. "Obiora! Bring your sisters now, now."

Decima runs with Obi and Arike. The compound is unrecognisable with people, goats and chickens in baskets.

"My husband. You the head of this compound, no one leave before you tell them. We must run to save life!" Mama Toni cries out running back and forth to the house fetching her children and provisions, her torch light diminishing.

"We must to go now, now! I feel this for many days. We must go! We must get out of here now or we will all perish!" She waves her hands about in a hysterical craze again as the flame becomes a smoulder.

"Fool!" Ozo retorts. "All you are good for is to panic! Did you not hear that I have already told you all to flee? Instead you cause more fear."

Mama Toni runs into the house with all the drama she is known for, before she rushes out again with another child strapped to her back. She continues ranting and waving her arms over her head.

"If driver, you no drive out now o! I take my children and begin walk," she yells. "Why we no listen to *dibia*, I never know."

"We, we, a-are all going to p-perish! Mama, Mama T-Toni said. We must run a-away," said Obi, breathless, standing between his sisters. "M-mama Toni s-said everything is bad.

What sh-she says always comes true." The night was hot but Obi's legs trembled like a naked child in the cold. "I not wa-want to die."

Obi looks at Mama Toni, she is squatting, about to toss another child over her shoulder onto her back. He watches her tie her wrapper around herself, ready to leave. Clinging to his sisters, he looks on at the rest of the bewildered adults huddled together. Mama Toni glares at them.

"Talking, talking! Waiting to see what Ozo do next! The enemy guns will soon come meet you." She cussed and spat into the darkness. Obi feels the fear in the women of the compound and looks to his sisters, who offer him no words of reassurance.

The driver cuts through the chaos, his eyes on Ozo. "This is why you keep me here. I cannot accommodate the entire village."

As more continue to arrive both men stand face to face, Obi stares at Eze; he has never known anyone other than his wives to interrupt his uncle before.

"Other lives are important. It is not only this compound in this village," said Ozo in a calm voice.

At the back of the truck Lady Ani lifts Decima into the vehicle first. "Go and sit in that corner. Do not move from it until you arrive where you are going. Do you hear?"

"Yes Aunty." Decima squeezes through the cramped vehicle, followed by Obi and Arike. Obi watches from the open-backed truck, his eyes still on Eze, who rubs his head, irritated he kicks stones and twigs from the ground around him.

"This engine is not cooling. Water! I need plenty of water! I have seen it before, it will be ugly. I am not prepared to wait any longer. Owerri will not be under Biafran defence; Enugu will fall at any time to the Federal Forces." Taking out his damp handkerchief he wipes his brow. "You must run from your homes before you are all butchered to death." He says facing the commotion, in utter despair.

Nothing changed.

The old man with his walking stick speaks up. "*Biko*, my brother; where you want our people to run in this darkness? With your own mouth you have informed us of our destiny."

Eze ignores the weary man to inspect his truck; he pours water into the radiator, shakes and pulls at various parts of the vehicle on his round.

Mama Toni stands before Ozo with begging hand. "My husband; *Biko*, I beg you give your children money for food." Obi watches Ozo separate damp notes from his bundle and hands her some cash before she turns to walk out of the compound. On her head is a metal trunk; on her back are two of her youngest children, and the rest follow her with heavy bundles on their heads. "*Biko, Mek* I begin walk. I return to my own village."

Obi and Toni share a moment held by a gaze as the entire family proceed past the loaded truck towards the woods. Obi looks back at Ozo to see if he would intervene, but Ozo's eyes silently follow his family walk out of his life and the compound.

*

In a democracy many things are considered, a good leader will not react to panic during crisis; Ozo was in a difficult situation.

From the crammed belly of the eviction truck, Obi could still read his uncle's face. A man defeated, perhaps flawed for not putting his family's safety before others. During war morality is often compromised by self-preservation, but not so for Ozo.

"Aunty! Where is my aunty?" searched Obi in a panic from the corner of the truck. He was off before his sisters could look up from counting the money Lady Ani had hidden in the cloth bag for them. Obi squeezes through the packed passengers in the truck leaving his sisters oblivious. Clambering down the truck Obi runs towards Lady Ani's summer kitchen at the side of her veranda.

"Come Aunty, come. We go, we must run away now. Quick, Aunty, hurry!" Obi pulls and tugs at her long arm but she doesn't budge from her seat.

"Obi my dear, I am too old to run anywhere. Running is for the young." Obi listens intently, separating her voice from the chaos left behind him.

"May the unseen continue to protect and walk with you; remember me to your mother?"

Obi's chest pounds with her words of goodbye.

"I no leave you, Aunty."

Lady Ani smiles, "Your sister will tell you off if you don't speak good English," in an effort to lighten the moment.

"You are not leaving me; I will always be with you in your heart. Go now, you must look after your sisters. Do not take your eye from them. Now go." she dismisses Obi without looking at him.

Drained by his tears Obi pulls her with all the strength in his body, but to no avail. Lady Ani prizes his clammy fingers from her arm. No matter how much she struggled to sever the cord, Obi wouldn't let go, not until he hears his sisters' screams from the truck. Obi runs from Lady Ani's side, back to his sisters, his throat tight and flaming, his T-shirt drenched.

Lady Ani walks towards her veranda and into her house.

11

Farewell

Obi settles on his sisters' laps, pulling his catapult from his pocket.

"We should be already gone from this place," Obi hears Eze say making his way back to the truck.

"Federal troops will wipe out everything that moves, anything belonging to an Ibo will be destroyed, starting with our boys. This place will look very different by the next sunset!"

"This vehicle is overloaded" Eze tells himself, holding onto the metal framework of his truck, supporting himself up onto the tyre to untie a rope. "Nothing will be as it was. The same happened to my own village. I have lost everything and everyone. My mother born three sons and four daughters; I am the only one that remain." He clears his hollow voice and refocuses on the task ahead.

Obi scans over his darkened compound for the last time. The wives' kitchens, which he had known so well over the years, were abandoned. His eyes rested on Lady Ani's kitchen.

"You are people of the cross. Pray now," Eze continued at his silent passengers. "Holding your breath is no use to anybody, you are not looking at a slow passing serpent."

"This road is like a new bride. I must be careful. Take the guard!" Eze commands his monkey who sits on the passenger seat next to him. Obi's ears prick up on hearing Eze's words. Obi struggled to find space to turn around to take a peek on recognising the tiny squeak of a little primate. He couldn't believe his prayers had been answered; even under such difficult times. He is finally with a working truck monkey and not jumping on a verge trying to catch a glimpse.

Completely detached from any sense of their situation, Obi somehow scrambles to look into the cabin. A capuchin monkey no bigger than a starved puppy jumps out of the front cabin, around its neck is a red beaded necklace. He saw the animal run sideways off towards the back of the truck; dodging between legs that must have appeared like a forest. The monkey picks up a block of wood from under the back wheel and dragged it towards its master. Obi could see into the driver's cabin with worn seats, under a big black steering wheel covered in black leather, partly laced together.

Eze's hand rests on the long-angled gear stick which danced to the vibration of the engine. After it had stowed the block under the dashboard, the busy monkey leapt onto Eze's shoulders, its skinny body curled around his master's neck. Obi was in the midst of an unimagined reality, as he watched the monkey sniff its master's face, tapping at the pearls of sweat on Eze's face with its thin rubbery fingers.

Taking a deep breath, he wonders how the monkey stayed willingly untethered.

Obi remembers the situation and drops back down closer to his sisters; perched on Decima's lap he could feel the trembling of her knees and unresponsive limp arms. Her hands were cold when he lifted them across his stomach, and she didn't hug or hold him.

Obi narrows his eyes adjusting his gaze in the darkened vehicle. He sees mostly mothers with children in arms. He spots a few girls his age and boys younger than himself. He saw some toothless women elders and a few *adas* who he recognised from Lady Ani's hair days. Obi wondered what the next evacuation truck would be like when it arrived for the others. He considered that he should be in that truck with the other boys his age, but he kept his thoughts to himself. He knew it was best to be with his sisters.

"When this truck decides to leave this compound, our village will be finished," one of the mothers said.

Obi leans back into his sister on hearing her words. Decima did not complain, even though she could not move any further back. He tried to find Arike's hand but she was sitting on them, ignoring his demand.

"Our mother and father will not be able to find us if we are not at home." He told Decima, and his head starts to roll with dizziness.

Decima tightened her arm around him, sensing her brother's agitation. Unable to shake off all his usual what-ifs from his head, Obi clings to his sisters as if expecting to be pulled away from them, much like he'd imagined had happened when their mother left. Thoughts of her and of any chance of ever seeing her again drift in and out of his mind. Helpless, they all sat waiting in silence as the truck chugged, ready to leave the safety of a life they were finally about to give up. There was no time to mourn another separation. No time to say goodbye to friends, or make a last visit to his secret and favourite places like the hollow tree he loved so much. It was a 'state of emergency'. Their lives and survival were firmly in the hands of God and Eze.

"This night is cooler than usual," a mother said from the crammed truck, her baby asleep on her lap. Her fear and panic had turned to a philosophy of what will be, will be. "We are not all going to perish from this war." She continued to mutter. "Some will survive and tell our story of what has happened to this village this very night. Oh, what a night. What a terrible night." Leaning over her sleeping child she wipes her eyes with her wrapper and says; "Oh my dear."

Eze jumps out, walking around his vehicle for the last time. Unrolling a tattered canvas over the metal frame of the cargo area, he releases a plume of dust upon his passengers.

"Long life, long life." Different people wished the sneezers, as dried leaves and dead insects fell upon them in the dark.

Quickly he fastens the canvas to the main body of the truck. There had been no time to break *kola* nuts or offer libations and prayers for a safe and careful passage.

"This is a sign of things to come. The men must pray and ask our ancestors for our protection. We need every prayer," said the gentle woman's voice.

"We are leaving, please make space so that we can proceed," said Eze to the people surrounding the truck as he stretched his arms to grip and lift himself back into his seat again.

"We must make chance where there is no chance," he told himself, pressing down on the accelerator.

Obi's grip tightened around Decima's arms.

"How can any of us imagine our life will change in one night?" another voice wept aloud.

The disarray distracts Obi from crying; he no longer felt the pain in his throat. He leaned back and hid his face against his sister. They sat quietly at a time when others were not. It was not the time to behave like a small child, he told himself. His attention drifts to his few treasured items, which he kept safely under their bed.

"Goliath!" Obi snaps.

Without hesitation, and before his sisters had realised, he was off, again squeezing between other passengers who stood in the packed truck, tiptoeing over the legs of those seated and those on the floor. He pushes his way out as the vehicle reverses, ready to go. Obi jumps from the bolted drop-back of the truck, braking his fall on his hands to run into the darkened house before anyone could stop him. The truck engine roars, crunching into first gear with a jolt. His sisters scream after him and try to make their way out of the truck. Arike was by the edge about to jump when a hand grips her shoulder and pulls her back. Furious, she turns and bites the hand, before it was followed by a heavy slap on the side of her head.

"Do not touch my sister!" Decima cried out; her voice evaporated into the heaving cargo. The woman had a firm hold on Arike as she screamed for her brother. Obi ran into the house, past his uncle's room, where Ozo was counting cartridges. Obi entered his bedroom and dived under the bed. He grabs two guavas, and a transistor radio. He pulled his blanket from the bed and left the room.

On his way out, Obi rushes into Ozo's room, he embraces his uncle from behind. Outside he releases Goliath from its pen as the truck pulled out of the compound. He chases the truck as fast as he could, while the passengers cheered him on with outstretched arms. The driver couldn't hear his passengers shouting stop within the commotion – stop, stop – of his truck; he continued driving.

Obi's broken radio, in its perforated brown carry case, dangled on its strap as he ran. He refused to let go of his blanket which dragged along the dirt track. Knowing his village well paid off when he cut through familiar narrow pathways and with only a short distance before the truck arrived at the main road and was out of sight, Obi sprinted like he had never before. He caught up with the truck as it wobbled in and out of the last ditches and the cavernous recesses of the dirt track he knew so well. Stretching his arms out with his belongings towards his sisters who were shouting at him to run faster, Obi let go of his belongings safely in the hands of his sisters before the women begin pulling him up into the loaded truck. His sisters weep squeezing their way back towards their corner.

"If you do something like that again, we will leave you and go," Decima told him while holding his hand.

"Sorry, I wanted my radio. I thought I would be back before the driver was ready," Obi said.

"Do not do that again." Arike whispered after she pulled her brother onto her lap before Obi gave the guavas and blanket to his sisters and shuffled his bottom so he was more comfortable on both his sisters' laps.

"I released Goliath," Obi told them under his voice.

"Don't worry Obi he will be fine," Arike offered some support.

Having their brother back delighted the crowded truck and they could not be upset with him for his deeds for long. Obi cleaned and polished his radio against his shorts. His sisters smiled in the darkness, relieved to have their brother back. The truck rattled and rolled as it smashed its way through the bushes and smaller trees. Obi's jaw dropped at seeing that the driver had removed a square piece of board from behind his cabin, giving him a clear view into the passenger area. Eze looked behind him through the opening at the weary passengers and shouted.

"Hold tight, it will be very rough and I do not want to lose any of you. This road is like a virgin bride!" he repeated.

The overloaded vehicle bumped its way through the numerous potholes of the village before joining the main road under similar conditions. The exhaust pipe bellowed plumes of black and grey soot while the tyres scattered trails of dust and sand from a life they once knew.

In the mayhem Obi had forgotten all about the little monkey and was surprised when he heard it shriek and clap his twig-like hands in excitement. Obi turned to peer into the cabin and saw the monkey peeling a small banana that the driver had handed him.

"I must leave road," Eze told himself suddenly swerving, leaving the main road at speed. The dirt track was barely wide enough to accommodate the truck. The craters and potholes did not deter Eze, he accelerated through knowing that his passengers would be tossed against each other, but under such circumstances there was little choice but to drive with haste. Those that stood banged their heads against the metal frames as the vehicle hurtled down the rough terrain, while the seated bounced like over-inflated footballs. The passengers enquired of how the driver could see where he was going, especially without his headlights, although they knew why they were switched off.

"It will take only one rocket to end this journey!" Eze interjected, "I have been driving behind enemy lines, unseen, since the beginning of this war!"

Obi felt the tight grip of his sisters' arms around his waist. They looked at each other in the dark and wished that no matter what, they would remain together and survive despite whatever lay ahead. They remained silent, each lost in their own thoughts. From that moment, everything would fall on Decima's shoulders to take care of her brother and sister as the eldest. Obi could feel the increased beating of her heart against his back as she held him closer, he turned to Decima almost nose to nose, his forehead to hers.

"Are you sad, sister? We will see our mother, she will come to find and take us, you will see."

"We are alone, Obi. Do you not understand?" Arike nudged him.

"*Biko*, Arike, let him be; of course he knows what is happening to us. Why do you think he ran back to bring us his blanket?"

"Where are all the rest of the people from our compound?" Obi enquired. "We do not have our mother and father to protect us so we have to look after ourselves." He examined his radio.

Decima and Arike rest back against the uncomfortable hard wood of the truck. Obi's head bobs up and down on Arike's shoulder as they travel in silence.

"I remember a story from when I was smaller. It was about when me and my baby brother chased a chicken around the compound because we wanted to eat chicken," said Obi in the hope of escaping the dark, heavy atmosphere of the truck.

The hours passed, each one seemed longer than the last. An orchestra of sounds and human noises played out unnoticed by the mass of bodies. Unfazed by the knocking and bumping of the rough roads, everyone fell asleep; even Obi became part of the mass of heaped bodies around him, when the movement of the truck lulled him back into slumber. Being a light sleeper, his ears focused on the whining sound from under the truck. The constant noise reminded him of the times he ran about the village wheeling his steel ring dodging in and out of people and objects with the skilful twists of his hand. Looking out through the various holes and slits of the canvas cover, he sees a different world by the morning light which seeps into the truck. Parts of his land he had never seen or imagined.

The sun nudged its crown over the tufts of fluffed-up white clouds above an unknown village as the truck sped past. Although it would have been too early for people to start their day, Obi could see that the village was devastated, levelled to the ground by an unwelcomed force of evil that had moved on to consume another community. Broods of unconcerned hens explored the deep tyre tracks for their breakfast while chicks pecked behind mothers who scratched and raked the dry, cracked earth. It was not a war of fancy folktales with heroes and spears, slaves and kings in a distant faraway land. It was the beginning of a real war, their war, a war for the survival of their new country, Biafra.

Obi wipes the sweat from his face with his damp T-shirt. Despite the dangers of the evacuation he smiles to himself delighted that he was riding in a truck, without having to go to the roadside and wait for trucks with the truck monkeys. He is actually *in* one, and with a monkey. Obi could not believe his luck and nor could he remember a time when he rode in a vehicle before. Even the stories of his wealthy father and the cars he drove no longer rested in his mind. It didn't really matter why he was in the truck; only that he is being driven in one.

The worn out slits and pinholes in the canvas covering caused tiny rays of light to criss-cross over each other like sharp lasers. The beams of sunlight brightened up the stuffy cargo of people. "Sister, I cannot stretch my legs," Obi whispered, as tingles fused his cramped knees together.

Decima managed to shift her legs and open her eyes for a second to peek at her brother. She smiles at him before she turns to rest against Arike's back. Distracted by the beams of sunray, Obi peeps out of a slit in the canvas near them. He could see a enormous open landscape with huts and buildings scattered in the distance against a clear blue sky dotted with tufts of white clouds. Seeing the vastness, the trees and hills, such as he had never known before, he gasped and looked around to see whether he'd woken any of the passengers. The trees looked inviting and easy to climb with low hanging branches, unlike the ones in his village; their roots rose like giant arteries pushed forth from the earth. He tried to recall all the names of the trees which his uncle had taught him; his mind went blank.

"Trees look unclimbed," he whispered to himself. And he thought; *the trees would be home to many animals which were not afraid of boys.*

"Baboon! Sleeping baboon," Obi shouts in excitement, forgetting where he was and that others were still asleep in the truck. He respected how much people of his village loved to close their eyes under any condition.

"Elephants, big elephants!" Elated, he shook his sisters from their rest. "Look through the holes."

"What! Where is baboon?" asked a woman, startled out of her sleep.

"Sorry Ma. My brother sees different animals in the clouds," Decima said.

"Too early in the morning for that kind of thing. Does he not sleep?" the woman asked, nuzzling for a better position for her head.

Obi watches her wipe a trail of saliva from her mouth; with eyes closed she kisses her teeth before falling off to sleep upon a woman slumped next to her. Obi's eyes are heavy; he drifts in and out of sleep, lulled by the motion of the vehicle. He can't help subliminally tracking the life he is leaving behind by the second. Even the last few days at school when no one knew would be their last.

*

The truck had not stopped since it left the compound during the dark of the morning. Obi and the driver are the only people awake; he thinks about the evacuation. Obi hears a tiny squeal from the monkey, but no chance of getting up to check for the crammed bodies strewn everywhere. Obi adjusts back onto his sister's lap having lost his sleep to memories of Lady Ani and uncle Ozo who he's left behind in his village.

If what we do today affects tomorrow, then what we did yesterday must also affect today, a confusing thought that he heard his teacher explain in class fleets through his mind.

Their journey seems unending. Obi struggles to stay awake

and sleep all at the same time; his head pops up intermittently like a fatigued soldier on watch. He continues to recall the past: the fireside stories he loved so much and how each tale could have different meanings for every person sat around the fireside.

Life is like a breeze in the way it comes and then it vanishes. Before you know it was there, it has gone my dear, an elder once said beginning his folktale.

During times of celebrations, musicians travelled from compound to compound playing to whoever felt like dancing. Obi and his line of friends waited for the right time to jump into the dance circle, which would have been teaming with old and young alike. The celebrations often culminated in an epic dance carnival in and around the village centre. Obi and his peers watched how the older boys jumped into the dance circle, but they did not have the courage to try to dance like the senior boys did.

Dancing is too important to make a fool of yourself in front of others, Obi remembers an *ada* telling him and his friends once.

All they wanted was to know how they could dance as fast on their feet like the older boys. Mothers, *adas* and the elders dance around in a formation, swirling arms and colourful protruding bottoms, swaying like flamingos on a merry-go-round. The tempo increased with the beats of congas, beaded calabash, cowbells and talking drums. The boys watch with open jaws, nudging each other, not quite brave enough to be the first to jump into the circle.

The passengers continue to make up for the previous sleepless night and Obi's mind is overrun with thoughts of the past.

He thinks of when he and Peter stood side by side aiming their catapults, sending fast pebbles high into the trees towards the bats. Eventually a stone sends one of the enormous bats to the ground, like heavy bread dough passing through the layers of thick leaves. Engaging another stone ready to shoot, Obi ventures into the woods to find the bat. Over the dry crunchy leaves amongst the dark undergrowth as evening closed in, Obi moves with caution, toes pointing before his feet touch the ground, one foot carefully before the other, suspended in mid-air perfectly poised like a praying mantis. Obi searches for his fallen prey, the further he pushed into the dense wood, the darker it got. He had forgotten that Peter was waiting for him; discharging a few random shots into the curled leaves in case of movement beneath them, especially snake. Looking down just in time he sees the camouflaged animal as it struggled, unable to escape. With twig-like claws bent and pointed like fishing hooks, the bat lay slumped. *Do I pick the bat up alive so we can keep it as a pet, or will it bite me and fly away?* Obi was undecided in his dilemma when his sharp ears picked up a slight and unfamiliar sound from the tree above. To take his eyes from his prey could result in losing it, but what if there was a baby monkey up in the tree? His heart hastened.

When he looked up, he saw Tabooless instead. He didn't know why they had been warned to stay away from that man. *What was he doing up in the tree with a woman?* Entwined and partly naked, they resembled the branches that supported them. *Women that size did not normally climb trees*, Obi thought. Tabooless's piercing red eyes look down at Obi on the ground. Raising his spear-like black finger to his pinched lips, Obi did not see who the woman was but understood Tabooless's warning; what mattered was that he moved on and said nothing to anyone. Obi had not seen that woman in his village before.

It was not too long after that Tabooless was involved in a big fight with the woman's husband. Although the husband brought his spear to warn him, Tabooless would have killed the man with his bare hands had some of the strong men from the village not intervened. Despite the heavy restraints, Tabooless took the spear from the man and snapped it with one hand. That was when the women elders chased him out of the village shouting: "Never return to show your face here again! When you have your own wife, a younger boy will take her." Obi thinks of his city cousins that always said that village life was dull and dirty, he wonders where they are.

12

Life and Daydream

Decima's cheek is glued to the top of her brother's shoulder; his clammy body damp against her dress as the truck chugs along a dirt road. Exhausted and still unable to sleep, unlike his sisters and the rest of the passengers, Obi squeezes his tummy remembering they hadn't eaten for a long time. He was used to being hungry and hadn't thought about the food that Lady Ani had given them for their journey, besides he'd never eat without his sisters, who were still asleep. Struggling to keep awake, his racing mind drifts to the various stories he'd heard over the years about his parents, especially his mother, how she used to run off to school without eating her breakfast; but it didn't bring a smile like it often had in the past. He remembers Lady Ani's words when they sat on her veranda shaded from the sun and heat while everyone else was asleep; she'd tell him lots of stories.

As a child, your mother waited until her father returned in the evening so they can eat their traditional evening meal of fufu together. In the morning, her mother begged her to drink some milk before she ran off to school.

"*I am not a cow baby,*" *she protested, before disappearing through the bordering woods of her land.*

Obi always laughed aloud when Lady Ani mimicked his mother's stubborn mannerisms.

The heat, humidity and the constant whirring of the engine is lulling Obi to sleep; not wanting to give into it, he hums to himself the John Bull song, and likes the vibration it creates in his throat.

"Obi, where are you all going?" the melodious whisper of a girl's voice brings a smile.

"My name is Obi."

"Shh, you are a boy? Boys cannot come here. How are you here? You have to go back. Go back now before they find you."

"Who are you, I cannot see you. Are you a ghost?" Obi looks around.

"I am here, right in front of you."

"Where is this place? Why is everywhere dark?" Obi protested.

"When you open your eyes, you will see that it is not dark. You should be out of sight in here, come. Papa's guards are all too big to come and check in here. You can stay for a while. My name is Rani. Who are your people?"

"I am Obi. Why are you praying?"

"I already know that."

"I live with my sisters – Arike and Decima. We live; we used to live in my uncle's compound."

"Compound?"

"I am seven, I think."

"I was not praying I was greeting you with respect." said Rani.

Obi puts his hands together under his chin, and her plump cheeks rise as she smiles back at him.

"Why do you not know how old you are? Everybody knows how old they are."

Obi scrambles to his feet as Rani approaches on the back of an elephant. A tiger walks with them.

Astounded, he couldn't believe his eyes between the haze and his vision. Beside the rows of sprawling trees Obi sees what looks like a white bull. Rubbing his eyes it becomes larger and clearer.

"I heard you singing. I could not find John, but I found a bull."

Rani looks down at Obi, smiling, she offers out her hand. "Come, ride with me."

Obi is weary but happy at the same time; actually calm instead of panicked or fear stricken. His face beams with joy on seeing Rani and her animals and the enormous bull with a bell around its neck and garlands around its horns.

"Don't worry Obi; I think your mother will find you wherever you are. Mothers have magic towards their children." Obi has completely surrendered to sleep on his sister's lap, dead to the living world in the humid vehicle.

13

A Memorable Journey

Except for his picture of them in front of his father's car, he had no recollections of times spent with his family when he was younger. Those memories were neatly contained within a colourful tin box of photographs. He has a few favourites: his father standing next to his car, himself as a baby in his mother's arms, him standing with his sisters in front of their father's car and another on his tricycle; this was when they lived in Minna. One of his aunties had told him off for using the hard, serrated edge of a photograph to demonstrate to his friends how the edge could cut leaves.

When he first heard women of the village talk of the 'big man' his father was; Obi thought he might have been a giant, not knowing they were referring to his father's expensive taste and lavish lifestyle.

The villagers were in awe of their bank manager son, so much so that a road was built in his honour; that stretched from the compound to the main road. They named it: 'Road of Benjamin's Car.'

As the truck drove through the daylight, Obi continued to think of his village and what he would be doing had he been back there.

"No food," he whispered.

There was a stagnant atmosphere under the canvas and the tall trees in the landscape outside no longer engaged him. The driver remained off-road, telling them how unsafe it was to travel or be seen anywhere near them. Most, if not all the passengers, had never ventured so far out of their village. The mothers and their babies sat fixed in the same place, staring into empty space with fearful eyes upon waking, and Obi noticed how they did not blink very much. It was unusual for the mothers not to greet one another on first sight. Bodies swayed silently with the motion of the truck, mother's grip on their babies loosened as their heads wobble from side to side, while others suckled holding onto the edge of a wrapper for security.

"What will become of our husbands?" a passenger broke the silence. "What of our sons?" she continued.

"My dear, I do not know. By God's grace, they are in another truck," someone else replied. Obi tries not to stare at her puffy face with angry bloodshot eyes; the intensity of her gaze left him wheezing. As much as he wanted to, he could not look away.

"You are Obi?" she asked him in a thin wiry voice.

Obi nodded and looked away in the direction of his sisters. His restless limbs twitched unable to stretch for lack of space.

"If we ever return to our homes, it will be a miracle," said a younger woman. "I doubt whether God even knows where we will end up!"

"*Biko*, my sister, let us not bring more difficulties upon ourselves, please. Watch your mouth; there are small people in here without their mothers. Ha, Jesus Christ!"

Sporadic conversations happened but mostly women talked amongst them.

"During this war of course you will doubt the existence of Christ," the young woman mumbled under her breath.

Women talked about Ozo and other elders from the village who refused to escape in the truck or to leave their homes to run.

"Run where? Where will they run?"

Silence descends once more in the sweltering truck, as the women closed their eyes unable to block out their fate.

Obi overheard how the Federal Army did not take prisoners of Ibo men; he worried about Ozo, wondering if he would be using his rifle to fight the army.

"They are animals who kill everyone in sight, the young and the old, everyone slaughtered by their bayonets!" said the woman with red angry eyes.

What is bayonets? Obi wondered, trembling, listening to the woman mumbling to herself; but her fury could be felt and his sisters were still asleep, though he wasn't convinced.

"How is it that a man can feed his brother faeces and urine at gunpoint? No woman is safe. They will rape us all and cut our unborn babies from our stomach." Although she mumbled, every word was heard.

The woman next to her retched and in no time another vomited into her wrapper from hearing such detailed account.

"Young lives, long memories. *Biko,* my sister, I beg you remember that there are children in this bus, I beg you control your tongue." Obi did not look to see who was talking but he knew it was an elder.

"Big mama, no *mek* you tell anyone what to say in here. We are not in your compound now," said a high school *ada,* not much older than Decima.

An argument erupts in the truck when others join in to chastise the *ada* for her rudeness in challenging her elder. Decima and Arike hold one another in their corner trying not to be seen watching the commotion, until Eze's fist thumps several times against the wall of his truck startling them before the women stop. But not before the young student had sucked her teeth into the stale air.

A few moments later she continued again: "My teacher spoke of God's grace in letting him get out alive from Kaduna. He said that Kaduna Radio sang praises of the evil they were releasing on Ibo people."

"Dear child, by escaping with his life, your teacher has shown us that God has not totally abandoned the Ibos, we must take heart and remember to watch over each other," one of the older woman explained.

"*Biko*, Mama, I am sorry. Please find it in your heart to forgive my disrespect." said the *ada*.

"My dear, you are young. Of course, you have a right to be much afraid. The news spoken by your teacher was correct. Is it best these children learn from us what to expect, before it is too late and they will not know what to do. We have not yet entered the snake pit and already we are fighting with each other. However will our people survive, if this is how we behave?"

Decima, Arike and Obi listened to the variety of conversations bounce around the agitated truck, mostly about the Ibos and how they will fare alone in the war, nobody really cared that there are children listening as they spoke of the horror, the gore and their ultimate fate.

"Who would believe that they are not orphans? Look at them, their father was a big man. How could he not take his children out before?" a woman from Obi's neighbouring compound whispers, but not very quietly.

"What of the boy?"

"I am speaking of the boy most of all, he will not see any of his village friends again."

"Then what of all the other boys left behind?"

"If they have not already been slaughtered by the Federal troops, they will now be conscripted by the home army."

"Did Eze not say that the boys will be following in another truck? They will be safe, by the grace of God!"

"Amen sister, Amen."

Obi shudders, hiding his face behind his sister.

"It is pogrom on our people," the girl said, looking in Decima's direction. Arike looks back at her with angry eyes.

"We lived in the north before we come back home. My father was killed when he went to collect me from school. It is true; I have seen many slaughtered by the army in the north."

Obi squeezes but could not huddle any closer to his sisters, who by now occupied one seat between them. Eyes shut, hands to his ears, he tries to escape the tense atmosphere. He'd always hated such circumstances when people didn't get on and now he struggles to think of Rani, his mind is everywhere. An old image of a time when his grandfather rode an enormous horse into the compound was the best he could muster. He was very small at the time, he ran with the other children to greet them. To his surprise, he was scooped up and lifted up to the saddle by his grandfather before they rode away. Obi started counting to pass the time.

The women calmed down again and closed their eyes returning to solitary thoughts. He pokes a finger through one of the slits and sees that they are in the grounds of a school or church. There are people everywhere but he cannot see other boys of similar age. The chaos outside reminds him of the tension when they first climbed into the truck to leave their village.

After Eze switched off his engine, the faithful truck juddered like a feverish beast before it settled into a well-deserved rest.

"Bam Bam!" Eze shouts and bangs the side of his vehicle. Obi hears the monkey's tiny voice screaming as it left the truck. He could not believe how he had forgotten all about it.

Eze begins to untie the canvas at the back while his passengers find their feet, trying to regain their balance on their cramped legs. A deluge of dust, twigs, leaves and dead insects from the cover rained on everyone as it is pulled away.

"Our new world, let us pray to survive this one," a voice emerged from the heaving truck.

Silent in total disbelief, the passengers take in their new surroundings. The hatch of the truck drops with a slam, alerting their new hosts of their arrival. Squinting, the passengers rub their eyes and shade themselves from the blinding glare of a fierce sun. The hot breeze is a familiar welcome that they have not left their motherland and the sun sanitises the odious energy and pent-up frustration of an unknown journey. Some of the elders remained seated, their heads bent forward with despair but gently, like chrysalises, they start to unfurl themselves under the hot sun.

The monkey set to work; it leapt back out from the bush and into the driver's cabin. The small creature scales up, over and around the truck in seconds. Obi watches it performing its duties obediently; throwing the wooden guard under the back wheel to stop the truck rolling. His master rewards him with a small fruit.

"Why does the monkey always eat with two hands?" Obi asks his sisters. The primate's activities captivate him to the point of distraction of their uncertain future. "How can he eat so fast?" Obi asks himself. The animal's head moves side to side observing what is going on around him, not sparing a second on any scene. Obi tries to count the seconds to see how long each movement takes before the next but the monkey moves faster than he can count in Ibo. Absorbed by the small creature he overlooks that the truck has arrived at their destination.

"We have to get out, Obi," Arike whispers in his ear before he snaps back to the present. Between the last few remaining legs he steps carefully and looks out into the vast open ground beyond the truck. Contained and unaware that his grip was hurting his sister's arm, he doesn't rush to see the mass of people.

14

First Base

Nudged to his feet it was time to disembark. Reluctantly Obi looks away from the monkey to see what the commotion in the new land is about. The open wasteland of patchy ground is littered with people. He scans the area and sees different types of buildings dotted around: a hut with a big cross, painted in his favourite colour red on the door, caught his attention.

"Where are we?" Obi asks his sisters as they prepare to leave the truck last.

"Jump out! Get out! Hurry, hurry!" a man barks from the grounds and Obi wonders why the man's eyes are red.

"Why are the people harsh?" Obi asks in a quiet voice with his head down.

"We have to do as we are told here, Obi," Arike replies. "You must stay close. We must not be parted. Do you understand? You cannot be lost here; no one will look for you. We are not in our compound anymore."

"I will not get lost, my sister," Obi promised. "What is this place?" he enquires, still standing at the back of the truck that he had grown rather fond of.

"This will be our home now, dear boy," an elderly woman told him. "Everyone here will have had their own sufferings.

You have been a good boy Obi; you must always listen to your sisters and know where they are. My dear, we are in wartime." Cautiously she makes her way down the steep descent from the truck towards the scorched ground of the refugee camp. Losing her balance, she lands and remains down on her knees, as if praying. Obi rushes, jumping off the truck to offer his help, but another woman was already helping her back onto her feet.

"Thank you *ada*, I do not know why I am holding on to life, I have seen the best of this world. My dear, this will be our life now." To steady herself, she grips hold of the girl's hand with her frail grey fingers.

"Go! Bring a wooden box or stool to help the elders get down from this truck," Eze orders the red-eyed man. "Do you not have a brain to know that for yourself, or were you born foolish? These people are not soldiers; how you can expect them to jump from such a height? Fool! Go now before I use you as entertainment and beat you in front of everybody." Eze assists the rest of the elders, mothers and their children out of his truck. "Oh! Are there more than one of you, my dear man?" Eze asked Obi, who had got himself back onto the truck.

"I no leave my sisters sir!" Obi said with a smile.

They look into each other's eyes for what seemed a long time. Eze held out his arms. Obi leaps towards him like his monkey. They hold on to one another as if they were reuniting father and son. Obi grips tightly around Eze's neck, his legs wrapped about his waist. Obi burst out crying.

"*Biko*, forgive me for bringing you to such a place. We no longer have the choices we had before the Devil visited our lives," Eze said. He saw that his passengers' eyes are downcast with despair. "I would have liked to take you all to a better place, but under these conditions, it is difficult to find any safer place than this, in our once-blessed country."

Looking at Obi, who was still clinging to his side, he told him that he had heard all about him from Brother Joseph. Obi jolts his head back to look at Eze.

"Is Joseph here? Where can I see him?" Obi asked, so excited that he momentarily forgets where he is.

"You did not know who I am?" said the driver. "Joseph was my junior brother. We are all Ibo brothers in the army. No, he is not here; we think Joseph is lost in action."

Tears run down Obi's face; his body shakes with the grief as he hides his face into Eze's neck on hearing the devastating news that Joseph is lost.

"In war, everybody pays. You and I have both lost our brother, because we do not know of his whereabouts," said Eze. "The story I hear is that Joseph was captured just after his arrival at Port Harcourt. We received news of his disappearance some weeks ago, but that was not corroborated officially. Then, shortly after, more news arrived of his escape." Obi listens intently to Eze's account. "He joined our forces behind enemy lines. It is only because I am an officer that I know this secret information." Obi hides his face against Eze's shoulder.

"OK. Stop crying. We are at war and you have duties also for the war effort." Eze puts Obi down. "Do not cry, my boy, we still have hope that he may still be living.

"You and your sisters should find a corner in the building to rest. I will come and find you later to finish my story about Joseph."

The light started to fade as Obi and his sisters head towards the former school, they walk in line with Obi in the middle looking back at Eze.

"He is going to leave," he sobs. "Why must everyone go away?" His salty tears dry instantly on his face upon contact with the heat.

They stop before the building, Decima and Arike look at his flooded face and agree he could go back to Eze if he promised to run straight back to them after the story was over. Obi thanked his sisters, promising to return as fast as he could run. With those words, he ran towards Eze with his aeroplane arms. Eze stood to catch Obi as he dived into the driver's chest, almost sending them to the ground.

"A big man like you still likes to be carried!" Eze laughs and Obi holds tighter to his thick, sweaty neck. "Joseph would want you to survive this hell of a war and to live a good and long life. I will try to look for you again Obi before I move. Now you must stay close to your sisters and do as they say. You are a good boy, the man of your family; you are blessed to have such sisters that look after you, especially during these difficult times."

They both walk to the edge of the open ground where a fallen tree lay, they sit for some time without talking until Obi settles from the sniffling and hiccuping from his crying.

"Have you more stories, uncle?"

Eze smiles and looks around the camp ground. "There are many stories of this war Obi, but one thing you must not forget is the might of our Biafran soldiers. No one outside Biafra will ever tell you truth of the bravery of your people. No one of our warriors receive payment for fighting for you. Our General uses his father's money to pay for the war."

Eze smiles, reaching into his pocket taking out a dried piece of red cola nut and throws it into his mouth. "Your brother has turned out to be a hero of the Ibo troops," he continues.

"A good 'Barefoot soldier', another of our names. I will now tell you more about this war. If Joseph has been killed, he would not have gone without a good fight. Did you know he was a good fighter?"

Obi looks down at his feet and shakes his head. "He told me not to fight with anybody and I made him a promise not to fight with anybody. Fighting is not a good thing to do, because people always get hurt," Obi replied, unable to control his sobbing again. "He did not keep his promise, now he is dead. Will we all die in this war? Why did he go to fight?"

"He fight for you not to be killed; after he finished his first training, he was posted to Backwater Port, I think. Do you know Port?" Obi shakes his head again. "I think your family lived there some time ago. We think he became disillusioned; the fighting was not progressing to save innocent people, like the people of your village. And no, everybody will not die. You and your sisters must make sure you stay together and survive, otherwise it would be another war when your mother returns and does not find you. You have to live and remember the suffering that war brings. His fellow officers said that he was a brave and excellent soldier, guerrilla fighting behind enemy lines. They said he did not think the war was ever going to end, so he struggled with his own war, inside himself."

"Uncle, why is it his own war?" Obi asked.

Eze continued as Obi listened in awe. "He hit the road after the news that Enugu would be falling into enemy hands. Nothing could stop him from going. He wanted to return to the village, the home and people he loved. 'I must see Obi,' he said. 'I have to save him and his family.' He was still in uniform when he was captured by the military police at Umuahia and thrown into the back of an army vehicle. He was then taken to Agara where he saw and met General Ojukwu several times, addressing his officers and giving everyone courage and blessings. General Ojukwu asked why Joseph was in the back of the vehicle and why he was a runaway soldier. 'General, I have to save my friends and family in Enugu,' was Joseph's reply. But Ojukwu did not hear him; his attention was diverted by other officers who had pressing questions. Before he moved on to his next engagement, Ojukwu told the men to lock Joseph up in the army engineer's office because he was a deserter.

"Joseph was a highly trained soldier in guerrilla warfare; he escaped into the forest that night."

Several boys from the camp arrived to listen to Eze's story.

"What happened next, uncle?" one of the boys asked.

"Joseph jumped into a truck to Agara Junction, this time in civilian clothes, where he met a woman and pretended to be with her. He was again captured and locked up, but gave them another slip during the morning fatigue."

"What is morning fatigue uncle?" the boys asked, reminding Obi of Lady Ani's hair days.

Eze looked with smiling eyes at the inquisitive faces and explained.

"Well, Joseph's disillusionment and loss of heart came when he realised how many senior officers were saboteurs."

The boys gasped on hearing the word saboteur, it had become a word that could seal the fate of anyone mistakenly accused. The war had turned people more suspicious than ever before, even village boys.

"Joseph loathed the wearing of dead soldiers' clothes, especially the ones he had killed. He became tired of smoking lemongrass and pawpaw leaves wrapped in paper. He was a young man who liked palm wine straight from the trees of his village." Eze laughed and looked at Obi; his head thrown back, eyes closed as if he had remembered a funny event but his voice bellowed. "His officer called him belligerent, because he refused to take native gin, which other soldiers drank to keep them high and their hunger at bay." Pausing for a moment, Eze continued, "My dear, although it would seem that Joseph died from this war, there is hope that he may still be living. We live with hope, side by side with the ravages of war."

"Obi!" Decima calls from a distance.

"Uncle, my sister is calling me; I must go now."

Obi stood up from the fallen tree trunk and set off towards his sisters who could see him from the steps of the school. They watched him running, weaving in and out of the mass of people arriving from all directions, carrying their possessions on their heads and on bicycles. Decima and Arike were not surprised when Obi switched direction and ran back to hug Eze, before running back to them again.

15

Strafe

Explosions sent buildings up into the air and limbs fell like branches ripped apart by angry winds. Cloudless sky crack open revealing sharp silver darts that crisscross under a familiar blue heaven. The complicit midday sun camouflaged the metallic jet fighters racing towards the refugee camp, on a mission of complete annihilation.

Like migrating wildebeests, children, women and old men get trampled in the frenzied stampede for shelter towards the forest's edge. Obi swiftly moves to higher ground so that he can scan the place in the hope of locating his sisters. With all attempts failing, he squeezes himself behind a broken cupboard in the darkest corner of the old school building, praying for them to find him. Closed eyes and clenched fists over his ears, he wants the nightmare to stop, when finally Arike and Decima's voices drew him out like a root pulled from damp earth.

"Come out of there," said his sisters in unison. "You will die there." The three run out of the building not sure which way to head as people scatter in every direction from the camp.

"I-I- know," Obi shouts, petrified, competing with the mayhem around them; grabbing their hands in the panic, running towards the trees for shelter. The ground resembled an assault course, strewn with mutilated bodies and ripped debris upon the earth splashed with blood. As buildings caught fire, smoke bellowed out evicting those that hid within its corners. Arike let go of Obi's hand when Decima tripped over a dead child, partly covered by a piece of corrugated zinc that had once been a roof. Separated, they continue running into the woods.

Obi was already taking cover behind a tree before he realised that his sisters were not with him. The sea of people all looking the same, running in the same direction, seeking the same hiding places didn't help. He knew they had become entangled with the mass of refugees desperate for cover. The trees in these woods were tall, prickly and unfriendly. Obi's panic morphed into fear for the enormity of finding his sisters was becoming an impossible task. Lady Ani's warning to stay with his sisters started to haunt him; it was their first day in the camp and he had already lost them, his face and armpits were a deluge of sweat. About to brace himself for a run against the tide, he sees what looks like Arike and Decima running into the woods; not chancing any more misses he screams out for them and runs at the same time.

"It is already half past one, they always bomb us at one o'clock." he heard one of the old women say as she limps into hiding.

They make their way further into the woods before they huddle like baby birds under the thicket awaiting their parents return. Only they were not birds, and there will be no parents that would look for them there.

To the shiny fighter jets they would have appeared like ants. Like sharp arrows their noses aimed down at the trees and at them. Obi watches from the gaps in the foliage of their hiding place, although there was nothing left to destroy they returned to honour their command.

The injured did not cry out or moan and the babies stared wide eyed upon their mothers' backs silenced by fear. Day became night under the canopy of the trees, the ground remained moist devoid of sunshine; fortunate, as it gave them hope to hide away in the undergrowth from the angry jets, praying that they would be less persistent in scattering their rockets onto unseen targets. Obi was glad that the old trees stood up to the unwelcomed warriors of the sky, and he didn't try to count the people he could see huddled behind them like he would have in the past; it wasn't the same life any more, he wasn't a bystander in a village. His former life could have been a million years away in history, his own history. Before the war; trees provided them with food, joy, shelter and much else; now they are protectors, stubborn against rockets that ripped their old limbs apart.

After the raid Obi watches in the distance, the flames travelling up the trunk while next to him his sisters rest with their backs pushed against the century old tree with knees to their chests. The burning dead split like pigs on spits, their flesh puffed and fat oozes out around them. The MiG's onslaught of rockets and bombs on the camp were accurate although not swift; the blue sky gave itself up to the grey smog and black poison. Behind the ancestral trees refugees sat tight and waited, the earth beneath them a comforting reminder of better times.

Decima, Arike and Obi did not rush out of hiding; they waited at the foot of the aged trees that had stood their ground against modernity. Obi had spied out the silver jets against the pristine sky through the tangle of leaves from where they nestled. For a solitary moment, despite the doom that had surrounded them, a warm smile lit across Obi's face and his sisters might have thought he'd been with Rani, their mother, or Lady Ani in a dream. He had always been fascinated by aeroplanes, especially how they manage to stay up in the sky without flapping their wings. Nothing about war was pretty; Obi had become accustomed to a war he knew nothing about until it was forced upon them.

Following the weary mass back towards what was once a camp, Obi and his sisters walk away from the safety at the wood's edge, they gaze into the burnt-out ground ahead of them. Frozen and confused, silent cries struggle not to be carried away unheard by the wind. There are no birds in sight, no crickets chattering, but most of all there are no reassuring arms to hold them. They hold each other.

"Our mother abandoned us," Obi whispers echoing the words he had heard others say.

It was early morning by the time most of them had emerged from the wooded area around the campsite. Obi thinks he hears the jets returning again to finish them off, but he is unsure of anything any more as hunger bites deep in his belly; especially seeing the mass running toward the wrecked food distribution area in the hope of any pickings. He couldn't remember when they had last seen anything edible.

"You must run for cover." A figure darts past them almost unnoticed. "They return to finish us."

The voice of a mother returning from the bombed-out camp warns them as she disappears into the woods with all the food she had found in one hand and her child in the other. Obi stares at the three fingers of blackened bananas within her clutch; he had forgotten all about bananas and how much he loved their sweetness. He and his sisters watch the woman push her back against the bushes before they closed in.

Confused about what to do, they look around holding onto each other, balanced upon the dirt mounds left by the smaller uprooted trees at the edges of the camp. The jets opened fire before their noise caught up, sending more bodies to the ground like wet washing from a broken line.

16

Biafran Pogrom

T he children copy and do as the others do. They follow the mass back into the same woods that had saved them from death. Walking the narrow path being created for them by others in front of the exodus, Obi and his sisters know they have to keep up because no one will carry them if they can't manage. Everyone a stranger within what has become a strange land, Obi no longer recognised his people, a people he had come to know as good people that would not trade their child for God. People he'd known to care for children that did not belong to them. It had all been a lie; his teacher could not have been a good man to have taught them such nonsense about Ibos and Iboland.

He didn't want to look at the once full and beautiful faces of his sisters, it made him sad to see their gaunt faces while his had not changed much over their time as refugees. Whenever they had to 'take cover' near a roadside as army vehicles passed, Obi made sure to have his hands free to help his sisters back up, the effects of starvation was merciless. Although the body was the temple of the soul it still needed looking after, most of all with food and water, no one had either.

When they stumbled onto a patch of green leaves, mothers found the energy to lift up their wrappers to run and pluck them to eat. Obi stopped his sisters when he heard another woman call them fools for eating animal bush. As everyone would know, bitter leaves were sublime when dried and added to soup, after most of the bitterness had been boiled out. The women vomited until they could no longer walk and they lagged behind.

Obi looks back until he could no longer see them. The first group of people was beginning to fall around them as tiredness took hold and the cushioned decaying ground became soft beds to lay their heads. The pace quickened and rejoicing voices that had been silent began to praise the Lord for his mercy of leading them not into enemy range but to salvation. It was becoming dark when they stepped out of the bushes and into a new camp. Spotting a mass of children with rusty bowls and cups, Obi and his sisters walked towards them. The children had been eating *gari* but there were no traces of food around their mouths or clothes, not a single grain amiss. Obi remembers the hungry dogs in his compound and how they longed for crumbs that never appeared. A mother came towards them from nowhere. She screamed, lifting her hand to shoo them away like unwelcomed stray animals.

"*Biko*, auntie, we need food," Decima begged with open palms towards the angry mother.

"You tink maket bi here o? *Biko*, na disturb children. Food na be here o." The woman tuts and kisses her mouth towards them.

Fatigued they try to enter the building, but the same woman rushes in to obstruct their way. Although she wasn't a centurion she stood in front of them as if she was, behind her were a mass of people sprawled out and unconcerned. It was clear that no adult would come to their rescue and welcome them into the hall.

"No!" said Arike as Obi tugged at her to join the others outside. Arike had had enough of the woman and her ways; Obi didn't want his sister to fight a grown up but it was too late.

Arike's eyes pierced straight through the crazy woman's cloudy grey eyes before she sent her crashing to her bottom from one almighty push. People shuffled out of the way just in time like scattering ants to avoid being squashed. Almost immediately after the woman landed on the floor she curled her legs up and made space for them to pass. Decima had spotted a clearing big enough for one of them. What usually happens is once a space is occupied, they can somehow accommodate more by squeezing and shuffling around. They fall asleep on the floor the minute they took the weight off their feet.

Obi was first to wake, he sat up between his sleeping sisters like he used to before the war. He noticed that other children, mostly babies, were sitting next to their mothers who were still lying down. Looking towards the doorway he could scarcely see the morning light for the number of new arrivals that had clogged the opening. Without looking he shakes his sisters; others began rising to their feet, heading towards the crowd dispersing from the doorway. It was like God had whispered in everyone's ears at the same time that food was being distributed outside. As soon as his sisters knew what was happening, Obi took their aluminium plates from Decima's bundle and ran, dodging in-between the grownups, struggling at the bottleneck at the doorway. But being slim and small he squeezes past the sweaty bodies holding his nose.

At first he wasn't certain which direction to head for, but it was unmissable, there is only one unending food line. Hundreds of starving people snaked around the former school ground praying the supplies would hold for them. At the serving table women scooped cupfulls of what looked like pottage onto whatever was presented before them even onto bare begging hands.

One of the women serving saw Obi mingling with the crowd, making friends and skilfully making his way to the front with his plates but pretended not to have noticed him after their eyes met. When he presented the two plates in front of the woman in charge, she threatened to send him away without food. She called him greedy and told him he must consider others. With just a portion of serving on his plate Obi pushed his way out from the crowded refugees; meeting his sisters further down the queue along the way. He walked beside them staring at the plate of food, disappointed that he couldn't get his sisters portions for them, and thinks *this is what it must be like to be a beggar.*

"Go sit over there and eat your food Obi," Decima tells him.

"I eat with you and Arike." said Obi, moving closer to them. They could see that the people in front of them had given up queuing as the line thins out.

"Food na empty," drained voices echoed on passing down the long line of famished refugees.

"Irish church no have more food."

Obi understands what no food means but he doesn't know what the first word is. He makes his way with his sisters to a concrete boulder, where they sit to eat. Unlike when they ate from the same bowl in the compound, no one was rushing to eat the most. Decima stopped eating after several mouthfuls and Arike soon after her. It wasn't long before Obi looked up. After he had divided what was left on his plate into three, with an adoring smile he named the meagre portions D, A, O, before his sisters' smile and play along, licking each finger clean.

As they finish eating, more food arrived; this time from the hands of the woman who had served and told Obi off. She greeted his sisters and handed them two small packages wrapped in dried banana leaves. She asked them their names as she stroked his sisters' faces.

"Is your father not Benjamin? You have one uncle; I think he is calling himself Austin." The children are stunned to silence.

No sooner had she finished talking, another air raid began, sending everything into a state of chaos.

"It is the midday killing," the woman said cowering, placing her arms around them. "I must go find my children," she told herself, checking for a good time to run.

The air raid did not last long, it was only one MiG. Reassembling the camp each time took longer, carrying away the casualties, burying the dead and covering thick pools of blood with dry earth. Their lives continue, living amongst the stench of death and destruction. Obi and his sisters sit out in the open for the rest of the day, not knowing if or when food might arrive again. Obi was becoming fed up with having nothing to do all day; he couldn't even find any kind of rubber to mend his catapult with, so he was unable to hunt rodents in the woods. Again he couldn't see many boys his age that were willing or able to play with him, everything and everybody was serious. The days continued to pass slowly and his sisters were able to relax and learn from the mothers at the camp.

When evening came Obi didn't want them to spend long hours with the women, he had seen how friendly some of them were with soldiers in the dark.

Once daylight waned darkness engulfed everything, all form of light was banned; even the fireflies had extinguished their tail lights and the stars withdrew their glow. Obi put away his broken radio on seeing his sisters making their way into the hall; they had finished chatting with the women. The camp enjoyed a calm and restful night without the sound of distant fighting.

The cold morning chill saw early risers running to the surrounding bushes. It reminded Obi of the kind of mornings he would rather not remember in his village. Leaving his sisters still asleep he sat alone at the edge of the school building in a lotus position, his knees grey with dust and dryness. Between his crossed legs he polishes the tiny perforated metal surface of his radio against his shorts. Obi wished that the radio would magically speak and sing songs again, but he knew it was broken, why else would his uncle discard it. The shiny surfaces and the mechanical wonder of the gadget still amazed him. He wasn't alone in not knowing what day of the week it was, it no longer mattered. Neither school nor Sunday Mass played a part in their lives anymore. He wanted to ask his sisters what they talked about with the women at night, but was beginning to understand that some questions do not always need answers.

Obi wonders which part of Iboland they were in now or even if they were there at all; the endless journeying and running has left him disoriented and lost. He even thought of asking the kind-faced woman who offered them food of their whereabouts; it had been a long time since he'd asked any questions. The cold seasonal winds had no sympathy on his dry skin as it split the corners of his mouth and lips. Finding it unbearable, he went back to huddle between his sisters inside the hall.

Decima and Arike woke when Obi sprung to his feet. "Tortoise face," he said almost in a whisper to check standing by the window. He was right; it was a Volkswagen making its way towards their camp. Obi recognised the distinguishable sound of a VW. It was a sound he had not forgotten since the last time the car arrived to take his brother and sister away before the war. Just like then, people started to gather around the humped back silver car.

"It is our uncle," Decima said, turning to Arike.

Obi did not wait for permission before he set off towards the car as it came to a stop in the middle of the grounds; it was his uncle, his father's brother. He wiped sweat from his temple with a piece of an old towel before he opened his door. Obi pushed his way through the curious refugees and jumped up to grab his uncle around his midriff; but his uncle did not return the affection. He merely unwrapped Obi's arms from his damp body before he barked instructions at him.

"Go, bring your sister, Decima!"

Their uncle told them that Ozo got news that they were in his region and instructed him to bring them to live in his house. Obi watched his face wrinkle as he spoke, showing his displeasure at having to look after three more children, but could not disobey his elder brother's request.

The silent drive to their uncle's home was not as long as the one in the truck, the route took them deeper into the woods until a walled compound emerged. Obi stared at the tatty gate propped by a boulder as they entered through it. He'd never been so excited and contained at the same time before. He imagined what seeing and playing with his cousins would be like after so long, the last time they visited his compound was long before the war.

"Close my gate!" his uncle snapped, sending his nephew's heart out of his T-shirt. "No touch my window!"

The sisters' eyes met without words. "Yes we will stay away from your house too," said Decima with a painful throat that was just about able to squeeze the few words out.

Admiring the pattern created by the gate scraping against the dry ground, a neat quarter circle, Obi tugged at the black metal frame, pulling and pushing with care not to break it any further until he closed it. After his uncle snapped at Decima and Arike to get out, he locked his car and made his way towards the house; stopping abruptly to face his brother's children who also stopped close at his heels.

"Do not come any closer, go that way," their uncle said pointing towards a side entrance. Banana leaves slap against their faces and skinny bodies as they push their way through discarded rubbish along the slippery side path of the bungalow. All the windows were shut as Arike mumbled that maybe nobody was home. Obi stared at the window shutters which were covered in thick green paint that had dribbled down against the wall.

"Walk around to the back!" a voice barked from inside the bungalow, startling Obi from his gazing.

The pained voice was that of their uncle's wife; Decima bent her knees and nodded, paying her respects, in the direction of the unseen voice. Her family followed swiftly along the narrow side path to be greeted by a mound of litter in the backyard and their auntie standing outside the back door. "Look at them now, the bank manager's children," she tuts to herself. "Go into that room!" she points to a windowless construction, stepping away from her door. A single stained and torn mattress was propped against the outside wall.

"When my children return from school I do not want you to speak or touch them, you hear me?"

"Yes Auntie, we will stay in our room," said Decima.

"You do not own room. Now come throw away this waste water into the bush. Where is your mother now?" she bleated as she scraped earth from her feet before walking back into her home slamming the door behind her.

After dragging the partially mouldy mattress into the small room of a similar size, Arike picked up an inch of candle from the corner and blew away the cobwebs; beside it was a box of matches. Due to their uncle's untimely arrival, they had missed the day's food distribution so had not eaten all day.

Darkness was setting in when Arike lit the candle. Obi was sitting at the foot of the mattress playing with his radio, his head against the wall; his sisters whispered together concerned that he might overhear them. "The room probably belonged to a previous servant during better times."

"I can hear you," Obi said. "If she doesn't give us food, I saw where her kitchen is so I will wait until they are all asleep." He continues to play with his radio.

The smell of fried food drifts towards them and into their noses when Obi stands and walks towards the door. Pulling the door open he sidesteps out and into the backyard, his sisters whisper to him to come back but it's too late.

By their back door, Obi stands listening, he could hear the family on the other side.

"*Come away from the door*," his sisters tell him and he obeys. No sooner had he returned, their auntie's voice followed.

"Your food," she bellows before she walks away.

Decima opens the door to find a small aluminium pot with a broken handle and dents which doesn't allow it to sit up no matter how much you try to balance it on three rocks.

"It is not good to put your ear where it is not invited," Decima tells her brother and he apologises. In the pot are three eddoes, and a blue plastic jug which is broken off at the handle, so only half full with water.

After washing the eddoes outside, the sisters watched over the pot of their evening meal. When it was cooked they peeled and ate the slippery vegetable on its own without salt, before they went to sleep. Obi and his sisters are kept busy around the uncle's home: they clean, wash and press clothes with the coal iron before returning to make their food with whatever their auntie spared them. Decima cleans the floors and Arike tidies whatever mess was made by their uncle's children who they never saw. Obi heard their uncle's wife telling her children to stay away from them because she didn't want them to catch any refugee diseases.

"I cannot eat this without salt," Obi retched. "Auntie has plenty of salt; I have seen where she hides it. I will get you some." Obi was resolving his problem.

"We do not steal food. It will harm you; it will rot in your stomach if you eat stolen food," said Arike.

Even before the war started, eddoes were not amongst

Obi's favourite vegetables. He didn't like their slipperiness but ate them nonetheless. He would not have imagined how different he would feel about them in starvation. As the days wore on he had got used to eating unseasoned eddoes on their own. It wasn't miserable living in their uncle's garden, especially because his other duty was to clean his uncle's car. He loved to stand on the running board, stretching over the hot roof with his cloth to dust off the top. He didn't mind that he wasn't allowed to clean inside where he could tilt the front seats back and forth and back again. Walking back along the side path he recalls how they had struggled to walk inbetween the overgrown plants when they first arrived. It wasn't clogged with rubbish anymore; he and his sisters had cleared it thoroughly.

It is early in the morning when Obi is awakened by the spluttering sound of his uncle's car. Bolting upright he rushes towards the door.

"Go back to sleep, it's too early to get up."

He was out the door before Decima had finished what she was telling him. The house is silent when Obi runs through the backyard; he peers through the side window into the kitchen before he runs to the front. The gate is open and the car gone, the tyre tracks lead Obi's eyes into the distance ahead.

"They have gone," he whispers to himself before jumping onto the front veranda to pull at the shutters which were bolted from inside. Running to the backyard he checks the door, he sees the big padlock that hung from its bolt. He races back to his sisters who were still curled up on the bare mattress desperate to ignore their brother's racket.

"What is it Obi?" Arike asked.

"They have left," he sobs.

"What are you talking about?"

"They have gone. They have driven away and left us. They have abandoned us," his voice trembles.

The sister's jump up from the mattress and run to the front of the house where Obi points to the tyre tracks.

"Obi is right," Decima said.

"We can't stay here," Arike agrees running back to collect their cooking pot, blanket and some water in a small container without a lid. They set off in the same direction of the tyre tracks. The faster they walk the more the water spilt, until Decima told them to drink it before it is all wasted. Obi passes the container to Decima after his drink but she handed it to Arike who took a small sip before handing it back.

"Finish it Arike, I am not thirsty."

"We don't know how long it will be before we can find more water," said Arike, but her sister had already walked away. "*Biko*, Decima, drink a little water. We don't want you to suffer."

"Why do you have to argue with me, I am older than you?"

"Sorry," said Arike.

They continue on their way as Obi follows along the narrow line of dead and crushed grass behind his sisters. But no sooner had they entered into the tall grass did they hear the noise of army vehicles heading towards the direction of their uncle's home. The bushes hid them from being seen.

Walking behind his sisters Obi drags his feet; he stops thinking of how long they had been on foot. He thinks back to his village before the war and how men and women entering the compound when the evening meals were being cooked cheered aloud when the cooking pan sizzled and the tomatoes hit the hot pan. The sweet smell of onions and scotch bonnets wafted out of the compound, signalling that food would soon be ready. The visitors' cheers would be met with laughter from a wife in her kitchen. This was a compliment to the household because good cooking was a sign of permanency in a marriage, some would say.

Obi remembered the fireside stories "My dear," they often began. Before long, a big circle formed as more people arrived to share different experiences of their day. When *apacati*, chatting, of the adults was over, the children liked to sing and whistle to *No condition is permanent*, which was Obi's favourite song at that time. In fact, all the children and adults, too, liked the song. Everyone sang together at the tops of their voices before the visitors left for their own homes and the hosts retire into their rooms. The song could be heard trailing off into the dark following the guests as they made their way home under the moonlight.

Respect for the night was ingrained in every child in the village.

"This is the time of the spirits. It is not for whistling. The spirits will hear the sounds and come out," children were told for as long as any of them could remember.

During the night, the children stayed close to the adults for protection from spirits. When the youngest children sat in front of the fire with their backs to the darkness, fear gripped them that a ghost would touch them from behind.

The evening folk tales that followed the grown-ups' accounts of the government and their difficult day's dealings soothed Obi and increased his appetite for more. He loved long stories best. Traditionally the tale of Imbe, the cunning tortoise, was the favourite. Tom, Elizabeth and the Giant Bird was another popular tale which children enjoyed. When stories ended for the night, a pail of water would be emptied over the fire to rest it as the compound fell silent. The boys settled quicker after they shared and retold the events of their day to themselves, laughing like grown men.

Obi likes remembering his friends and family in the village and all the good times, though it brings him pain to know that it is all in the past and he may never see them again. He runs up and reaches out for Decima's hand holding it gently as they walk.

17

Another Path

They emerge into a small clearing beneath a tree with thick ivy along its trunk. The soldiers and their vehicles were out of sight and their engine noise overridden by unconcerned birdsong. Arike stopped; the pot rolled from her hand hitting the earth before she fell to the ground too, like a canary shot by her brother's catapult. Seconds later Decima collapsed with the same exhaustion next to her sister. Obi checks to make sure his sisters are okay, rolling out the blanket he lays it down for them to sleep upon. Sitting beside them he listens to the chirping of the happy birds; it has been a while since he last heard birdsong. He remembers the eddoes from their meal but was confused about which night that had been; it wasn't long before he was between his sisters asleep against the tree.

Startled to their feet they see large birds of prey circling above them and Obi pulls his broken catapult from his pocket. He tries to fix the fraying rubber knowing full well that it will snap the second he pulls at it.

"If we start walking they will let us be," Decima said as they set off in an unknown direction.

"Vultures," Obi mumbled, abandoning any ideas of shooting the man-eating birds.

Decima led the way through shrubs and dunes of the parched land; it seemed they may have been walking in circles all day until Obi spots what looks like the same tyre track markings of their uncle's car. The tracks danced in parallel lines before his eyes until they fade and disappear into a road, playing tricks under the raging sun til they all become a blur. Exhausted they continue, recklessly walking alongside passing trucks that ignore them and their dusty bodies. Gaunt faces with haunting eyes look back at them from the crammed open truck. Almost unable to lift his feet any more, Obi no longer looks for working truck monkeys. Under the desert conditions they shuffle forward without water and food. It was Obi's turn to carry the blanket and Decima's to hold the pot as Arike led the way along the side of the road. The orange sun was halfway down a flat landscape of Iboland when another overloaded truck passes them the same way, unnoticed and uncaring, turning off into the same road ahead of them.

They arrive but watch from the periphery of a camp as evening sets; hesitant, if they would be welcomed without an adult by their side.

"Biafran war refugees," said Obi, pacing around his sisters.

"We have to go in," said Decima with laboured breath, "we have to find food."

At the turning of a path they join the migration, the swell of people are just as desperate for everything; immersed into the crowd they jostle along staying close together. Even though the sun had set, the sweltering heat intensified inbetween the masses, people were dropping to the ground like flies especially when those that were helping them had moved on. The stars tremble when distant ripples of jet engines drift towards them in the dark, and people scatter, running about the ground aimless and unsure which direction is safest. They bump and collide with one another in the darkness in total mayhem. Obi and his sisters watch not knowing why everyone was running about like unearthed ants.

A vicious bolt of thunder tore through the sky a moment later as the frail refugees ran into the bushes near them. When the piercing screams of mothers for their children hit Obi's ears, he froze between his sisters. An explosion landed, scattering sand and debris around the camp, he trembled and clung to them like a cold bat on a twig. They watch as people emptied from the buildings into the woods; no one can hear themselves amongst the ripping noise of devouring Russian jets.

Arike tugged Obi's hand to run. He couldn't move, he just wanted to sleep, but they both grabbed a hand each and pulled him along into the bordering bushes. It seemed that everything was angry, even the dried twigs that scratch his legs, not until he freed a hand to brush something off from his shin did he realise his sticky fingers were red with blood. The trees obstructed the stars above the dark clouds of an African evening making it more foreboding. Arike took the lead after Decima's slipper snagged on a rock and slipped off her foot.

"We have to stop, we have gone too deep," said Arike, "we will be lost again."

A strange smell of crushed beetles became overwhelming, they slowed their pace, and Obi looked back unable to see the winding trail of ruffled dead leaves behind them.

Opening their eyes to the streams of sunrays through the trees and dancing leaves, they get back onto their feet. It was morning when they re-emerge from the woods into the dappled sunlit field. They may have been abandoned yet again, but surviving another day away from their uncle's uncaring words and left over food and cousins they will never know or recognise was a triumph. Who cares? In hindsight they are able to appreciate that, had they not left when Obi alerted them of the situation, they would probably be in the soldiers' company and Obi would either be dead or conscripted, depending on which side got them first. Life may have been harder than impossible, hanging by a thread, but when they count their near misses and still being able to wake up together to greet another day, they know gratitude was the only thing in order.

Before them lay a vast clearing in the ground where several large buildings were dotted around.

"There is nobody here," said Decima.

"Are they Ibos?" Obi asked.

They decide to remain within the safety of the woods, at the edge where they can keep an eye on everything.

Decima eases herself to the ground, her eyes roll up to the sky and flicker between wakefulness and sleep, looking like an unwanted kitten. Arike couldn't free herself quickly enough of the pot in her hand before she collapsed. Obi dives to his knees to attend to Decima, but he doesn't know what to do next.

"We have to find water," said Arike, looking closer at the community ahead of them. "I'm going to ask them, stay with Decima, do you hear?"

"Decima said we must all go," Obi relays to Arike.

"We don't know who they are," she replied, helping her sister to her feet with Obi on the other side.

They limp from the hedge towards the clearing, spotting others also heading in the same direction. Emaciated bodies covered in blood and cuts emerge dusty from unwelcoming hedgerows. Obi remembers his injury but the silent conversations of others around them keeps him alert while he walks with his sisters. Careful not to step on them, they move around the dead and dying bodies, those who couldn't quite make the last journey to the new camp.

In a foetal curl alone on the cement floor outside the building is an elderly woman. On seeing her Obi freezes, his sisters stop to look at him. He shivers, terrified of the woman, and his sisters struggle to move him.

"She is not Magdalene, Obi, she is not a ghost." Arike pulls and tugs at his arm before her brother follows them in. On passing the woman, they hear her say;

"I never know our land hold so many people."

The children thought how similar the camps looked. A darkened gloomy space of unfamiliar and unfriendly atmosphere, where no one raised their heads in acknowledgement of new arrivals, or to see what was going on, nor did they move out of the way for them to pass.

Hesitating at the doorway for an invitation no longer served them. Stepping over all kinds of bodies on the floor, Obi turns his face away from the stench of the hall to face the doorway for fresh air. In the past he would have held his breath to avoid such bad smells of the injured and unwashed people. His sisters pull him along when his pace slowed; it was difficult to keep an eye on everyone and everything around them at the same time, making sure not to trip. Obi never liked being pulled along; it usually made him cry because he'd believe he had done something wrong.

He spots a floor space and makes a quiet dash for it before it got taken. Strangers exchange stories comparing their sufferings with anyone who listened.

"*Mekam* hunger no kill you *o*," said a mother curled around her baby who may have been dead or asleep.

Her dark face was *even darker than Tabooless*; Obi thought as they walk carefully over a tangle of legs that belonged to whoever claimed them.

"Pain and anguish." Obi catches a segment of another conversation along the way. "*Anguish*," he whispers to himself, and repeats the word in his mind before adding it to his collection of unknown English words he stored in his head.

"There's not enough space, we should go back," said Arike stepping over people.

"We are all refugees, there is nowhere else to go, we will remain where we are," Decima told her in a stern and breathless tone. They bedded down on the spot Obi had found earlier; before long the smell of food wafted in from outside. They looked around the large darkened building where the odd lamp flickered, struggling to stay alight. Obi covered his nose hoping to block out the heavy odour of sweat and unwashed bodies.

"*Biko*, no come sit here." The woman said in her scornful harsh voice, she did not have to repeat herself to be understood. Numbed into silence by the cold rebuke, it was enough to turn them around and out of the crowded doorway, her words following them out to look for another spot on the concrete steps outside the building.

Obi didn't want to look at her when they walked past but could not resist. Her face was as sour as her words and it sagged like heavy black velvet in Mr Emanuel's tailor shop. Obi could hear people arriving under the cover of darkness into the camp, he remembers that Mama Toni was the first to leave the compound with her family.

"Where is Lady Ani, where is Mama Toni, where is everyone?" Obi asks his sisters, his eyes sting welling up with tears. Everyone has had enough of the war.

Arike instinctively lifted a corner of her dress to wipe the tears from her brother's face, while Decima placed an emaciated arm around her sister's bony shoulder. Pain stuck to the back of her throat as another realisation of loneliness and abandonment sunk in that they were truly alone in this war. Darkness had descended when the orange sun played above palm trees in another far-off horizon. Beauty dances in the face of a cruel merciless world where children with empty bellies and painful eyes sat huddled next to uncaring strangers.

Obi remembers a group of children with gaping mouths choking and rubbing their eyes which stung from the smouldering fires around the airless hall. Their mothers, bent forward on their knees barely able to blow energy into leaves that refuse to ignite. Obi and his sisters didn't know how the camp worked, or how and where they could get food or water. Decima looked around in the hope that she could spot a friendly face in the midst of the harshness to ask for help.

They couldn't remember when they had last eaten. No shops, no hawkers, no traders of any kind to be found anywhere. Folk tales and songs that once concluded the day and fed Obi's imagination vanished without warning. Obi saw a large, moth-like insect that a mother had placed on top of her flickering embers to roast for her children.

"*Yuck*," he whispers, recognising the fat insect was one that he and his friends back in the village avoided at all cost, especially because those grubs smell like baby vomit and tastes like gone-off snail meat.

"Do not look at others and do not mock their food. At least they have something to eat," his sisters remind him.

Looking up into the evening sky Obi checks his pockets for his catapult, but to his horror he saw that other refugees outside were lighting bonfires. "The enemy will see us, we will get killed," he panics tugging at his sisters.

"We can go there." Decima points to a long concrete step at the side of the main building, Obi runs to check the area first.

"Stop!" Arike calls, but her brother was already there and waving towards them. He pats his hand on the warm concrete for his sisters to come. Once they are seated Obi squeezes in-between them and looks at Decima, noticing that she is short of breath again.

"*Water pipe,*" he whispers randomly, snuggling inbetween his sisters making himself comfortable, he falls asleep with his head and arm resting on top of Decima's lap.

After the cold uncomfortable night on the step, Decima agreed they can't suffer another night outside. Early, even before the cock would have crowed in their village, she led them towards the crowded hall again. They walk in with some of the new arrivals. It was evident that these refugees had also travelled for days; their scanty clothes sagged laden with dust and dirt. The daylight revealed some of the healthiest adults they had seen over the eighteen or so months; they must have evaded death on the run. The stronger more able-bodied refugees lead the procession, the weak and frail shuffle along behind them.

"*More people but no boys my age,*" Obi tells himself.

"They are all dead," a lone woman cries from a corner, "They are all dead," repeating her sorrow. She starts humming a hymn; with eyes closed she rocks her head to and fro, her arms crossed against her shoulders. Obi listens, paying more attention on hearing her remembering all the family members she had lost along the journey. He realised that she was the same women from the night before and was sorry that he had imagined that she was a ghost.

"We have to find space inside," said Arike looking at the long queue of new refugees.

The foul humidity of the hall sends Decima collapsing to the floor, Arike and Obi help her up and her feet brush against bodies on the floor.

"There is no room," a woman groans stretching her legs out to block the way. Obi hesitates; he's never liked confrontation or going where he doesn't feel welcomed. Arike pushes the woman's bony legs aside and out of the way. They look for a clearing, walking deeper into the stagnant hall with blacked out windows and stained walls. The floor heaves with a sea of distressed and confused bodies. Old men and women with sick babies lucky to be alive; on seeing them, Obi remembers the bats in his village with leathery wings and clawed fingers. He felt Decima's limp hand trembling over his, her hand slips away with the heat of the hall and he tries to get a firmer grip on her clammy palm again. He tugs at Arike with his other hand. She did not look back; she'd spotted another small clearing by a door. Obi tugs again before she stops with her back to him.

"I know," she replied. "We are almost at the end. I see somewhere."

Obi holds Decima's hand tighter as Arike led the way to a small space on the floor by a closed door. Arike frees her hands to hold and break her sister's fall. Decima had collapsed.

The unventilated hall was odorous, with a constant hum of ill and dying people. Yet none of that mattered, war presents the inevitability of silent acceptance for the victim. Smells of urine, perspiration and unwashed bodies came from all corners, and Obi desperately pulled back the urge to vomit. This was one of the things he dreaded the most: being surrounded by bundles of excrement wrapped in old newspapers, the product of the night lay dotted around the floor next to their owners.

"There is no other space for us, all the good spots have already been taken," Arike said. Arike carried their meagre possessions of blanket and aluminium pot; Obi, his broken transistor radio and his catapult wedged in his pocket. Desperately they look around for help but no one acknowledged their presence, they could just as well have been invisible.

"My sister needs help," Arike begs the hall, but no one listened.

Not knowing what to do, Obi offers an unripe guava towards his feverish sister's hand. She didn't respond as tears engulfed his eyes.

"She needs water," said Arike, wiping her sister's brow trying not to let her brother see her tears.

Obi was halfway over the bodies and dodging the paper bundles before Arike could look up. She cradled Decima, telling her that Obi had gone to fetch her some water. When she looked up, he was gone. She sat with her sick sister, as others in the hall began to rise and pick up their bundles.

"Your brother will soon return," an old woman next to them whispered. "The sleep will heal her. Don't worry, take heart, it is not her time," continued the woman in her attempt to console the wretched madness. "No worry, he will soon return. He has gone to fetch water," the woman reminded Arike.

Obi stops at the uneven ledge of the school wall, he looks towards what he thought was a water tap. The midday sun arrived early, greeting his face, shielded by the back of his hand as he looked about the field of scattered people over the sandy ground before jumping off its ledge, towards a small outhouse at the edge of the camp. He runs towards the small building in the hope that it may have been a toilet for the school, but it is an empty doorless room similar to where they had lived at their uncle's back yard.

Still frantic he runs around the camp looking for water, lifting big leaves to check for any trace of condensation. He is too late. The greedy sun had already sucked up all the morning dew. Recognising the wooded area from where they had entered the camp he races towards it. But once he arrives at its edge, he could no longer recognise nor find where they had created the pathway through the tall grass. He runs up and down the boundary of the hard, mud mounds; Obi feels his body overheating and trembling at the same time, although he had not drunk any water for a long time, sweat engulfs his body and he remembers the fear he felt on seeing the wizened old woman towards the roadside of his village before the war. He thought of Lady Ani and what she would say to him if she saw his scratched legs and dirty feet; he struggled to harness his thoughts.

Tears fill his eyes when he thinks of other directions through the spiky hedgerow; going into the wooded area was his best chance of finding any kind of moisture. He pushed himself backwards through the twigs and green foliage, bright beams of sunlight illuminate the forest. Birds and other small creatures sing more noisily than he had ever heard before.

Obi ran under the cool and shady trees where he was calmer, he no longer felt the heat of fear in his body. He remembered the people from the first camp where Eze had taken them; they carried water in gallon containers. He hoped to find one inside the woods, perhaps discarded by a falling body. Deeper he looked, to no avail, it was hopeless, he can't save his sister and dreads the result of returning empty-handed. Obi tries to recall a geography lesson when his teacher told the class that water can be found in the ground if you dig deep. On his knees he begins to rake the dead brown leaves aside. He digs and rips at the surface roots of small trees until the ground becomes too hard for his fingers.

Tapped on the shoulder by a miracle, Obi looks up from where he is on his knees, he sees a woman sitting away from him. Camouflaged by the bushes which had grown in and around her, he gets to his feet daring not to take his eyes from the tiny woman. He doesn't look at her face but wants to believe she is fast asleep when he walks towards her. She remains static where she sits. Next to her is a bundle, wrapped in traditional red, yellow and green patterned cloth, with rain-splattered earth around it. Instantly he recognises that the edge of a tin that juts out of the threadbare cloth is sardine. The large flies around her scatter sending his memory back to the time he was engulfed by blue flies on the path to the roadside of his village. His sisters had told him that it is not good to steal, especially food because it always rots in the thief's stomach.

"Auntie, *biko* can I have water?" he asked.

Her wiry hand is on the ground, in it a small container of water. The woman did not respond to his plea so Obi repeated his question. "Auntie, *biko* can I have water?"

With closed eyes, her head tilts down to the ground, but Obi didn't want to think she was dead, although he wasn't scared. He took the water and thanked her, mindful not to disturb her rest as he preferred to imagine. His ears prick up at the rumbling noise of a distant jet. Like an animal caught in the glare of the headlamps he is still for a moment before looking around the ground before him. Picking up the few tins of sardines from the ripped bag beside the tranquil woman; he pushes the fish into his already stuffed pockets without looking at the slumped woman again.

Getting to his feet in front of her, he thanked her, cradling the goods in his T-shirt before making his way out.

At the edge of the woods in sight of the encampment Obi stops to check the tins he had wedged into his pockets, he wasn't taking any chances by keeping everything together. The distant jet noise did not come for them then. From the doorway of the hall he saw his sister asleep. Carefully negotiating his feet trying not to drop any of the goods from his cradle or pocket he preceded towards them.

"Obi," his sister smiled half-asleep.

On his knees with his back to the hall of people, he reveals his finds. Arike looks around the hall before she takes the water from the pouch of his T-shirt. She cradles her sister's head to her lap before she pours a little trickle of water into her open mouth. Decima is too weak to respond and falls back to sleep.

"Decima, please open your eyes. Obi has brought us food and water."

Obi's eyes drill into Arike's eyes for reassurance. Gently she shakes her sister's shoulders before Decima wakes up and takes a sip from the container.

A commotion outside sends people clambering to their feet towards the doorway, food has arrived they hear others say, rushing out of the building. A childless woman next to them wants to get up but she is too weak and she flops back to the same warm spot of her floor. The hall is almost empty but for them and a few elders. Obi prizes a tin from his pocket and offers it to the woman with both hands as a mark of respect, and she snatches it without thanks. Arike unclips the metal key at the side of the tin; uncoiling the strip around the key to open the fish feast. Next to them the woman eventually sits up, her once cream blouse is the shade of cleaning rag. Obi is fascinated by her, she also opens her tin of sardines. He tries not to watch her crinkly lips on the tin as she sucks the tasty oil first. Unconsciously he smiles to himself on seeing the lid; he likes the deep red colour behind the picture of a black fish on the lid.

When the night's darkness sealed them in, Arike thanked her brother for what he had done, finding them water and food. Obi let out a sigh of relief when Decima woke and drank some of the water. He sits cross legged opposite his sisters, happy that he wasn't taken away by his Uncle Harry with his other brother and sister before the war. Obi got up and threw his arms around his sisters with such force that he knocked them over; they laughed in a heap on the floor like there wasn't a war.

"That boy is a good one," the grateful woman smiled and tucked into her meal. Obi watched her scoop out her food with two fingers; she licks her entire hand certain not to waste a drop. When she tilted her head back to drink the last drops of fish oil, Obi saw that her neck had a deep cut under her chin.

"War is a terrible thing," she said, as Obi looked away. He moved closer to her and offered her some water.

"My dear child, no waste your water on me. God will always bless you and your sisters."

"Obi, please let her rest," Arike said gently.

Obi moved closer to his sisters from where he watches the woman fall to her side.

"She sleeps now," he whispered.

Random conversations could be heard in the dank darkness of the hall.

"Because the jets cannot find our troops in the bushes, they like to empty their bombs and rockets on refugee camps, churches, and market places. They cannot see our faces from the sky, they cannot see we are afraid for our lives," an elderly man vents his frustration before nodding off.

"*Ogga*. Sir, let us rest o," pleads a voice in the dark.

Burps, snores, and other bodily sounds echoed periodically in the darkness. The smell in the hall continued to intensify and linger by the floor where everyone lay. Obi and his sisters were asleep wrapped up in each other's arms until they were startled by a deep voice over them.

"Small children, you have to move to another position. There is a reason why this space was unoccupied. People come and go by this door, both day and night. You will not get any rest if you remain here," the man warned.

It took a while before the children came around; Arike was the first to wake. Their new home, the spot by the doorway, can no longer be their space.

"There are no other spaces for us," Arike said with a lump in her throat.

"It is too cold for us to remain outside for the entire night, I am sorry, sir," she pleaded to the man respectfully; they stand helpless and exhausted in the dark.

Because the door backs onto the bushes at the rear of the building it becomes a busy access point to the wilderness for toileting. The door remains closed because of what is on the other side of the wall. Obi felt squeamish even if he was half-asleep, he wanted to throw up for the smell around them.

"You will suffer if you remain there; the smell will make you unwell. Are you orphans? Has your *moda* perished? Has no other *moda* adopt you? It is because you are three; divide and join with different *modas* or you will not survive this war." The man seemed concerned for the children's welfare at first, but then he became a barrage of questions that neither Obi nor his sisters cared for.

"Have you not heard of what is going on?" he went on until someone thumps against the door from the outside; it frightened them, they had not seen it in use before. A woman pushes her way through; she slammed it shut much like villagers who closed car doors with all their might. Obi watches her walk several paces before she turns around and hobbles back towards the doorway. She left patches of excrement dotted along the floor next to them when she made her way to the edge of the step where she scrapes it from under her feet. Obi retched from the smell. The doorway gets busier, wafting in more stench and trails of disgusting mess around the children's space, forcing them to move. Obi and his sisters watch the man make his way out through the main doorway while the others come and go as they needed with their paper bundles and resettle back into their spaces empty handed.

"*Biko*, my daughter is no more, I no need space for her belongings. Come, rest here," a pleasant looking woman with sunken, hollow eyes called out to them.

Obi and his sisters couldn't believe their luck, though Obi wondered, *what if they sleep on the same spot where her daughter died*; quickly realising that she was never in the hall, it was her belongings which the woman carried that took up the space next to her.

"Thank you, auntie," they all said in a chorus looking at each other for reassurance.

Desperation made acceptance of many situations inevitable, war tested everyone. The days and nights of walking and hunger took its toll; at least for now they didn't have to be on alert, this brought a sense of safety for the time being; there were many in the same situation.

Obi was half-asleep in front of his sisters when he checked his pockets for his catapult and transistor; before he snuggled up together under the cover, the same grey blanket which he had retrieved just in time before the truck left his compound.

"Thank you for bringing our cover," said his sisters, curling up in foetal positions behind him using their palms for pillows.

"How is Rani? You don't mention her any more," Decima mumbled in a dreamy state.

"*We are going to marry one day,*" Obi whispered, half-asleep.

"I didn't know you still see her when you sleep," said Arike.

"Rani." Obi smiled.

"It is late, be quiet, we have to sleep," said Decima.

The hall had settled for the night as Obi and his family lay huddled like newborns. The past few days on the move had taken its toll.

18

Fever

Obi's body twitches now and then, he dreams of Rani's garden. The flowering fruit trees sway in the palace grounds, the leaves and branches quiver when the elephants quicken their pace to greet him. He runs, skips, and waves his arms up and down to greet them. *Where is she?* Obi thinks excitedly, his arms jolt his sisters from their sleep.

"Shh, don't disturb him. There is more space for you over here."

"He will be frightened if he wakes and doesn't find one of us on either side."

"Yes, that's true."

"Goodnight sister. Thank you."

"Go to sleep now," Decima tells Arike before they settle back to sleep.

The night passes without bombing and evacuation and no early cockerel calls to signal a new day as early risers begin to file out towards the bushes.

"My dear, the enemy know we are here. The MiGs will continue to empty their bombs around the camp. It is only a matter of time before they see us." A woman breaks the silence from somewhere in the hall. Her scrawny body could have been mistaken for a discarded cloth on the floor.

Obi is awake and doesn't want to look at the woman who seems to be sleep talking. He remains curled up on the floor, with the blanket over his head; his ears alert to the morning noise in the stuffy hall. He remembers yesterday's conversation between some men on how the war had been progressing. It continues to run rings in his head: they said, "Why would foreign Egyptian pilots, in Russian jets, want to harm us?" The new words: 'Egyptian, pilots' and 'Russian', ruminating, he memorises them to ask his sisters later.

New refugees continue flooding into the camp during the day as others loiter and wait for aid which was rumoured to arrive that day. Obi informs his sisters that the rations were distributed twice a week from behind an enclosed area of the camp and only by joining the line very early in the morning would they have any chance. Obi asked to be woken so he can join them, but when the time came it was Decima and Arike at the queue because sleep was too sweet so early. Upon waking Obi ran to join them, the queue was still static and they were in front of the building.

"That woman said that if we are lucky and not at the back of the queue, we will receive powdered milk and *gari*." Obi whispered to his sisters.

Before the war Obi and every other child in his village liked eating *gari* soaked in water with honey or sugar cubes added. Now they ate it dry not even imagining how delicious it was when made with hot water for swallowing with okra or *egusi* soup.

It was frustrating for the children when they got to learn of the pecking order of the food distribution line, the people that had been longest at the camp were at the top of the chain and of course those who were friends of the distributors. The new arrivals had no status if they didn't have cash. People in the early stages of starvation had lost all hope for nutrition and nothing much could be done for them.

"You are lucky to be alive," some of the well-fed food controllers and distributors snapped at the starving who begged for more rations for their sick children that couldn't join the line.

Decima hoped that after a while they would no longer be the 'newcomers' and last in line; although they were grateful for whatever supplies they received. Obi had powdered milk for his breakfast, which his sister mixed with hot water if the water pump was working. When they did not have water, he ate the milk powder dry, awkward as it would stick to the palate of his mouth. He found it unusual at first because children did not normally have milk other than breast milk before being weaned off, however tinned condensed milk was enjoyed by many.

Expectant mothers preferred to eat *enzi*, a satisfying chalk-like rock said to be high in calcium. Obi would have liked to have some *enzi*, especially because it reminded him of his favourite smell after the rain when the ground and walls were damp.

On hearing about the unfairness and bribery that went on Arike whispered to Decima, "We have to fight them."

"*Biko*, Arike. You always ready to fight. No!" Decima was stern holding one of her shoulders back.

Obi wraps his arms around his sisters burying his face between them.

"Move! Obi, move before I smack you." Arike fumed.

"Arike, we are all hungry and I do not like what they do. We are not as big as them and we have no strength to fight anybody."

Arike leaves, shaking her hand off from her weeping brother's hold; ignoring the line of complaining people she heads towards the front, leaving Obi confused and Decima still standing in line.

"Obi, go stay with Arike." Decima tells her brother.

Obi runs off to the front of the long line of people. He doesn't know why he's short of breath and unable to run as fast. Thinking he should see Arike by now, he continues and the sand swallows his feet and energy. In all his life he has never seen his sisters fight like that before, he really was lost for what to do next. Tears fall to his chest, he can't see Arike. Obi pushes through to the other side of the line and still does not see his sister anywhere.

Obi circles back when he hears Decima's voice from the end of the line. He breathes long and deep when he sees Arike and Decima together standing away from the line and he sees food in Arike's hands. The heaviness inside him is lifted.

Back in the hall, they sit down to unwrap the newspaper of food which they struggled to recognise, it was a mixture of leftovers. Decima set the meal on the floor in front of them before saying grace and giving thanks.

"Decima, I am sorry to argue with you but those people will not give us any food if we do not push them." said Arike.

"We are only children to them and they know that we are alone." Decima looks over to see if Obi is eating before she scrapes the remnants of food from the paper it came in and ate it; that was her meal for the day. "You are right, but we still have to be very careful," Decima agreed with Arike.

"Did you know that when the food aid arrives that they hold a lot of the stock to sell and pass on to their family and friends first?" They continue talking quietly while they eat.

"I also heard the same," Decima acknowledged.

It has been over two years of living like rodents, eking out what they could for food. They had become accustomed to the different ways of how people treated one another in times of extreme hardship. The good qualities every teacher and elder taught them about the Ibo ways may have just been another fireside story.

Together they huddled over a small portion of *okporoko*, dried cod fish crumbs, which was the debris left when the sack was emptied: scraps mixed with strands of natural fibres and grit. After Decima picked most of the visible grit out, she used the dusting to flavour her soup for the *gari*; nothing went to waste and people at the camps were grateful for the distribution even though the portions could not sustain them.

"Decima, *biko*, no let them break teeth. Swallow, don't chew the food," a mother warned them and Obi's mind instantly travelled to his village before the war and how he and his friends used to extract loose teeth for each other by tying a thread and pulling at it.

Months of taking cover from the continual air raids, the children settle into how things were done in the camp and Obi was beginning to get back to his old self, where he goes to look for food in the forest with his catapult. As a child he had perfected walking without making a sound on the dried leaves when in the woods. There were no warnings against entering the woods because soldiers had not been reported in the area. The moist leaves soothed his feet on entering the cool woodland. His attention was upwards amongst the branches in the trees; that was until his foot knocked against a pile of leaves, revealing some massive snails.

Obi wedged his catapult into his pocket before he starts to collect the snails as big as his fists. He didn't have a bag so he took off his T-shirt, and bundles as many as he can and carries it like a knapsack on a sling. He quickly maps out his direction back before heading off. The shells knock against each other as he walks reminding him of the hollow musical instruments the young *adas* played during ceremonies. He wants to run but not at the risk of smashing the shells, they gradually start to escape climbing up his shoulders and down his bare arms and chest. It makes him shudder to feel the cold slime, pulling and tugging at them with difficulty he removes some but others remained stuck to his skin. By the time he arrives back his body glistens from the dried silver trails.

"I am going to complain about the unfair food distributions," Arike said with clenched fists in front of Decima.

"Do you think anyone will listen, Arike? It will not help us to get any more rations."

Decima reminded her of the people who were refused rations by the food monitors because they dared to complain about unfairness. Even those who had officials that stood up for them at the food distributions saw a different side when their support was gone. These officials were often army officers who visited women with gifts of lipsticks and powder compacts. Arike lowered her voice after realising that they were being overheard.

"See how they hold our food," said a mother, under her breath.

"Watch them carry food back to sell to those still with American dollars," replied another in a whisper.

The jets' targets had sharpened again, sending fatigued bodies and buckling legs along the narrow path into the dark woods. Obi runs with his sisters after they managed to collect their few belongings. He watches them from behind as they sprint ahead dodging trees, lagging further behind in the dark, hearing the sounds of other petrified feet he begins to panic on losing sight of his sisters.

The woods cleared and people dispersed in all directions; Obi lets out a sigh of relief when he hears Decima's drained voice calling him. Alone in unfamiliar woods was no longer a frightening experience for them, they had been there before. They continue down a worn pathway following the exodus. Obi drags his feet looking like a sleepwalker, Decima and Arike do not fare any better. They had walked the whole day and not caught up with the others, each sister taking his hand and pulling him along but their efforts did not add to the pace. They came to a main road just in time as night was setting in; they followed on mindlessly along the dirt tracks running parallel.

"A vehicle is coming," Arike warns, but not in time.

No sooner had they seen the headlights, the vehicle arrived; it was too late to hide. Tiredness had betrayed them when the army truck stops close by with its engine still running. They started to shuffle back towards the woods when a uniformed soldier jumps out.

"Stay there. No run," the officer commanded in Ibo walking back to open the rear of the vehicle.

During the war they had not seen such healthy Ibo soldiers. Obi's eyes fixated on the long metal torch in the soldier's grip. The beam of light blinds them, intensifying the darkness, before another man jumps down from the back. Obi could not believe his eyes; he was looking at a real life white person, an Irish priest in shorts and short sleeve.

"I will help them inside," the man waves summoning them to come to him. Obi was about to go when he felt the distance of Decima's hand.

"*Biko*, I no wait if you no come." said the impatient soldier.

"Can't you see? These children are afraid," said the priest.

The kindness of the stranger's face gave some assurance that they are not in danger. Just like when the evacuation truck came into the compound in the dead of night, the man lifts them into the truck. This time the vehicle was not filled with refugees, it was full of boxed items all neatly stacked.

"Take this," the stranger handed Obi some sweetbread which he had broken from the loaf.

"Thanks Sir." Obi holds the bread until Arike and Decima have theirs.

"Dear Jesus, these children survived alone with your love." said the priest blessing each of them with his hand on their heads.

"Drink this," he gives them a tin of cream milk. "*Biko*, drink it slowly, it will be enough for you all. We will drop you off at the next camp where we unload these supplies and then set off to the next. Jesus has been with you so far, I pray that he continues to be," said the priest as he shifts the boxes around the truck.

"Thank you, Father," said Decima and Arike before they took the first mouthful.

The truck continues along the road for what seemed to the children a short while because they had not finished eating. The vehicle moves slowly avoiding the crowd arriving at the camp. The priest gets up and unfolds the tarpaulin to reveal the mass of congested people all trying to get into the camp.

Obi's eyes darted everywhere as starving faces looked back at them and the food in their hands.

"Obi, don't stare at people," Arike reminded him.

"Jesus, Mary and Joseph" the priest crossed himself, and so did Obi. "I think we have to let you off here. This checkpoint will take long to get through."

They were about to join a new camp and it no longer fazed them to become one of the masses. They did not know why they weren't allowed in; the entire line was being held up at the makeshift gate. Obi noticed that the barrier wasn't like the checkpoints he was used to; the type where a soldier pushes down on a bamboo pole to raise the barrier. Obi was fascinated by this gate, made of old logs and planks suspended between two ribbed metal barrels. A quarrel erupted between mothers who wanted to pass their children to others to take through, in case they were not allowed in. Women spat on the ground and cursed at one another as Arike squeezed past, pulling Obi and Decima forward through the barrier. Obi saw the familiar red painted cross with a circle on the larger tent; he had seen the symbol before. This red cross was tatty with paint peeling from its edges and cracked at the centre. A man with a wooden rifle posted himself in front of the tent as people filed past. Obi wondered what the purpose of guarding with a wooden rifle would be; mesmerised, he stares at him when walking past in tow with his sisters and notices that some of the younger women with red lipstick smiled at him as they passed.

The clouds moved over and the sun shone intensifying everything as they made their way to the main building. Obi noticed how much healthier the people looked in this camp. Stood at the entrance was a group of people arguing forcefully about the lack of space in the hall when the sisters pushed straight through into the building. Obi is impressed and remains silent.

"Call yourself a man! Why are you not fighting with our men?" Obi could see the red rage in the women's eyes as his sisters pull him along.

Inside they find a small clearing of floor away from the back door. They spread their blanket and go off to sleep, grateful that they didn't have to look for food due to the kindness of the Irish priest and the Ibo soldier.

In the morning, when Obi opened his eyes, his sisters were gone and to his surprise he didn't panic. He was too tired to acknowledge any fear, he accepted his fate as sleep engulfed and sent him back to the floor.

"Obi, are you not well? Do you have a fever?" Rani enquired, blowing a soothing air across his face and watching the pearls of sweat evaporate from his forehead. "Don't worry, your sisters will be back, and you will be fine."

Disturbed by the smallest sound in the hall, Obi opens his eyes and sees his sisters walking towards him carrying something in their hands. He staggers to his feet to greet them, wanting to run, but he falls in a heap, his legs too weak and his head in a whirl.

"Drink this, Obi, it is *ackam*," Decima told him when they were all sat together on the floor. Obi detested *ackam*, it looked like pus and left a slimy feel in his mouth afterwards. Nonetheless, he drank his *ackam* and felt much better. He asked if he can go out and play with other children. But no sooner had he thought of play, his body collapses in a heap back onto the blanket. Decima and Arike look at each other before they agree to find someone to help their brother, knowing also that their chances are slim as every adult they've come across looked after their own. His forehead becomes saturated with sweat as he sleeps fitfully. Decima covers him with the corner of the blanket.

They watch over their brother as he becomes delirious with the heat raging in his body; crying, laughing, talking gibberish all at once. Arike rushes out, praying that she finds some water, she was ready to beg, steal or fight. Letting out a sigh, her heart smiles and lights up her face, it had been raining and she went to collect the tin cans she had hidden, just in case. She pours the water into their aluminium pot and puts the cans strategically back in place camouflaging them.

Both sisters take turns to give him sips of water and place cold compresses on his head with the dampened corner of their blanket, mindful of dirtying their ration of water. Two days and two nights his sisters sat watching praying and tending to their brother.

"I saw Rani, the girl in the garden, the one with long hair and elephants and lions, she said something," were his first words on waking, and reaching out to find his sisters hands and clasped them feebly.

Emerging from the hall he sits on the concrete steps of the building and observes his surroundings, enjoying the warmth of the sun he throws his head back and savours the silence which was rare.

"Obi! Boy, *biko*, come fetch my stick, *mek* I go bush to urinate."

Puzzled, Obi wasn't sure whether he had imagined his name being called.

"Obi! Boy, *biko*, come fetch my stick, *mek* I go bush to urinate."

The same voice beckoned him a second time, before he sees an old man waving, gesturing at him to come and see him. Still unsure Obi looks around in case he was calling out to someone else.

Obi remembers the wizened old woman again making his way to help the old man. He looks up from his seat asking Obi to hold onto the stick while he grabs it to pull himself up.

"Why you be afraid of the old?" the man asks limping towards a tree to relieve himself. "Stay there, I soon return," the man looks over his shoulder and orders.

Over the next coming days, Obi befriends the old man, and others at the camp. He makes them laugh when he proudly tells them who his people are.

"I am from Uboji village. My uncle is Ozo," Obi introduced himself to the elders. "Do you know my Ozo?"

"We have too many Ozos in this land," a woman elder said. Obi settles back within the camp, Decima and Arike also make friends with mothers and grandmothers that show them the kind of vegetables they must not try to cook. The kinder women help to mend their dresses by pulling out frayed strands to use as thread to sew their clothes with a rusted needle.

Obi was again firm on his feet running about the camp ferrying news and messages for them. He likes that he was allowed to stand in the food line for them and proud to be able to carry several plates at a time. His face would often be screwed up in tight concentration while he walked slowly to the elders trying with all his might not to spill or drop any food.

The events of war saw him no longer squeamish about other people's excrement and when they were too weak to go into the bush, he brought them big leaves to use for their toilet and he'd dispose of it for them. "I will come to help you when the jets come," he tells his new friends. His fondness for the elders saw the energy back into him. Obi tries to teach them the drill for escaping the bombing in case he was not about during an attack, knowing that the elders could not escape in time because they could no longer run as fast for cover.

Obi found out that he wasn't the only child in the camp, there were many, only most of them remained close to their mothers because of sickness.

A woman rushed at Obi, she grabs his head and pushes it into her chest.

"My son, my son," she cries before Obi's sisters pull him away as he trembles hiding behind them. People watch and shouted at the crazy woman but she persisted in claiming that Obi was her lost child. When she tried to go around Decima for Obi, Arike took hold of her arm.

"My brother is not your child!"

The crazed woman did not stop as she tugs and pulls at Obi's arm with all her might.

"My son, my son!" she continued as Decima and Arike held firm before eventually others came to their help.

"Move! Fast!" a woman in military trousers orders. "Go in there." She points to a building having subdued the frantic grieving mother. She leads the distressed woman away to the Red Cross tent and returns to check on Obi and his sisters.

"Come, take this!" She hands them a package wrapped in oil-soaked newspaper and bound in red string. Obi could not believe his eyes when he saw the *akara* doughnuts. It has been years since they last ate such a treat before the war. They stood and ate them on the spot, being ever so grateful.

"Thank you, ma," they said all together.

"Go inside, if you want to sleep inside this night, the sun will kill you," the woman told them. "Take this." She hands them three roasted corn on the cobs and half a chunk of freshly-washed white coconut to eat with their corn. They could not believe their luck from someone they had never met.

"Thanks, ma," they said as they watch her walk away in her tight green khaki trousers, an unfamiliar sight for the village youngsters.

"Call me Antie," she said walking away.

When Obi looks up from eating, he sees that his sisters have put away their food.

"Try not to eat too quickly because it could make you sick. I will wash your shirt when we have some water," Decima told Obi.

The atmosphere in the camp had lifted; almost joyous for there have been no signs of air raids in the few days since their arrival. Obi enjoys discovering the grounds and more so the trees because he can climb them and he imagined a small lake nearby, swimming with his friends; it has been a long time since he was up a tree.

As the days and weeks pass, he and his sisters settle into their new environment. A nurse called Veronica visits the camp; she was Vero to the adults. Obi had never seen a nurse before and wondered how the white of her uniform stayed so clean.

"You are a big man, Obi, with skills for survival. Many children your size are fighting in the front line, why you no go?" a woman said sweeping sand from the veranda of the building.

"*Biko*, mama, Obi knows about the war and that other boys are being killed," Decima stood in Obi's defence as she had overheard about the loss of her two sons in the front line and resented all those that were alive.

Obi was growing up fast with concerns beyond his age and the daily thoughts that he may be taken to fight; he is not alone in being robbed of his childhood.

Obi heard the distant arrival of enemy aircraft before anyone else in the camp. "Take cover! Take cover!" he screams. No sooner had the words left his mouth the rockets whizzed overhead, exploding off target into the trees sending the settled camp into hysteria. Over the years they have been fortunate not to have lost each other during the air raids.

"They will return and empty their bombs on the camp next." Obi reminds his sisters from where they were crouching against the building. "Come, there is a bunker we've been digging; we go hide in there now. Let me see if the elders need help?"

"We need to go now Obi, there's not many left in the camp." The girls insisted. They were surprised at how grown up their little brother had become. Obi sees his old friend with the stick and helps him to the bunker, but his friend refuses to get in in case he never makes it out again. Waiting out the onslaught in the heat and wet of the bunker became claustrophobic but it is still safer than hiding in the bushes like they have been doing.

Ibos are known for their joyful celebrations through song and dance, even at near-death when there was little else left but hope and faith the women emerged clapping and praising Jesus for his mercy. The chorus and tempo changes to 'Biafra win the war. Their songs the only gift left for them to give to the almighty.

Another vicious attack followed which hit at the heart of the camp.

*

Exhausted from having cleaned and cleared baskets of broken concrete, bricks and the splintered debris from one corner of the camp, the sisters were seated against a gum tree and Obi sorted stones for his catapult close by. They watch mothers collecting their scattered belongings, utensils and any possession which went unclaimed. The air raid caused horrendous devastation, probably the worst they had experienced since the war had started. The nurse's tent was splintered and blown up on one side and it seemed plausible that the soldier with the wooden rifle deserted his post, running for cover, during the attack.

Obi heard Veronica's voice in the distance and wondered what had happened.

"Where is your junior brother, she came running; is he OK?" she asked Arike. "Boy! Obi! Come. Come assist me find this foolish excuse for a soldier." She did not have to repeat herself, Obi scrambled over to her after he'd gotten his sisters' nod of permission. Obi checks all the possible places to the north of the camp to see if the soldier is there and Veronica investigates everywhere else. It became evident that the soldier was nowhere to be seen or heard. It was only when the vultures started to gather on the treetops and pieces of bloodstained clothing fell to the ground that people became suspicious.

"Why are vultures here?" Veronica wondered at first.

His name was Moses; he hadn't abandoned his post, an explosion had landed near the tent and propelled his small thin body into the air and the trees.

Obi vomits on the spot, heat rising in his head and he starts to tremble with fever, ready to faint, when his sisters lead him away walking in silence.

Veronica held a bamboo that was long enough to reach up to the branches where she sees his remains which are still wedged in the tree; she pushes and pulls his clean bones to the ground. Other women come and help her collect the remnants and tatters of what was once Moses into a brown cardboard box. It was not large enough; a mother watching from nearby who no longer had her child to carry on her back gave her best wrapper to cover all the remains. The older women of the camp said long prayers over Moses' remains that were laid to rest at the outskirt of the camp. Obi did not open his eyes for the entire burial; they had seen enough dead bodies during this war but not a fully mutilated human laid to rest.

"God rest his soul, amen," were the women's last words as they walk way.

Obi and his sisters stood looking at the grave marked with an ordinary rock that was no different to any other.

"His name was Moses," Obi whispered. "What of his gun?"

Obi thought he should ask Veronica for the wooden gun to watch over the camp. He knew his sisters would tell him off and that he was too small for such responsibility. Obi thought about how he could approach the subject with his sisters and Veronica.

"I am no longer afraid. I must fight and be a man," he whispered to himself.

"What are you saying Obi?" asked Decima.

"I was not saying anything."

"Yes you were. We heard you," Arike told him.

"Veronica said that no army will come here and take boys to the front line because they are not well enough to carry a gun." Obi shared the information with his sisters before he walked towards a clearing to practise his manoeuvres.

Alone he marches with his knees up to his chest, and on the ground he crawled like a lizard, and mothers stopped to watch him drilling and mimicking the Ibo troops he'd heard so many heroic stories about.

"*Biko*, stay out of the sun." said a mother walking past.

Decima and Arike had settled in well with the women of the

camp and followed their advice on how to cook and sell food to the soldiers. Temporary shelters were built after the last blitz when most of the buildings were destroyed.

Obi was comfortable within the camp and with its residents before Decima agreed to accompany the women to help them at the roadside trading posts. Obi watches them leave, disappearing out of his view. At first he wanted to run after them but the elders told him to 'go sit down', a common Ibo telling off.

One morning Obi made up his mind that he would follow his sisters and the women to the roadside, remembering his own roadside trips before the war and the many experiences he'd come to treasure. How he longed to see a truck monkey and watch people going about their business from a tree. As they left in the early hours to catch the hungry warriors, Obi waits a while before he trots after his sisters, keeping well out of sight. He watches how the women and his sisters dodge the army vehicles on the road until they arrive at the small clearing of trees to set up their market. Obi found a tree with smooth branches for the morning. He climbed as far as was safe to see and not be seen, and fell asleep on a sturdy branch.

When he woke he saw that everything had been cleared away and that his sisters had gone without him. Climbing down as fast as he could without slipping he ran disoriented in a direction he guessed may have been the way back to camp. Not wanting to be trapped in the woods at night, Obi ran like a thief in the market place, leaping over fallen trees, broken glass and debris as he went. His eyes catch something that fascinates him under some decaying leaves; it is a red bottle top. He picks it up like if it's a precious gem; knowing exactly what he is going to do with it. He'll flatten the buckled edges with a rock then look for a nail to punch the central holes; it will be a spinning wheel, Obi marvels.

The light was beginning to fade and he had let his excitement distract him; he turns three hundred and sixty degrees and there is nothing recognisable, Obi surrenders to the fact he is lost. His sisters would not know where to find him. His knees went weak and he finds himself wiping away fat tears feeling sorry for himself, imagining that he would not see Decima and Arike again, he didn't know what to do or how he would survive the night alone; he started wheezing. Hearing the hoots of an odd owl didn't help. Twilight was beginning to give way quickly as darkness started to close in, Decima's voice sounded heaven-sent when Obi heard his name drifting in from behind the trees.

Decima did not have time for entertaining her brother; she had work to do with the other young women of the camp for the following morning's trading before it became too dark to see what they were making. Whatever supplies they received prior to the last bombing raid did not last the day, it had become even more dangerous for any relief to get through to the ravaged refugee camps of Biafra. Mothers had no choice but to strap their children to their backs in order to try and make money to feed them before they died.

"Obi we have to leave the camp to try to make some money for food," Arike reinforces to her brother. "*Biko*, Obi, stay and play with your spinning top. Don't leave the camp and if we see good rubber we will bring you some to repair your catapult, OK?"

Obi felt his pocket and pulled the catapult out and looked at the broken elastic band dangling pitifully.

With more time than they cared for, and news of how malnutrition was killing more Ibos than bullets, Decima and Arike knew they had to be proactive. They wake early every morning to make biscuits with the mothers and by the time Obi is awake, his sisters are finished and packed for the roadside stall. Obi's fear for his sisters' safety was second nature to breathing;

no matter how much he tries to conceal his anguish he fails, they know him too well.

"What will happen if you don't return, or if a raid separates us?" Obi cries pestering his sisters, tagging along until the boundary of the camp. "You must run away if the enemy soldiers come. Don't sell them your biscuits." Obi stands and watches his sisters disappear into the distant horizon.

19

Young Lives,
Long Memories

At the camp, Obi and the few friends that were able to walk pretend to be soldiers and march around the grounds. Obi dresses them with sticks he collected for rifles, and places them against their shoulders. The children barely have energy to stand, let alone play but their despondent mothers push them forward like stubborn cats.

"Go enjoy with Obi," they would say in frustration, and they joined one by one in the singing procession led by Captain Obi, who preferred to share the captaincy with others in fairness. The boys mimic the Biafran troops as they practise, waiting to be called to the front line.

> "Armoured car, shelling machine,
> Fighters and bombers, kaboom!
> They will never beat Biafra.
> Biafra win the war!"

The boys' brigade sing for as long as they can until their emaciated bodies are ready for collapsing. Grown-ups joined in, singing in merriment for a moment's laughter until they remembered their ailing children and disappear to be by their side. The parade dwindles and Captain Obi marches alone, unaware of his solitary voice.

Obi was shocked, elated and confused all at once, which wasn't a good thing for him. How was it possible for Mr Uwani, his school teacher from his village to suddenly appear at the camp? He wanted to run and greet him, but he froze; where are his school friends, IK, Peter, what about his Auntie Ani and Ozo? He looked for the rest of the refugees as they usually arrive in droves but there's no one, except Mr Uwani. Obi went running to find his sisters for answers. They had no answers either of how, when, what or why?

As it was, almost everybody in Iboland was suspicious of everyone as they may be working as spies for the enemy. Mr Uwani explained to some elders how he had escaped capture from the Federal Army, but when asked why he was not fighting for Ibo people he seemed evasive. The thing was that even if he was a spy, nobody in the camp other than Veronica had the strength to challenge him.

Mr Uwani remained at the camp, he continued to teach and preach to those that listened, and he was a storehouse of information. He started by telling them that, "Ibo troops have little ammunition and they lived rough in the bushes with little food and no boots to cover their feet. Whereas the Federal troops are spoilt and want for nothing; the news of the mishaps of the Federal troops boost our morale and give us entertainment," he'd repeat at any opportunity.

"Even in war, a teacher will still do job," a woman said aloud and sucked in air through her closed mouth in disrespect.

"He is not too old or too young to fight," another mother commented, as anxiety descended on the camp.

Most corners of the camp were posted with lookouts to warn of any troops or deserters, and yet no one saw him arrive or knew how he managed to escape conscription and starvation. What if he is a saboteur? The entire camp will be in grave danger. The teacher looks around at every occasion when he talks of stories he has heard; stories of a miraculous time when weapons had fallen from the skies at night and into the laps of the Biafran soldiers.

"Federal arms suppliers had missed their targets and supplied the Biafran Army instead of their own troops. During these fortunate times, the 'barefoot warriors' of the Ibo soldiers rejoiced in the name of Jesus: Even God is on our side they cheered."

"Hallelujah!" everyone cheers, forgetting their suspicions. The teacher told them to take heart and to believe that the intelligent and creative Biafran Army were outsmarting the Federal troops.

"*Anu ofhia.* Animals," he curses and spits to the ground while he looks around to see if people are looking at him.

"We thank God! If God is kind and merciful, why is there no food?" a woman challenged him. She told him to stop filling the children's heads with lies and propaganda, before she leads her child away.

The discussions continued into the night as Obi sat listening and his sisters slept on the floor next to him.

"Biafra is building its own fighter planes with guns, battery cell mines and its own armoured vehicles." The teacher stops talking when he hears some of the elders discussing about Biafra having a light aircraft which would not stand a chance against the mighty Russian MiGs. Obi knew the stories well because he'd heard them all before, but he continues to listen.

"Federal Air Force has all the fast jets, and Biafra has none. What is light aircraft?" Obi asked himself and thought back to the story of the black gold of Iboland, oil. *If good people witness evil and do nothing, then how can they not be part of that action?*

He recalls a previous discussion between the men and wishes they had new stories.

"Our country rests on top of the finest oil, and yet our people don't have any say about where it is sold or distributed. We do not have say about the distribution of money either. Why must the Ibo people suffer and remain without power?" The discussion continues into the night.

Obi repeats every word of that conversation back to himself. He knows it is important even if he doesn't understand all of it. Completely baffled as to why people had to die because of oil from the ground. He couldn't see the connection he knew nothing of adult economy.

"You must not visit that gathering, Obi. It is confusing you more and more each time you listen to those men. When we are at the market, you must try and stay with the mothers and their babies. We have already asked them to watch over you," Arike told him.

"I have to go to the camp school. That is where we get news. And I must practise marching with the others."

"Look at you, Obi; your eyes are sunken because you are not sleeping. Your mind is causing unrest when you should be asleep and you are agitated because of the things you hear from those men," Arike said as they sat to eat. "People in the army do much more than practise their marching you know; they kill and expect to be killed themselves. Is that what you want Obi? To be killed by a grown-up soldier who is the age of our father? We do not want you to die. We have to stay alive to see our mother and father, do you not remember?"

"No, I do not remember them any more. I don't want to die. Young boys are not supposed to fight in wars, sister, I don't want to fight a man and be killed by him in the bushes."

Tears trickle down Arike's eyes as her brother cries, and Decima looks away because she too has started to cry. His sisters had noticed the changes in their brother; his capacity to remember and memorise the things he's heard about the war was taking its toll on him.

"Obi, please lay down. It's the middle of the night, you have to sleep."

His fascination with the war and his need to know more details about what was going on was extraordinary in someone so young.

"How can we keep him from listening to everything?" asked Decima.

"We both have to be at the roadside every day. We cannot take him with us in case the army snatches him away."

"Do not remind me of what I already know," Decima snapped.

"I am sorry, my sister," Arike apologised.

"*Biko*, let us find some sleep this night," said an elderly woman who could hear them. She begs them for stillness and respect for the night. "Is it not enough that most nights we must sleep with open eyes, waiting for the bombs to start falling? You keep the whole room awake listening to your foolishness. Why do you not join and fight? *Biko*, allow me to sleep this night."

Obi and his sisters fell silent.

Early morning, Obi looks at his sisters asleep on the floor next to him; it was becoming colder with that familiar morning chill they had come to know so well. *It must be Sunday,* he thought, and gently covered his sisters with the rest of the blanket that he had dragged over to his side during the night. He rubs his eyes and stands up carefully, negotiating his way around the mass of sleeping bodies on the floor. The cool air made him shudder; the sunrise no longer had its brightness and hid its warmth behind the grey clouds. He looks up at the distant sound of a passenger plane above the clouds and takes out his broken radio from his pocket and begins to play with it. He twiddles the serrated edged dial and presses the various buttons. He walks to the tree and drops to his bottom without checking the ground. His mind drifts back to last night's conversation with the men.

This made them invincible and invisible to the might and rage against them, David against Goliath. Biafran troops put out the lights at the airfields when the MiG fighters came to bomb them, and then put the lights back on when the food supplies came in. We also practise this blackout in the camps at night when the MiG jets fly low to drop bombs on civilians.

Obi snaps out of his thoughts when five lizards run across the empty ground in a line one after the other. He looks at the small creatures as they scurry into the undergrowth at the edge of the campsite. He watches without reaching for his catapult and lets them escape. As much as he knew, no one ate those small orange-bellied lizards, which was a pity, because he was hungry. He looks forward to food distribution days and no longer hunted. "I am idle to hunt," he mumbles. It wasn't idleness, he reminds himself, but simply that he's not been able to fix his catapult.

On the occasions when supplies arrived when his sisters were out at the market, he was allowed to collect on their behalf and when they were about, he kept them company in the long queue. It was almost expected that Obi would entertain his sisters and others at the line by showing them how to march like an Ibo combatant and how to crawl on the ground like a lizard, a crab or a scorpion. People in the queue would laugh at how high his bottom stuck out in the air when he was a scorpion.

"Make sure the enemy do not shoot your behind, Obi!" the refugees laughed.

The weary and famished appreciated his endeavours in taking their minds away from hunger and the idle waiting.

As the war progressed the enemy jets found their targets more readily on the ground. The years of living in fear of death had become second nature, when humanity represented a time when children are trampled, ignored in place of self-preservation.

Obi had heard that some of the refugees were heading for different camps such as Ozu Abam and Orlu which he had never heard of before.

The food relief no longer arrived and his sisters could not find maize flour to fry biscuits to trade any more. Arike kept safe the valuable *kobos* they had earned from the roadside trading. It was the only money they had and they intended to use it well.

News about what the soldiers were doing to civilian mothers and sisters continue to find its way to Obi's ears. He was afraid whenever his sisters left to look for food that they might not return; he didn't want to tell them how he felt because he feared the words might come true. In turn, Decima and Arike were at a loss for how to help their brother. They could see how petrified he was at the thought of losing them but they couldn't risk letting him tag along with them; boys his age were not seen unaccompanied by adults and neither was it safe for them to move around on their own; no one was safe.

He sat at the roadside after seeing them off and often remained there waiting to meet them on their return. For hours he occupied himself at the edge of the camp scooping fistfuls of soft arid sand, watching it trickle through his tiny fist, completely absorbed by the golden grains.

"Why do you not talk of our mother or of our grandmother and Joseph any more, Obi?" Decima asked.

"They are dead; if you talk of the dead, their spirits will come. I don't want any spirits to come now." Obi fidgets and struggles for breath as he speaks.

Arike put her hand on his shoulder, "Our mother is not dead, she will come to find us, remember?" she told him.

"This camp no receive relief so more people will die," he whispers under his breath.

"You say *don't*, not *no* receive," Arike corrected him. "We try not to leave you alone but it's safer for you at the camp instead of the open road where soldiers might see you," Arike continues in a calming tone. Obi hunches over in a tight ball covering his ears and squeezing his eyes closed, not wanting to hear her terrifying words. He screams, unaware of the noise he is making. People run to see what the matter was but he was oblivious to everything. It wasn't long before Obi opens his eyes and sees the people gathered around them; his nightmare slowly dissolves into inconsolable hiccups.

"These are difficult times for all of us, dear boy. Thank God you are still with your sisters. Others your age are dying every day at the front line and you scream like a baby. Be silent!" a woman scolded. "Where is your catapult? Instead of gazing into the woods like someone who has lost his mind, go find and bring birds. We are starving here. Are you not a man?" the bony woman told him.

"Auntie, our brother wants to hunt but his catapult is broken. *Biko*, no scold him for being afraid, are we not all afraid?" Decima told the woman before Arike had the chance to retaliate.

20

Beetles and Termites

Obi's time alone playing with sand wasn't all idle play; he calmed himself down while watching the soft flowing sand drain from his fist. He thought back to his life before the night of change when the truck arrived and made them refugees. He thought of Vasco and what he might be doing and whether he was fighting in the war. He remembered the games and mischief of his past life and all the animals and bugs that he so loved; creatures he could no longer find during the war, especially all the beetles he'd played with in his village.

No matter how much he delved, there were no sad memories from his village, even the likes of Vasco taunting him no longer seemed cruel. Only fond recollections remained. The Benjie beetles, how they hummed suspended in mid air hovering round the boys' heads. The peaceful shiny green bugs were not fast flyers therefore easily caught in mid-flight as they laboured through the air. The boys would dexterously pierce the hard protective outer wing with a needle so that they could harness the beetle with a thread. But not before begging and pleading with one of the mothers for an arm's length of sewing thread.

"Is repairing your dress less important than wasting my thread by breaking it and giving it to you for nothing?" A mother would be guaranteed to scold the children before breaking a piece with her teeth.

The beetle's soft silky inner wings remained closed until it was launched into the air from the palm of their hands. The children gasped in amazement, the fine green wings unfolded in flight and the airborne benjie flew, humming frantically in front of their faces still attached to the string.

Proudly the boys took turns to hold the thread whilst they walked around the village with the bug in flight above their heads. Shop keepers came out to cheer and clap from their empty shops, and naked children who had been playing in the sand got themselves up to follow the procession. Occasionally the boys let go of the string to watch it create a haphazard pattern trailing in the air and the frightened beetle tried to escape. Often a fight would erupt when the fragile wing detached from its body and the bug escaped, traumatised and flying up and away from the boys' reach.

Obi could not get enough of the armour-plated type of creatures. He would sit for countless hours waiting for one of the larger beetles with serrated hook-like claws to move. When he got too impatient with the insect playing dead, he'd poke its head and force open its claws with sticks. Once he offered his finger and it accepted and locked its jaw on his flesh making him cry out. Obi observed what he could about beetles: how they would balance perfectly on their thin, pin-like claws and hold the same stance all day with their head, claw and body raised, ready for defence. Even when he picked them up they held the stance; he knew how strong those grippers were and that they would rather lose their heads than let go. Some time ago in his village a child was bitten on her Achilles heel. Even when the insect was detached from its head its grip remained locked until her father returned and smashed its head between two small rocks.

The boys, for obvious reasons, did not have much interest in catching or playing with dung beetles, instead they watched spellbound.

"How do they know how to do that? The shit is wet but does not stick to the claws." The boys inspect the beetles closely.

"That's because, when they roll it around the ground all the sand and dirt get on," IK proudly replies. They watched in disgust as the bugs rolled and pushed dung the size of tennis balls up the hilly dirt track, intrigued that those little creatures can move things ten times their size and weight. It was always happy memories from before the war.

Never would any of the females from the water fetching party during those early morning jaunts have imagined that Obi would one day look back upon the memories with such fondness. None of the other boys ever went to fetch water with the women; Obi could only think that they missed out on a wonderful experience.

"Is there another way to Oche?" Obi asked rubbing his eyes.

"It is the same way as you always go, dear child. When the minister agrees to help us bore a hole for water in our village, you and I will not have to make this journey each morning before you go to school."

"Okay, Auntie," said Obi as he washed the sleep from his face and found his water pail for the journey.

By the time the water party arrives at Oche the cable carts already start moving high above their heads carrying cargos of coal that rocked like a baby's cradle. It is a picturesque place by the canyon near the pointed rocks where the sluggish metal baskets travel through the air to and from the quarry. Obi gasps every time he looks up at the line of rusted cable carts overhead, validating how close they are to the clouds. It was early morning and the sun was not being merciful; even their long shadows stretched away from them as their backs burned. Exhausted under the heat, the water party trace their steps carefully back, in silence around the jagged rock face. A fall down the steep hill would be fatal; the edges were like broken bottles cemented to the surface of a boundary wall. Even though he wanted to, Obi didn't risk looking back; unlike his first trip when he saw the sheer drop, and his legs gave way under him. He started lagging behind as the adults pushed up the hill and further out in front. He no longer notices the animals around him as they hurry across his path. It wasn't until he hears his name being called by the women that he realised he had strayed off in a different direction. His bucket has sloshed half its water out as he struggles to carry it with both hands.

"You are not the same as the lazy boys, Obi. You never complain, you always do as you are told. Never mind, the journey home is always quicker. A time will come when this kind of work will help to make you a good man and husband," one of the women says while she waits for him to catch up.

"When I am older, Auntie, will I still have to carry water to the compound?"

Obi sobs, completely fed up with his chores.

Carrying heavy loads on top of their heads was as natural to the women and girls as washing their face first thing in the morning, but for boys such as Obi it was a different story. He puzzles as to how the women can do so many things with children tied to their backs. Meanwhile, he struggles balancing his bucket of water on his head without spilling all its contents before reaching home. As the gap between him and the other water bearers continued to increase again, one of the women stepped back to help him.

Obi places his bucket on the ground again. He notices that she has a larger bucket and manages to keep the water without spilling, all whilst raising and lowering it from her head effortlessly.

"This is how you carry heavy objects on your head," said the woman as she lowers her head support, a twisted bundle of fabric which starts to unfurl and stopped just before it touches the ground. She rips a strip from it and winds it into a circle which she places on Obi's head.

"Your *moda* is the one who should teach you, not I," she said.

Obi fought back his urge to cry.

During the journey back, he mimics the women and thinks, how funny they look from behind, when they walk. Their heavy buckets rest perfectly still upon their heads, their hips sway gently from side-to-side in sync with their arms swinging to and fro. From then on, Obi and other boys stopped trying to carry heavy things by dragging them. Even the grey metal school boxes were carried on top of the boys' heads just like the young girls had done for as long as anyone could remember. It was no longer seen as a thing that only women and girls did, it was a shameless understanding on the boys' behalf.

During the rainy season, there were fewer trips to Oche. The rainwater was collected from the edge of the tin roofs of the main house into an old oil barrel before it was strained and filtered, removing tiny squiggly insects before the water is transferred to the calabash inside the kitchen for drinking and cooking.

The women used fine head ties as water filters to clean the drinking water. Children were not asked to filter the water, particularly boys. They could not be trusted to take such duties seriously and nor would they be able to support the weight of the water barrels if they were tilted. The boys were happy for being allowed to watch how it was done; their main interest was in the squiggly baby mosquitoes. Hearing was selective for them; they seldom responded when their mothers called them to help with domestic tasks like washing the iron pots. They had better things to do like chasing beetles and termites instead.

When it rains, it sounds like pebbles were being emptied from the sky upon the tin roofs. The heavy rainy season is one of Obi's favourite times; at night the sound of raindrops upon the roof lulls him into deep sleep and he had no fear of hearing strange noises around the compound. He is always excited by the downpour and the first to be drenched the instant he steps off the veranda. He jumps and dances barefoot and naked in the deluge, oblivious of others in the compound. Singing and playing alone in the rain until other boys join him after their mothers woke them and told them to 'go wash'.

The mothers from the main house and the surrounding huts come out to watch Obi; they lean against their windows and doorways and enjoy seeing him in his element of total bliss.

They laugh and cheer along, "Obi, Obi, Obi," rocking their babies on their hips during the downpour and Obi sings out loud.

"I say come, you say go, you say work, I go rest, you want money, I no money, you want marry, I go run, pa-pa-pa-pa-pa."

Obi is in heaven with his singing and dancing, putting laughter upon every face in the compound as he merrily continues.

"I'm too young for you; I'm too young for you, I'm too young for you; you're too old for me..."

He'll be dirty in the muddy waters in one instance and clean by the heavy shower the next, the elders watch and clap from under the shade of their verandas as Obi entertains them for the entire duration of the deluge until the water wrinkled his fingers and toes.

Not only did Obi love the joy of dancing in the rain; he adores the smells that followed, especially when they saturate the earthen walls. During the dry season, he tries to recreate the same precious smell by throwing his cup of water against the wall instead of on the marigolds. More often the heat of the day's sun worked against him, drying the porous wall almost instantly before he's gotten a sniff of the wet clay. Often he got told off for wasting water when he was caught with his nose squashed against the house in search for dampness. The prospect of inhaling the moisture of the wet wall was worth any telling off.

During the journey back from school, the boys lobbed stones at targets which they set strategically; using their catapults to identify individual leaves on tall trees or rocks. His friends practised their skills on living targets when they saw them, therefore the birds around their village made themselves scarce because of the catapult shots from the boys and men alike. Their search for more creatures took them beyond their village; they wandered further out; making pit stops to build small fires to roast their kill and enjoy the feast with their friends before they returned home for dinner.

The numerous edibles amongst their catch often included various fat grubs, termites, beetle and caterpillar and birds, the red termites were easy to tease out from their nest, probably because they viciously defended their territory. Obi sent long thin strands of grass down the narrow holes into their kingdom, drawing them out was a joy seeing the dome-headed insects with razor-sharp pincers locked onto the green blade.

Along the termite mounds dotted around, some were kneeling and others flat on the ground on their bellies, in silent concentration the boys attended to their task. One eye peering down the hole and the other closed for a sharper focus, not much could be seen anyway but it made them feel more like hunters. Inevitably there was always someone slapping at their legs in an effort to shoo off the multitude of furious ants that had a habit of appearing from nowhere to fight. Before they amble back to their compounds the young warriors thanked their prey. Forgetting the nips to their tongues from the insects that fought back inside their mouth until the evening when the hot pepper of their mother or auntie's soup reminded them of their previous meal.

21

Silver Trails

L ondon 1969. The black-rimmed clock on the foreman's wall had not missed a second since Caroline started working at the meter factory. A full pay packet at the end of the week relied on how punctual she has been. When she was clocking out, she struggles with a snag in the lining of her coat sleeve to free her arm in time to pull the heavy door open. She shudders when the cold winter rain hit her face which distracted her from hearing the greetings from her colleagues as they ring their bicycle bells when they pass her. She looks about the dimly-lit road before making her way across it heading towards the bus stop. She cannot see any signs of one approaching.

"Why does the bus take so long to arrive when it is bad weather?" she said aloud, but the few people at the bus stop turn their backs without a word.

"What is the time, please?" Caroline enquires.

"The nine-thirty bus is late, winter journeys always take much longer," a woman's voice answered from the queue.

On occasions when she walks to the next stop in the hope of making up time, Caroline repeatedly looks over her shoulder like a child who has informed everyone that she is running away. But today she waits and wiggles her toes inside her flooded boots.

"Sister, you will be lucky if you make it in time for the ten o'clock news tonight," the conductor told her when she got on board. "This bus has been crawling all the way from North London." He spun the metal handle of his ticket machine in front of his waist and hands her a long strip of narrow paper. Her left foot was cold. The newspaper she had stuffed inside her boots before she left work has turned to pulp, and a squiggly white watermark ran over her damp leather boots. Her wig moved up and down her forehead when she scratches an itch and pulls it back into place before she rests her head against the window. Caroline listens intently to two women in front. They chat about the Biafran War when one of them turns and looks at her. But Caroline had already averted her gaze to look at the worn photograph of her and her children from her bag. Their eyes meet when Caroline looks up, she smiles at the passenger as she tucks a stray braid of hair back inside her wig.

"Our prayers are with you and your family love," the woman said, before continuing her conversation with her companion.

Even in London, others know your business, like in a village, she thought. Sometimes people are kind, but this time she ignores the mothers who tug and pull their children away from staring at her.

When she abandoned her night school to take on extra hours at the factory, she did not think it would take her so long to achieve financial stability. She hardly saw her husband as their paths seldom crossed. He steps out as she steps in. By the morning, when his night shift at the underground car park is over, she will be getting ready for the early shift at the factory after cooking and placing his meal on the cold shelf against the misty window that kept their milk fresh. On the unlikely occasions that they went out as a couple to an Ibo party, the police would arrive at the house when their quarrels conclude with a fight; Caroline did not appreciate the attention her husband paid other women at the parties.

Caroline's frustration developed into short temper which was further exacerbated by the thoughts of her lost children and neither did she believe that there was nothing she could do to be reunited with them. The news of the war on the television was conflicting with what she heard from the Ibo community, who were more connected with the goings-on in Biafra. Caroline's urgency to want to go back to find her children grew by the minute but she didn't know where or how to begin that journey.

On the bus, she checked that her savings account book and passport were safely wrapped in the clear cellophane bag that she re-secures with a red rubber band. Although she has travelled the same route five days a week for seven years, she still counts each stop like an anxious tourist.

"Next stop Caroline," the conductor informs her as they approach. "Mind your step love; it's a bit slushy tonight. Mind how you go." His grip tightens around the steel pole as he swivels around it on the open platform.

The passengers watch as she jumps off without looking back. She lands in a wet puddle gasping when the cold water penetrates her boots again. The reflections from the streetlights warn her of other hazards in her path as she runs along the street towards her home. She notices that something is different by the time she arrives at the parade of local shops that are normally open both day and night. *Why have they closed?* She wonders. *Is it their Christmas?* Caroline presses her face against the shop window and looks through her cupped hands at the clock above the counter. She sees movement through the line of light underneath the door that separates the shop from their living quarters. The clock said four minutes before ten when she turns to head home. She could hear and feel the squelching water from her soggy cold boots with every step.

"Even Ashok has closed his shop and is with his family; I don't blame him. My husband will have to come to buy his own egg to break into his morning coffee," she told herself.

Behind her, she hears the hollow rumbling of a sash window being opened.

"Hello! Who's there?" Ashok calls out.

"No worry, Ashok. Stay with your wife. I hope everything is fine with your family?" Caroline shouts, looking back up at him peering out of his window on the first floor.

Her words trail off behind her as she adjusts her steps avoiding the dog mess that's dissolved by the rain. She would have left work a bit earlier had her foreman not offered her overtime.

"I want overtime," she told him when she first took the position.

She hastens past the small parade of the butcher, greengrocer, off-licence, post office and hardware shop that offer 'green shield stamps', which she likes collecting. She flings open the wrought-iron gate to her house. It clangs against the wall before she rams her key into the front door and remembers that they have run out of paraffin for the heater, which would mean having to go out again to make the long walk to the petrol station on the main road. Keys in hand the heavy front door slams shut behind her under the flickering light bulb of the hallway.

A small packet of tissues falls out of her open handbag when she runs up the stairs to slide the key into the lock, opening the door in one single sweep. The bedsit was dotted with small piles of folded clothes. Caroline reaches over the table and turns the plastic ivory coloured knob of the television. The click of the set reminds her of the radiograms in her village. She bangs her fist on the box, it frizzles and warms up; the photograph of her with Obi, Decima and

Arike, which was propped up against the aerial, slides and falls behind the set.

She throws her bag at the unmade bed before she slumps onto it, pulling off her wet boots. The thin pink nylon eiderdown had almost slid off the orange blanket on the bed. A strip of patterned wallpaper hangs halfway down the wall, curling over next to her pillow. Caroline waves her hand about as if to clear a smoky room. The damp smell did not shift. The ceiling light flickers as she felt her foot on something cold and slimy. Looking down at her feet she sees trails of silver lines all over the red and green patterned carpet covered in the glittery slugs and snail trails that reminded her of strips of sellotape.

"*Tufia!*" She curses the slimy creatures after her foot accidentally squashes another.

The television finally came to life when the horizontal lines settle into a picture.

"That was a special report, smuggled out by our war correspondent from Biafra. Sleep well, and a very good night."

Caroline wept and fell to her knees against the damp floor. The television had taken too long to warm up so she has missed the news. She weeps for her children and begs God to watch over them wherever they may be and to unite them again. As Caroline prays she hears another click and darkness filled her room. The electric meter was out of charge. The communal telephone on the landing rings and she hears one of the tenant's heavy footsteps descend, a step at a time to answer the call.

"You have phone call," the voice outside her door said.

When she went to take the call, the man drops the receiver and goes back up to his room.

"*Caro. My sister, kedu, how are you? I think you have just returned from work. Our country is on this evening's news. They will show a newsflash before they shut down."*

The woman speaks hurriedly before the beep-beep-beep for more coins ends the call. Caroline put down the receiver and ran to her handbag in the dark. She ruffles about for her purse – leaving the room like an athlete. Flying down the stairs her footsteps were too fast as she disappears out of the front door. In front of Ashok's shop she calls up to him.

"Ashok! Come now to give me change for my electric!" She bangs at the door.

A head appears at the window above, and disappears just as quickly before the line of light from under the door floods the shop on Ashok's entry. Caroline watches him make his way to the front door and unlocks it for her.

"Did you see your country on the news?" he says opening his door and Caroline marches in. "It will be on again they said. Too many hungry children in your country Caroline." Ashok shuffles in his worn out slippers to the counter and Caroline takes a quick look at an aisle, her gaze falls on the eggs and tears fill her eyes.

"Hurry, you must not miss it," he urges her, counting out coins in the dark.

Caroline collected the change from him, she appreciates that he puts the money into her hands, unlike his wife who threw the change on the counter. But that was before they got to know Caroline after she had just arrived in England.

"I am not an untouchable," was Caroline's response to her.

"Take brown eggs, you don't have any, I know." he said and made his way from his counter to see her off. "Being hungry will not help your children."

Caroline stares into his soul before she remembers to go. She gave him no more words on leaving his shop, she knew nothing about his life and yet it seemed he knew all about hers.

"You must hurry, you can pay tomorrow." Ashok locks his door behind her.

She returns and feeds her meter but the machine is jammed, unable to accept any more coins, Caroline thumps it in an attempt to dislodge the trapped coins, but instead she almost wrenched the grey metal box with its loose screws off the wall. She wedges a few matchsticks into the wall to anchor the screws before she pushes the meter back against the wall.

"Too full," she complains, fumbling around for the box of matches on the floor; she lights the candle on the centre table of her darkened bedroom. The solitary sound of a single coin lands inside the meter illuminating the room; and crackling from the old television. *Hallelujah* she thought in her head, while she waited for the special news report. Her hands couldn't stop her knees from trembling, her breaths long and deep.

The report came from within a Biafran refugee camp. Tears cascaded down Caroline's face as she watched the screen. Engulfed by what she was witnessing, she reaches out to touch the faces of the stick-thin children before she saw something that took all strength from her legs to the floor, like a possessed body in a church. On her knees she wipes her eyes and moves closer to the screen.

"How can this be?" she whispers. Behind the reporter are hundreds of people within the densely populated camp. The camera pans across the mass of refugees, mainly children with flies on their faces. "Obi, my son, is this you? Where are your sisters? Where is Decima, where is Arike?" Caroline sobbed and sobbed, "I am coming. In the name of Jesus, I come find you if it be the last thing I ever do." Caroline is in a daze, she watches the Queen in her carriage along the Mall before the transmission service ends for the night.

"How can this be?" she questions the almighty. "Millions of refugees and you show me Obi. How great and merciful you are."

She stays on the floor till the television shuts down into a tiny dot of light in the middle of the dark screen. She prays thanking God for his mercy, tears leap from her eyes again, before they turn to laughter, she sits back on the floor. Her son is alive.

22

Hearsay

Biafra 1969. According to the various news that travelled with the war; the Federal and its supporting British Government had only expected the war to last a few days or weeks before the Biafran Army were expected to be crushed. Clearly they did not know or anticipate the Ibo spirit and determination of that generation. The war was heading into its third year, Ibos were driven out of their villages and towns; discovering their vast land, be it as refugees.

"This starvation is because of him!" Obi began; he referred to what he had heard of the Federal commander. He could recite the entire speech word for word. Words he had heard from a mother they walked with after their camp had been strafed one night.

"Our children do not know what to do if you give them food." Obi thought about that and remembered how a three-year-old child did not know what to do with a piece of food he'd been handed once at a camp.

"Food blockade by Gowan's Federal Government is the reason we are suffering like this," the mother moaned with her child on her back. "Ojukwu cannot trust that Ibo food supplies would not be contaminated with poison if the enemy intercept them first before giving the food to our people. It is senseless, it is important that our children all have an opportunity to know their history and all the suffering of the Ibo people." Obi hurried to listen closer in the dark but Arike pulled him back in line. "No one knows tomorrow; the Ibo death toll is increasing rapidly at the front lines and millions of civilians are dying."

Obi continued to hang around the various groups of elder refugees in the camp; he dipped in and out of their discussions. Out of sight, curled around a tree or propped against a corner of a wall. When different voices spoke, he could put faces to them. He particularly liked listening to the old women; it reminded him of the women of his compound and village. He'd sob into his hands so that he could not be seen or heard when he was homesick and missed Lady Ani. He wasn't as upset as before on hearing elders argue.

"Which other day!? You lie. *Biko*, go and sit down! Have you and I not been here since? If Ojukwu's concern is of our future why does he send our children to the front line?" an elder refugee woman said with bitter venomous spit of rage as she turned her back to the discussion.

"Biafra win the war!" a man stood and shouted before his legs became unsteady beneath him.

"Fool! Sit down. Look about you. Do you see us winning anything? Do you think our leader does not use propaganda also? Biafra win the war? Utter nonsense. As long as we continue to sit on a bed of oil which the West want at any cost." A male elder shouted the speaker down dismissing him with a wave of the back of his hand.

All Obi knew about oil was that it was used for cooking and for rubbing on hair and dry skin. In his village, he and his friends did not feel the injustice or the oppression of Ibo people, which over the years, he had heard many times. As the war progressed he came to understand that Biafra, even Nigeria, could have had the respect and power commanded by other wealthy nations if it had not been for the mismanagement of the state's riches. He absorbed every word just like he did before the war but now he didn't save them to ask or repeat to his teacher at school for the following day.

"We are going to give it to them at our own peril!" the man yelled again before he left the gathering, and Obi could still hear his continued disdain when the man limped past him and Obi held his breath so he didn't catch his odour.

"International banks welcome corrupt leaders with open arms! They accept the stolen money of foolish leaders like many who have claimed to be our leaders." He stopped before storming off from the discussion. "Do you know in England, it is big offence to accept stole items? Their banks accept stolen money." He continued in disgust from afar.

"Ojukwu know his people well well. He has only one choice, to continue the fight for our people. He knows that if he was to surrender, his fate will surely be an execution. Not by the hands of the Federal Government, but by his own people. After all that he has put us through I no blame him o." The man articulated from the open grounds of a camp nobody cared to call by name.

When he finished talking he stretched backwards and inhaled the hot air before he urinated into the bush.

"My urine dark o."

Obi watched the man returning. He walked close by him again and Obi held his breath and couldn't help but look at the man's chest, covered in a fatigued membrane of thin skin that pounded against his visible ribs which reminded Obi of a bird's cage.

Even though he'd listened over the years to every discussion and argument he could about the war, Obi never really understood what the war was about. The elders seemed to favour the word 'genocide' and used it more and more during their discussions. He knew what the grown-ups said about God being on their side when weapons intended for the Federals landed on the laps of Ibo soldiers; although he was no longer sure what side that was.

He'd heard on different occasions that Biafra had little international support, but he didn't understand what those long words meant; it was not a word he had learnt at school before the war.

Often he sat alone with empty hands; even the soft sand no longer engaged him and he stared into a void motionless. During the evening when there was nothing to do, he looked for the groups of older men or the womens group, he wanted to be invited to sit with them, but instead he eavesdropped. Unlike before, the children no longer sang and chanted the words of the campaign. They simply watched more people arrive in droves on foot by night. He was no longer one of the older boys; some of the new arrivals knew more about the war than he did so he tended to keep more to himself. Their eyes were dark and squinted, their lips pinched like the edges of a pie and they had no fear, ironically it was the adults who feared them.

"Be careful around those boys, Obi. They are said to have been soldiers who have run away from the bush," Decima warned him before she set off to sell her biscuits. "They do not want to make friends with anyone; they would rather fight than talk."

"*Ibos must fight*," the new boys repeated as they sat rocking on the ground.

"General Ojukwu is not only fighting an unjust war, he is

fighting a slander, propaganda war against him and his people!"
the boys shouted like zombies as their anger grew.

Obi didn't stop to wonder what slander or propaganda
meant; instead he made himself scarce as Decima had earlier
suggested.

23

Boy Soldiers

llah is most merciful and forgiving. Everything is permissible under his holy name, Obi thought, after he'd eavesdropped upon a discussion between the new arrivals. Although no one batted an eye to see him in the company of older people, Obi kept a respectable distance.

"Do not forget what your sisters tell you. You are listening to too much idle gossip from us hopeless old fools. Go find children of your own age to play with," one of the women reminded him.

Obi scanned the camp for familiar faces before he ran off towards the road's edge. He stopped at a new gathering he had not seen before.

"In England, I was a doctor," a man said from the small company of people. "Even the radio and television news in England reported inaccurate incidents. No one should believe what comes out of the world of news report. I ran from a town where the Federal troops shot down a Red Cross relief plane. The world watched in silent compliance; the camp starved because of no food!" The impassioned man banged his chest.

"Ha! My brother, I no know how such a thing can happen? And nothing of that evil was reported in Western news. So people in the West do not know that it is their government who is fighting and killing our people. How can this be so?"

"It would be an outrage over there if the English people know the truth," replied the doctor.

If good people witnessed evil and do nothing, then how could they themselves not be part of that action? Obi remembered from a long time ago. He did not understand all that he saw and heard of the war and its consequences, but he still liked to talk to his friends at the camp about the things he had overheard but they, in turn, did not understand the points he tried to make either. But it kept a futile communication alive. The exhausted camp community found it hard to distinguish any longer between their own needs and that of the children; Obi had seen far too much for a child of his tender age, as had his peers. He was grateful that he was not fighting at the frontline like other boys.

Whenever the camp came under attack and the food supplies and medicine diminished, people struggled to be patriotic in their understanding that General Ojukwu was doing all he could to ease Ibo suffering. Though it was a false sense of security, everybody at the camp still believed the hope that they had pinned on Ojukwu. The elders of the camp spoke about how Ojukwu visited the camps and villages to support and reassure his people; they also talked about the suspicion that he had already abandoned Biafra. Obi longed for General Ojukwu to visit his camp, and would wait for that moment seated upon a boulder at the camp's edge in case Ojukwu visited, but that never happened.

His thoughts of seeing his mother again were becoming a distant pipe dream as the war and its effects raged on. Ojukwu's encouragement became empty rhetoric for hope whilst the hollow bellies continued to swell. People at the various camps knew the risks that the relief supporters endured to help them. They brought far more than food, medicine and powdered milk with them when they arrived at the camps; they brought a different kind of hope, the hope that a good life existed outside the camps and that Ibos were important enough to be cared about.

A mother's desperate cry in the early hours of the morning meant only one thing, the passing of her child. Their grief shamed and frustrated the old men as they remained helpless. Powerless; the men had chosen to flee their homes or seriously injure themselves rather than face death at the hands of the enemy. Dependence upon international and church missions for survival was challenging for the upright and previously, stalwart Ibos; they had to come to terms with the indignity of no longer being able to look after and provide for their families and children. Such sacrifices were inevitable and left them feeling disempowered while, at the opposite end of the spectrum, the fact that Obi and his sisters were without parents did not seem to concern anyone.

"This is war," the women would say. "There is many children without parents."

Decima and her family were fortunate; they had so far managed to avoid illness and disease. Their bodies were thin but not bony with bloated stomachs known as *kwashiocor*, unlike some of the unfortunate children at the camps who were very sick and destined to die. Although most were numbed and shocked, traumatised by the atrocities of war and the abject misery of their lives, Obi's popularity around the camps remained consistent; to others, he was a bright spark in the dark.

"Obi, *bia, bia gwa m*, come, come and tell me, tell me of your family before the war!" beckoned a woman who was slumped against a tree.

Lonesome old women rang alarm bells for Obi, after all she may not even be human and he didn't want to be led away by a ghost as he could just about remember the wizened old woman of his village. He buried his face in his shirt until she went away. Obi's patience that day was finally rewarded when his sisters returned from the roadside trade; he ran and greeted them without informing them of the old woman by the tree.

Decima and Arike started to prepare their evening meal from the bartering they secured in the makeshift markets. They talked about their compound and wondered what had happened to the others who evacuated the village in the truck with them that first night. They recalled as many people as they could from the previous camps, remembering those who travelled with them before they became separated at various junctures of their escapes. Their attempts to engage their brother from the depths of his isolation did not always work. Obi's overwhelmed mind blocks out many memories, much to his sisters' concern.

"Obi, wake up. We have to leave now; most of the others have already gone as we slept." Arike shook her brother, who did not stir. The whole camp heaved with sweaty bodies which collided in the dark. Someone had heard a faint noise of a distant jet and raised the alarm. Everyone tried to get away before bombs lit up the already torn and bludgeoned landscape.

Arike returned to the hall after collecting what was left of her utensils and a few discarded items that had been spared by others as they fled.

They joined the last few remaining refugees in the dark; it was 3am as Obi rubbed the sleep from his eyes and Decima took a firm hold on his arm before they rushed to keep up with the others. Arike followed with their utensils, blanket and a stick clutched in her hand; ever ready to fend off any untoward offenders.

Dawn crept in from behind the hill tops of Iboland. A silent land where birds no longer greeted strangers from the tree tops. The eerie silence was broken when twigs snapped, forging through the darkness of a land they did not recognise.

Obi followed his sisters without a care; the only time when he was at ease. The years had been hard on them: he had lost the will to hope for an end to the war and misery and he'd forgotten the sound of laughter from his sisters. Decima's hand was hot and sweaty but she was not going to let go of him; she knew that Obi was losing his will and all he wanted to do was to curl up and sleep. They had been on their feet for over twenty-four hours. She prayed in her head and whispered to God to help them. She asked God to give her little brother the will to live and carry on for she could do no more than what she was already.

Obi watched Arike's long strides supported by her staff, stepping over large potholes and fending off branches that lashed against her from the people who walked up ahead through the bushes. He wondered at her strength and how come she didn't need to sit.

"Come on, Obi, not far to go, you'll be able to rest soon," Decima tried to encourage her brother, as his energy continued to flag. Obi heard nothing; he was shutting down, he barely had the will to check that his catapult, radio and stones were still in his pocket. Suddenly he shivered when he felt someone gently hold his right hand. He dared not look to see because there was no one beside him. Arike marched on, leading the way. Obi felt a surge of tingling energy run through his fingers, circling into his palm and up his thin arm into his shoulder. A familiarity that he could not put into words brought calm and acceptance, if it was death he felt ready to turn and look.

"*Hello Obi, I've missed you, I have been wondering where you were? Then I heard your sister was concerned that you weren't feeling well. So, here I am; what is the matter?*" said Rani, who looked as fresh as hibiscus dancing after a summer rain. Her red floral dress flapped with the wind and her long black hair bounced around her face as she walked. Obi held his breath, unafraid at seeing his friend after such a long time. But what if his sisters saw or heard her, what would they say? Thoughts and emotions raced through him; he was awake and yet he felt her soft palm caress his dry and bony hand. All dread abandoned his body and mind when he released himself from his sister's hold to skip on ahead to check on Arike and the procession before them. Decima looked at her brother, and smiled, "How come you are suddenly so happy? I like it when you are smiling." She wasn't alarmed, she knew that God always answered her prayers.

Obi was baffled that his sister didn't ask questions about Rani. But he was not going to worry about something that did not happen; instead he looked at Rani with a smiling face. He always had many questions for her but remembered none when he saw her. *She squeezed his hand and smiled. She said with her sing song voice, "No one can see or hear me, except you. Have you forgotten? My, you have had a tough time. Remember, whenever you need help or just want to see me, call me? I'll come straight away. All you have to do is call straight from your heart." Rani beamed a reassuring smile at Obi, before she gave him a hug and said "Bye!" With that she hopped onto her tiger's back in one swift motion after it lowered its head in her direction. The bright stripey creature disappeared with Rani into the woods.*

Rejuvenated, the woods reminded Obi of back home and he didn't feel sad at her departure like he might have expected, but ecstatic that his magical friend still visited him.

It wasn't only Obi who became unnerved when they noticed young boy soldiers, dressed in smart army uniforms with their stripes on their shoulders. It was a fleeting moment when the boy soldiers spotted them from the back of their trucks lined up along the field beside their military camp. *Small soldiers*, Obi thought to himself. All camp children knew the strict codes of obeying orders, as they often overheard in conversations between the elders.

"Every soldier must obey orders from a senior officer, no matter what. Even if he is ordered to kill his own mother or father, he must do it. Soldiers are trained to obey the orders of senior officers," Obi repeated, retreating back into the woods with his sisters. He had heard of the ruthlessness of boy soldiers, particularly towards children.

Obi mumbled in his sleep under the trees, turning and twisting in between his sisters before he bolted upright as others snored like toads in the dark.

"Death on the front lines," he blurted from a dream. Decima and Arike were lost with what to do or how to help ease their brother's suffering. Obi hadn't experienced the carnage on the front line but the front line was truly lodged in his mind from the times he had spent hovering around adult conversations about the war efforts.

24

Gifted Children

Decima did not imagine life would be easy for them to manage, let alone survive for as long as they had. Weather-worn and tattered, her only dress which she had left home with that fateful night in the truck, no longer fitted. The once bright floral patterns hung threadbare and close to disappearing under the patchwork of multi-coloured repairs. At thirteen she appeared a lot older than her years; her hair was grey at the roots with the dirt and dust of difficult times.

Quite often, on Sundays, when she did not go to trade at the roadside, she sat alone in a distant corner where she'd suck her thumb in isolation. She'd put her finger to her mouth whenever she felt troubled; but during the war she had managed to conceal the habit. She undid the threads from her hair and lined them on her lap like the *adas* in the village used to. She joined short threads together and twisted the ends into knots between her bony thumb and forefinger, her nails half eaten, nibbled from worrying. From a piece of oil soaked newspaper in which they kept some vaseline, she took a small amount with the tip of her middle finger to massage into her scalp with closed eyes. Obi would wonder what she was thinking during those times. Decima no longer knew what she looked like, or that her eyes had sunken with cheekbones jutting. Looking into a mirror was a distant memory, no longer part of a life she recognised.

When Obi's food was ready, Decima called him in from the grounds of the camp. He wasn't far; he'd been on the front steps of the building where he could see the older boys from a safe distance.

"Remember to wash your hands," said Decima, not realising that he was actually nearby. She placed his food on the floor in a feeble attempt to deceive Obi into thinking that she and Arike had already eaten. But Obi knew his sisters' tricks well and that they would never eat without him. Although he was famished, his sisters were also starving. No matter how small the portion of food was, he never ate without them. Obi had a mouth of gari and handed the plate back to Decima, with enough left for the two sisters to share. 'The miracle of God that the body can survive with little food', Obi always remembered someone saying. He could still remember many of the ingrained ways of Ibo people, such as before the war, whenever adults ate with younger people; they always finished first, leaving some food for the young to finish after them.

Arike was never the extrovert, however it didn't take her brother and sister much time to notice that she had retreated into a silent inner world, spending more time apart from them. Everyone had walked to the moon and back drained for the years of toil. Almost three years of patriotic loyalties left the Ibos dead, if not starving.

Even the trees lay barren and fruitless because they were picked to death as soon as any signs of buds appeared. Up in the tall trees, empty nests perched between the branches, with the twigs unbound and disintegrating. Even the swifts that once touched the clouds had disappeared altogether.

Obi spotted a black object in a distant corner and ran at speed towards it. He recognised it in an instant but couldn't believe his luck on finally finding a piece of inner tube. He picked it up, shaking off the dirt; he could at last fix his catapult. Delighted; no find could have been as precious to him, he sits and wipes clean the rubber. In the village one of his friends would have a razor blade, but in his pocket was his metal bottle top, which he sharpened against concrete.

Like an artist skinning a fly, he cut two long and four thinner strips of rubber. He didn't mind that the midday sun was on top of him, he was too engrossed in the task to notice why his eyes stung with salt.

After he'd tested his new weapon he ran off, forgetting to tell his sisters he was going to hunt. The sun had been harsh as it always was; even after it had sucked all trace of moisture from the fallen leaves. Obi had forgotten one of the most fundamental qualities of a hunter; calmness, as his feet crunched he would have alarmed everything in his wake.

"Boy. Why you no find anything in the bush with that catapult of yours?" said a dishevelled old man hunched over a hole in the ground. In his hand was a wire string with a noose at the end, ready to entrap any unfortunate animal. "Boy, do not be afraid. I am still living."

Obi was no longer concerned that the haggard old stranger might be an apparition. He was unsure of what to make of the man but he kept his eyes fixed on the dead rodents which hung by their necks from the man's waist. Obi stared at their gaping mouths that revealed their menacing needle sharp front teeth, and remembered when rats nibbled the feet of refugees in a previous camp.

"You no think to take and run with my food, boy?" challenged the old man with wrinkled hands and mean red eyes.

Obi stood firm and said nothing to the mistrusting man,

with a sizeable stone lodged into the pouch of his catapult, Obi looks beyond the scrawny man and stretches his arms apart, drawing his stone like an archer; the black rubber of his catapult is parallel with his arms ready to fire at the opportune moment. He discharges a shot into the bush behind the man and sees a blade of grass moving. His shot lands on target before he pushes his catapult back into his pocket and proceeds to collect his kill.

Obi whiffs the foulest stench ever as it enters his nostrils from the direction of the bush man, he continues towards his kill trying to resist the urge to throw up. He jumps back startled by the naked bush man who leapt in front of him to grab the dying animal. One of the dead rodents from his belt of rotting carcases rubbed against Obi's arm, leaving a smelly slimy fluid on him.

"Thank you, thank you boy," said the malodorous man, who clapped his hands in a joyous and grovelling manner. "You aim well. I have not seen one of these here before, it will feed a brigade." The man cackled holding up the otter which was still convulsing. He rammed its head against a tree, crushing its skull and Obi shuddered at the sound, still shocked by what was happening in front of him.

He watched the bush man fastened the dead otter to his walking stick and slung it over his shoulder.

Tears filled Obi's eyes on seeing that he'd shot an otter instead of a rat. The war had seen most of the wild animals hunted to near extinction for food; Obi would have wanted to keep the otter as a pet, but that would not have been possible and they would have been targets from hungry refugees at the camps.

Robbed of his food Obi watched on speechless before he engaged another stone.

"You no take my kill. *Biko*, Uncle, my sisters are h- h- hungry, we no have food to share. Each d-day, she no eat, she get weaker. I want to cry but I cannot because it makes her cry. She will become sick like the others. She, h-has give me a dress and said that if the soldiers come when she is not there, I must put the dress on, and go hide. They will not recruit young girls in the army. You m-must not come out of your hiding place, not for the Federal or Ibo troops, do you understand?"

"Shut up. In war there is no honest people and your good neighbours will sell you for a naira. See how it turns you crazy. I was imprisoned for many years until war arrived and explode jail. It free me; it is not only bad. Go! Run back to your camp; if I see you here again, your sister will not recognise you. Go! Foolish boy!" said the thief.

Obi stood, heels firmly dug into the ground.

"Idiot, are you deaf, did you not hear my order?"

"I want my animal!" Obi cried. "*Biko*, sir, my sisters are hungry. *Biko*, sir, I speak truth. My stone killed the animal!"

Obi was conflicted, he still remembered the old ways of his upbringing in his village where children never challenged elders; that seemed a million years ago and war had changed everything and everyone.

"You no witness, is I who kill the beast?" the man argued with a fast pace into the woods.

Obi's plea made no difference to the smelly stranger who stopped to face him in the lonely woods.

"You can follow me as long as you like. Idiot."

Obi stared at the tight wrinkled lips, no longer aware of the words that spewed from them. "It will soon be dark and you will become stranded inside this bush." said the man.

Obi took one last look at the limp otter that swung to and fro from the old man's stick. In his hand is his loaded catapult. The man has no weapon. Obi considers shooting a stone to the thief's forehead. The man looks at him frozen in a firing range as Obi pulls his best stone towards his ears, ready to shoot. They stand without words, in a bull and matador moment of truth. Obi knows his aim would not miss. Before he had lowered his aim, the man was off running for his life. Obi did not chase him but instead spat the man's foul smell from his mouth.

He returned empty-handed to the camp, he was inconsolable. His cry touched the mothers who came to see what the matter was.

"Obi, my child, *biko*, no cry any more. Your sisters will soon return." A mother embraced him with assurance. Obi realised that he'd been out for a long time and had missed his sisters.

Darkness had set in and his sisters were still out on the road somewhere. There had been rumours that the soldiers had been abducting women from the roadside, but no one knew if they were Federal or Ibo soldiers. Other news of checkpoint detentions that were common; normally the guards could be placated with generous portions of free food from the traders' baskets if they had some.

"We will all die from hunger like my friends," Obi said to the mothers who tried to reassure him that he and his family would survive the war.

"Why don't the old men go and get food from the woods?" Obi protested.

"All they do is sit and complain about everything. They told me that I do not know anything because I am a child and not supposed to be thinking and worrying about matters of the elders," he continued expressing his upset. "I heard them talk about no food for refugees and they said that everybody will die. The camp elders are not like the elders in my village. They just sit and look at each other. If my Ozo was here, he would not allow any of us to be hungry like this. He would make the useless men be men and go find food; instead they are afraid." Obi cradled his knees as the mother returned to her own children. He could not get his sister's words out of his head, he sobbed and hiccupped in silence, his breath becoming laborious and shallow.

"It is very dangerous outside the camp. You must not come out to look for us if we are late returning back," Decima told him sternly once. "You have to let us go sell the biscuits to the soldiers before they have all gone. If we sell our entire basket, we will bring you something as a special surprise. Stay with your friends and wait for us. Eat your *opa* when you feel hungry."

Obi repeated the words to himself as he obeyed his sister's instructions to stay within the camp. He'd sit alone out of sight; comforted by the feel of a tree against his back, he waited and fell asleep under it. Undisturbed, he remained alone until faint voices floated through the darkness, which woke him up with excitement. Pulling up his knees to his chest, he closes his eyes for a few seconds and adjusted them to the darkness around him.

He got up and ran towards a group of women who had arrived back from their day's work. Flickers of light from the kerosene lamps dotted around the darkened camp were enough to reveal the familiar sight of his adored sisters.

Obi had calmed himself, ready to settle for the evening, when he heard an old woman who addressed his sisters.

"*Obere nwanyi*, small girl," she said. "How the madness of this war has troubled everything and everybody. This should be your time to watch how the women put on make up and dress their hair. Instead, you and your sister go out on the dangerous road trying to sell food to hungry men. My dear, what are we all to do but our best? Your mother is truly blessed as God continues to watch over all of you." She continued her praise.

Obi had had enough of listening to old women and their words; thoughtful as she was Obi and the girls were too exhausted to respond. Decima unwrapped the food that they swapped for her biscuits and shared them out. They ate in silence; with no pots to wash they spread out their blanket and huddled upon it with their arms criss crossing over each other.

*

Morning came too soon, Decima and Arike had already left. Obi made his way to his usual spot and sat alone with his thoughts. Memories drifted back of a time he and his Uncle Ozo attended an Ozo's funeral. He had not spoken of the experience to anyone, even his sisters, in case something bad happened because he couldn't keep his mouth shut.

The story was when Ozo told him to fetch his stool and Obi instinctively thought that they were going to one of the Ozo meetings. Obi was always delighted whenever his uncle asked him to do anything for him, he never needed to be asked twice. As Ozo led the way, whistling into the air, Obi walked behind him with the small wooden stool. The funeral of an Ozo was unlike that of ordinary people.

"I want you to know how our traditions are observed, because you will be alive long after, when our people have lost their essence of who they are," Ozo said in Ibo.

"Okay, uncle," Obi replied, although he had no idea what his uncle was talking about.

"Had your papa been here, he would be making this journey with you."

They walked for hours as Obi followed hastily detouring in

and out of the woods and narrow pathways. Occasionally Ozo stopped and waited, watching him; on realising his uncle was looking at him, Obi dropped the leaves and twigs to catch up.

"Sing me John Bull," asked Ozo, leading the way again, knowing that Obi would try to keep up so he could hear his song.

When they arrived at the compound for the funeral, the celebrations were already under way. Hundreds of people singing, dancing and greeting one another with cheer and no tears of sorrow. Brightly dressed groups of mothers danced across in their direction to hug and welcome them. Obi loved the way they shuffled towards them like crouching doves in unison.

Ozo rested his staff against the wall and walked across to see the body of his childhood friend. For the first time, Obi realised that he had hairs which could stand on the back of his neck and arms when he saw the dead body. The former leader looked alive at a glance, dressed in his colourful *agbada*, robe, befitting the chief he was, but his face was grey and wrinkled like a chilling death mask. Why was he not in a coffin, instead of sitting upright on a chair with his arms tied onto the armrest, and his staff gripped in his right hand? Questions went through Obi's mind, he shivered at the thought of '*what if he got up and walked off?*'

When he heard the pitiful bleating of a goat from the dugout pit, deeper than a grave, he froze remembering Goliath. Obi moved closer to the edge and peeked down at the goats.

"Boy, you *na* wait till it is your time to go into the ground?" said a stranger after he'd pulled Obi back from the edge of the ceremonial grave.

Three goats lay head-to-toe at the bottom of the grave, their limbs bound so they could not move. During the ceremony, one of the women turned Obi's head away so he couldn't see what was about to happen next. But Obi saw everything reflected from the glass of the main house. He saw the dead man's mouth it was forced open to accommodate a long tubular rod down into his throat like a sword eater.

Obi's heart jumped when four strong agile men hopped into the grave; he thought they would be buried alive with the Ozo and goats. The large grave seemed suddenly small and crammed with activity; the dearth of space meant that the men trampled on the goats' heads and bodies which made them bleat even louder. Obi covered his ears with his little fists, clenched; while he watched the men guide the heavy carved armchair with the body down into the pit. One of the men arranged the chief's feet so that they rested on the goats like foot mats.

A solitary man stood in the pit holding the long metal pole steady while the others shovelled earth into the grave, filling it. Obi stared with horror, as the man was only visible from his waist up, until the men at the graveside pulled him out with one swift motion.

His eyes filled with tears when the bleating of the goats became stifled, suffocated alive; he reached in his pocket for his catapult and held it for comfort.

When everything was buried, only the hollow tube stood firm in the mound of red soil. The musicians sounded their drums, and the women sang out, young men jumped onto the ground from every direction and took their place around the grave; they danced their hearts out while the ground heaved with the pounding of the beat and dancing feet.

"For quite some time, palm wine must be poured into the tube and down into the mouth of the deceased Ozo," his uncle told him.

All the attendant Ozos were at the head tables with Obi seated on the floor next to his uncle while the villagers danced and the celebrations continued. Obi liked the perks that came with being with his uncle and counted the number of horns of palm wine his uncle had downed. Obi drank a small bottle of Fanta all by himself for the first time, and was glad they headed back home to their village long before the orange sun set.

"Now you have seen the customs of your people, you must remember them because our way is fast-changing and may be lost and forgotten for fear of the 'white man' church. Many years ago, slaves and servants were used instead of goats to help the dead Ozo in the next life.

My father was also honoured the same way when he passed; I was not much taller than you are now when I helped to bury his dead body in the ground," his uncle continued as they set off home.

*

Evening was drawing in, when Obi descended from the tree where he'd spent the entire day while his sisters were at work. He ambled about in the twilight with his hands in his pockets looking at silhouettes of bats flapping about in the evening air. It was a tease, he knew they were out of reach for his catapult. He circled a tree, caressing it with one hand around its trunk like he used to in his compound; spinning around, alone in the dark. He let go and ran to greet his sisters on their return to the camp, they looked exhausted. But Obi doesn't ask, he is eager to know whether they brought anything back for him.

The heart-wrenching cry of a grieving mother stopped them in their tracks, they knew her child had died during sleep. It was a sound that no one wanted to hear. Decima led them towards the mother to pay their respects. Obi watched his sisters curtsy and say 'sorry Aunty' before the woman.

"You have to rest, Obi. You will not die if you let yourself sleep. You are not as weak as those other children," Arike told him as he lay awake inbetween them.

Hours passed until he was finally able to close his eyes in the hall. It hadn't been five minutes since he closed his eyes, when he sat bolt upright, saturated in sweat. His terrified gaze fixed on the emptiness of the night and the thought of the woman who screamed for her dead child. Obi whispered the dead baby's name before he stood in the dark for a moment until his eyes adjusted. He picked his way out of the hall towards the mother who was still sobbing at the same spot outside. The full moon illuminated the dark of the concrete step; the broken-hearted mother was sitting with her dead child. Obi sat beside her, he said nothing, only sat. He couldn't help but look at the small bundle cradled on her lap, her child was covered in her wrapper.

"Dear boy, who is your *moda*? Ever since I arrived at this camp, I do not see you with your *moda*," said the woman.

"I don't remember my mother, she is in London," Obi replied.

The early morning light brought a chill of fresh air that swept over them and into the doorway of the hall. The mother stood up and tucked her child closer to her chest before she descended the step. "I go bury my child," she told Obi before she set off into the wooded parts of the ground.

"Sorry Aunty," Obi told her.

"My dear; where the wind is harsh the tree is strong. This wind of war has been harsh on us all. You will be a strong man as you are a strong boy." Obi listened to her words and watched her walk into the woods.

"If it is only your childhood that this hell has stolen then you and your sisters are forever blessed," the mother told him as she walked past on her return from the woods.

As the casualties of starvation increased by the day, Obi's fear of death returned and he stopped going into the woods. No one had the strength to dig graves anymore or to carry the dead into the woods where vultures sat and waited; the food embargo affected everyone.

25

Dream Child

A lmost three years had passed since that first night when the truck arrived and Ozo ordered the evacuation. Hunger and death trailed like an evil twin companion as the war raged on and they clung to life. The mantle of indifference and fatigue lay like a morning mist over the scattered tufts of Ibo grass on the camp. As children, they lived and survived, in an adult world that continued to threaten them with annihilation. Few would question the resilience of children; more so the strength of Obi, Decima and Arike.

Decima and Arike often watched Obi lingering around the elderly male refugees, running and fetching for them; remembering a lost moment with his uncle before the war. In silence he yearned for his father.

Under the sun, a child sits on scorching sand with cupped hands waiting for a drop of water from an empty tap; much the same way, reports of the war efforts trickled in from various new camp arrivals. 'Biafra win the war' campaign had seen better days; starved refugees had lost faith and no longer cared for the reasons behind the war. Sisters, mothers, fathers, brothers, husbands and wives had abandoned memories of their families lost along the way. Haunting images of their children serving in the army of an unborn state brought no sense of pride and yet they continued to live in the hope and trust of Jesus' redemption.

Nothing had been gained in the years of war except for sore hearts that had witnessed atrocities and fiery trails of death and destruction behind them. Rumours that the Federal Army had not wisened up to the cunning tricks of the beleaguered barefoot soldiers of Biafra no longer excited their imagination. The angry soulless years of war and poverty had taught the refugees about the double role that propaganda served. It worked both ways: the encouraging news may well have appeared biased towards Biafra, but it fed a lie that inflamed the wrongdoings that diverted the cause of justice.

The wrath of the Federal Army was felt more than ever before as they pushed to end their frustration with the cunning Ibo Army. The refugee camps received the full onslaught of the Federal Nigerian contracted pilots who took to the air; their rocket attacks persisted and landed closer, and on occasions on civilian targets. The sight of Biafran children with distended stomachs and stick-thin limbs, too weak to stand, brought tears even to the most hardened elder. They heard how those images had proliferated the British news and brought about an international outrage; mainly because the mass starvation of the Ibos was orchestrated by sanctioned food embargoed by the Federal Nigerian Government.

"It is a ploy to starve out a nation from within." An elder stood up with a tattered newspaper in his hand. He smiled through his tears at the realisation that the 'white' reporters who put their own lives on the firing line could at last tell the world about Biafra and their truth. The man handed the paper to Obi who had tugged at his shirt sleeve with patience, just to look at the writing, even though he could not read English. Obi recognised the heading 'Biafra' and imagined what if he was one of those sick and diseased children in the photograph. He looked away, dropping the paper to the ground and ran to help a boy who struggled to get up to take food handed to him by an aid worker.

"Idiot!" the man called out after Obi for dropping his paper.

Obi continued to find his way into the discussions of the elders who were mostly women. He liked that they didn't always talk about the war and what the leaders should and should not be doing. It wasn't that the women didn't discuss war, they did, but more so they talked about who had enough salt to lend them, and why new babies are still arriving. The company of women helped him remember the stories of his compound and the village when he listened to the chronicles of what had occurred many years ago.

The childhood skills Obi had learned before the war had proved more useful than play and continued to afford him much adoration from his sisters. Reaching double figures, he thought at ten that he was old enough to bear responsibility and be more helpful to his sisters and use his time better. He had found it increasingly difficult to sit and wait for them to conjure food from thin air; especially when many were weak with malnourishment.

Desperation was all around and Biafra winning the war became fictitious. Biafran soldiers were human after all; they too like the civilians wanted life, more continued to discard their military fatigues to linger in the outskirts of camps in hope of handouts.

Fear intensified, stories and rumours arrived of what the home troops were doing to women and girls. Mistrust of Biafran men increased. Obi wanted to protect his sisters and decided he was old enough. He'd waited until they had left the camp boundaries before he followed them with his catapult and pockets filled with stones. It hadn't been ten minutes when Decima spotted him after sensing his presence behind them. She sent him back, but not without a good telling off in which she made him promise to never follow them again.

Obi had forgotten his idea of being more grown-up until he took up the plan to follow them again from a distance. The tall grass had closed in behind them as Obi ran. He pushed through the growth against his face until he found himself at a busy clearing away from the main road. Startled at the sight of the women at the roadside with scattered offerings of various items of dead rats, cola nuts, alligator peppers, wilted bitter leaves. Completely absorbed with thoughts of the market place of his village, Obi did not notice that the women were shouting for him to hide because a vehicle was approaching. Not until he was pulled by Arike did he realise what was going on; they hid amongst the trees until the soldiers had passed.

"What are you doing here?!" Obi had never seen Decima so enraged. "Idiot! Did we not tell you to stay back?" Decima shook him by his shoulders.

Obi was in shock.

"I, I don't want soldier to trouble y-you."

"Shut up. You don't want; do you think you are my father?"

Arike stepped forward and puts her hand on Decima's shoulder. "Decima we have to leave him here until we have finished for the day."

Behind a tree, Obi sits and waits until the day's trading concludes and they walk back together.

"When did you last dream of our mother Obi, have you forgotten all about her now? You don't sing and dance in the rain or ask of her any more," Decima asked him one morning as they prepared their biscuits for the market.

Obi thought for a long time about Decima's question. "Maybe our mother has forgotten about us," he said after careful consideration.

Prophetic dreams came to Decima and most of them had come to pass. She didn't regard herself as gifted in that respect, nor did she pay any attention to them other than they were just dreams; except for one she secretly prayed to come true.

One morning, while Decima was preparing for the market stall, she began to tell both Obi and Arike about her latest dream.

"I am not sure if it was a dream or a vision," she began.

Arike took the aluminium spoon from her and continued to shift the biscuits around the frying pan, giving her sister space to talk. It had been a while since Decima had shared her dream. She seemed distracted and bothered that morning. She wouldn't look at Obi who had rushed to sit by her feet ready for a good story as Decima leaned back and rested against the wall.

"What has happened, my sister?" Obi shook her knee. "Are you not feeling well?" he worried, and looked to Arike.

"It's just the heavy smoke Obi, I am fine," replied Decima, in a whisper as she coughed moving her face away from the rising smoke from the stove.

"I do not think we should go to the roadside this morning," she said unsure of herself.

"Yeah, yeah, yeah!" Obi cheers and jumps up and down.

"What did you see?" Arike asked, shaking the biscuits loose from the pan above the fire.

Decima said nothing and watched as Arike lifted the pan off the heat and placed it on the ground next to her feet. They huddled around her; they knew when something was troubling their sister.

"Are you afraid of the soldiers; is it the soldier who wants to marry you?" Arike enquired.

"Is my sister going to marry?" Obi blabbered and jumped up to his feet. "No, no, no," he protests. "You will never marry a solider! I will shoot him with my catapult."

"Be quiet, others are looking," Arike told him.

"No, I will not marry; even if he said that he will make sure we all have food," Decima tried to reassure Obi.

"Okay. We will go and I will deal with him." Arike was ready to leave and she grabbed her staff, the one she had carried from their first camp.

"No, Arike, that's enough; it was just talk, he did not threaten me in any way. I have already told him not to bother me, and besides, I know a different spot where we can pitch and that is not the road he takes." Decima calmed her concerned sister.

"Okay, Decima. But I am still ready to deal with him, tell me and I will attack him with my stick," said Arike, as she swung her staff around and it missed Obi's legs only because he jumped out of the way.

"And I will use my best stone to shoot him, and he will not know anything." Obi looked at Arike with raised eyebrows before he scrambled and hid behind Decima; and Decima placed her arms around her brother and considered whether to tell her dream because she didn't want to give him false hopes. Decima placed the pan back on top of the fire and turned her biscuits over while Arike rested her staff on the ground behind her. The stick was smooth midway where Arike held it. Obi and Decima stared at the lifeless stick like they had never seen it before.

The fire had almost burned out; its grey smoke picked on Arike, engulfing her face and making her eyes water.

"We are too late for the morning's trade; the soldiers will

have all gone by the time we get there. That means we will not have any money for our food today." Decima spoke in a low and serious voice.

"Did you have a bad sleep sister; was your last dream a bad one? Will you tell it to us now sister, *biko*?" Obi persisted, as he beckoned Decima to sit back down beside him on the ground. Decima accepted Obi's invitation and gathered the hem of her tattered dress before she sat on the ground next to him.

"It was a morning just like this one. I was worrying about how I can find more money for our food. We had just finished making the biscuits for the market when our mother arrived at the camp."

Decima had not finished the beginning of her dream when Obi leapt uncontrollably off the ground with an excitement such as they had not known for the long years of war.

"Our mother is coming, our mother is coming. She will come to take us away, our mother is coming," Obi repeated, each time louder than the last.

"Be quiet. Stop it, everyone is looking," Arike told him.

"Sorry, sorry," said Obi, kneeling in front of Decima in anticipation.

"In the dream," Decima continued, "our mother arrived and told me that I must throw away the biscuits because we are leaving the camp to go back with her."

The entire camp evaporated around them for that moment. Arike moves closer into the tight bundle, a trio holding a secret, tears ran like a leaky dam down Decima's face.

She sniffled and continued with a fixed gaze; "She told us that she had come to take us with her back to England."

Obi was confused between joy and sadness for Decima's tears, he reached to wipe them with the back of his hand when Decima smiled at him and wiped her own face. Obi didn't know why he would be looking at the frying pan, right at that moment, but under the circumstances nothing seemed normal, if ever it had. Obi couldn't wait to hear more; he paced and fidgeted around his sisters not knowing what to do next. He wrapped his arms around Decima, forcing his face into her side squeezing her with his might before Decima managed to pull herself clear for air.

"Tell us again, *biko, biko,*" Obi pleads in a frenzy.

Decima and Arike watched, unable to reach their brother, as Obi danced and jumped about the cooking area until his foot knocked the pan sending the brown baked corn discs to the ground. Decima grabbed Obi; she cradled her brother who wept into her dress. "Our mother and father will never forget us Obi." She comforted him. When Obi calmed down in her arms they laughed about how life overseas might be. Rather than eating his breakfast of dry corn biscuits Obi wanted to hear the dream again.

"No more running or hiding from the bombing." Arike smoothed down her stained dress that had become thick with embedded dirt.

"We will not have to eat rats anymore." Obi pursed his lips and screwed up his nose and laughed at his impression of a rat, while Arike seemed to be smarting herself up for something. Decima watched in silence, she had never seen Arike concerned about her appearance before.

They had lived a dream if only for the few seconds where they could smell fresh air and taste ice cream for the first time. So real was the dream that Obi cried a howling "No!" when he saw his sisters about to leave for the market. The dream had crashed into the dirt beneath their feet.

"We must go and catch up with the other women, we are already late," Decima said, standing up ready to pick up her basket of food. She pacified her brother again and explained why they had to go and that they'd be back in the evening. She passed her hand over his short, almost shaven head and Obi stopped crying. He could sense that something was still not right with Decima that morning, but he didn't want to delay them any longer.

Before, she would have been dressed in her smart pressed blue and white school uniform. Her hair oiled and combed, neatly pinned back to a smooth finish as she made her way proudly with her school bag. Instead she was tired with the worries and responsibilities of an older mother. Decima squatted as Arike helped to lift the food basket onto her head. Obi continued to quiz her about how their lives were going to be overseas. Obi wanted them all to stay together in case their mother showed up like in the sister's dream.

26

London, 1969

There were no bombs going off in London, but the situation within the Agbo household would probably not have seemed emotionally misplaced to that of other warring relationships. Pedestrians looked at the house while they passed police vehicles badly parked on the pavement. Caroline's voice was heard in the neighbourhood, "Coward! You think I am afraid of police? Watch me. I will kill you this night. How can I be certain it is Obi I see on TV? Shame on you Benjamin, shame on you." Her bitter words explode like arrows from a bow.

Caroline's frustration was all around her; every avenue she sought help for her children was marred by obstacles larger than the Milken Hill of her town. She had exhausted all her endeavours of help from the television reporter. The government had warned against anyone returning to Nigeria and her husband was unsupportive of her idea of going into the front lines of Biafra.

There were members of one of the Ibo Progressive Union groups which met regularly to share news, stories and whatever updates about the state of affairs 'back home'. They attended rallies and demonstrations in London to highlight the plight of the Ibos and their genocide in the Biafran War.

When Caroline told the group of her plan to travel to Biafra and bring their children out, no one objected. Caroline wasn't sure what to make of their non-reactionary attitude although none of the members would have dared to challenge or question her. She hadn't at the best of times gotten on with most of the group members. She'd told them to their faces at one of the meetings.

"Anybody can walk. You think by demonstrating in London you will save Biafran lives?"

"It is a wonderful thing you are considering doing Caroline. It is difficult times; even here in the UK; we no have money to help you," said the Chair after they had all sat in silence for a long time.

"Did you hear me ask any of you for money?" Caroline retorted.

She was not deterred by such 'propaganda' as she called it. "As long as my children are there, I am going in to find them and bring them back with me," she told the group.

In preparation for the mammoth task ahead, Caroline worked as many shifts as she was given in the factory. She planned her solo mission in spite of the government warnings and Foreign Office advice against anyone travelling into the war zone of Biafra.

She set about reigniting old connections in Nigeria as she organised her entry and escape passage; determined not to be put off by the barrage of unforeseen obstacles. Her mission into Biafra soon became not only about the rescue of her family as news travelled within the Ibo community dotted around the UK. Caroline became aware that she was perhaps becoming a symbol of hope for those who knew about her journey.

Caroline and Benjamin could not have been more divided in their views, the news and limited coverage of the Biafran War began to play on their minds. For years Caroline lived with the guilt of having abandoned her children. At first, when she told Benjamin about her plans to go to Biafra, especially having spotted Obi on the news report, nothing was the same. Caroline could not think of anything other than her children, she stopped spending money, even on food.

"If our children starve, we will starve." Caroline saved all she could towards her rescue mission. She refused to consider her husband's point about the war ending soon and how difficult it would be for them to manage. No consideration could outweigh the fact that their children faced death each and every day of the war.

Squabbles continued to be a regular part of their life. As it was, they didn't see each other very much due to their work commitments. Benjamin's study and work contributed to his misery so he spent more time away from the home he shared with his wife. Caroline's jobs at the factory and office, cleaning at night, supported her absence, and she didn't concern herself with her husband's self-absorbed unhappiness. On the occasions when they were home on a Sunday, Benjamin attended mass without his wife. Caroline had become disillusioned with their local church and their opinions so she gave up going soon after she arrived in England, and they continued to fight whenever they were together.

"I am not a politician, Benjamin. You can stay in your room and listen to their empty words and let your children perish in that hell. I am going back to look for our children, no matter what you say." Caroline was resolute, she dragged her suitcase out from under the bed.

"You go, you will not be returning to this country again," replied Benjamin, equally unyielding.

"Fool! You are not a man. Coward! You cross me again about my children and I will finish you. Idiot!"

Caroline was never short of a plan; people gathered around and looked at what was on offer on her table after she had laid out a glittering display of her 22-carat jewellery at work during the lunch break in the meter factory.

Her good work ethics commanded high regard from her colleagues, men and women alike from various parts of the world.

"How much do you want for this one, Caro?" the men and women buzzed around as if at a charity function around her makeshift tabletop bazaar.

The women donned the dazzling pieces of jewellery with pride, not particularly worried that the African gold didn't bear hallmarks; they trusted Caroline not to deceive them. They were more than happy with the weight and the glisten of the yellow gold as they made their way back to their work stations.

"This'll do my missus," another colleague said aloud as he held up a gold necklace for others to admire.

When Caroline arrived home that night, there was no mention of the war in the news so she turned the television off and noticed for the first time how beautiful the row of horse chestnut trees opposite her window were. In her room she lingered by the window until the silence was snatched by the telephone and the heavy sound of a tenant thumping down the stairs to answer it first.

On hearing the receiver fall to the floor Caroline knew it was for her before the man begrudgingly shouted "phone" in his usual disdained Yoruba voice. The call was from her Ibo friend Julie who lived in North London; Julie had lost her entire family two-and-a-half years ago during the start of the war.

"Hello. My sister, yes, that was he, that foolish no good of a man. He is from the North. Me? Never! Watch out for what? I have already warned him to be careful of his mouth." Caroline shared her plan with Julie, also telling her how she had tried to contact the BBC to find out where they had filmed the refugee camp.

"No worry, I know my own country well and 'there are many ways to skin a monkey'. I sold my things at work today; yes, I make enough money to pay for my flight to a neighbouring country. I will pack the money well, out of sight. Yes, for plenty of bribes."

Although Caroline had not expected any help from the Ibo group, the women rallied round to offer whatever they could. Patricia called an emergency Ibo meeting in her house at Leytonstone and insisted that Caroline attend with Benjamin; she was the most senior woman of the group and had collected £15 in donations towards Caroline's trip.

The meeting was set for two o'clock so it did not clash with morning mass. After the group had bowed their heads in prayer, the host brought the food out and her husband opened numerous bottles of Guinness. When they had finished eating, Patricia stood in the middle of her sitting room and called Caroline up.

"Caro," she said. "Please, *biko*, know that we are not enemy of yours. Even as a child back home you always had a quick temper and believed that everyone was against you. Our sister; it is God's work what you are intending and we pray that the Lord guides you to find and rescue your children."

Handing the cash to Caroline, she hugged her as the others got up to offer their good wishes.

Most days after work, Caroline sat up till late and stitched secret pockets into her clothes and the lining of the suitcase.

Benjamin kept out of her way and engaged most of his time

267

with his friends and his studies. He continued to listen to the
news and political debates, believing that the war would soon
be over like the politicians had always commented, and that the
situation in Nigeria would blow over and life would soon return
back to normal. Although many thought him to be credulous,
a trait his wife hated, but Benjamin was a deep thinker and a
man who avoided most forms of confrontation. Like most Ibos
he longed to return home, though not penniless and without a
new car in tow. Caroline had admired his qualities of kindness,
but the more he helped others with their savings the more she
resented his ways.

Caroline wanted to withdraw money from their joint
account, but Benjamin's signature was too difficult to forge. She
would rather go without than ask him for money, and neither
did he offer her any such support which, for her, proved her
point that he cared more for others than his own family.

*

Caroline had abandoned her plans to fly via Cameroon which
would have been fraught with complications. Not wanting to
waste time, she decided on Lagos and made her way to Victoria
for the Heathrow bus in the morning.

Usually it would have been mayhem at the airport with
Nigerian travellers with overweight luggage, but the war saw a
more civilised check in.

In the plane, Caroline looked out of the window for the
entire duration of her flight, unaware of what lay ahead. She
didn't know that the air hostess stood over her asking if she
wanted a drink before her meal. The plane echoed with the
laughter of wealthy alcohol-filled businessmen and Western
press officials. When the plane landed, Caroline waited as the
businessmen disembarked with women they had met on the

flight. The women would be expected to return the favour for a trouble-free entry and ease through customs.

Over the years in England, Caroling had forgotten the once familiar and murderous sun of her country. Greeted by the heat which engulfed her as she disembarked onto the rickety steps to the tarmac, she followed in the direction of the arrivals hall. The merry making and chitter chatter of the passengers had been silenced by the conflict of war, except for the distant whining sound of a jet that could be heard around the airport. Caroline took her place in the short queue and exhaled, relieved at having set foot in Lagos. But looking around she sniffed palpable fear and suspicion; her eyes were everywhere. Caroline knew she had to keep her temper under check when the Federal soldiers questioned her at length. She could see people being led away with bayonets pointing within an inch of them. Her legs trembled but she could not see a lavatory.

"Sister, only those from UK smell like you," the Chief Officer commented. Hanging from his shoulder is a machine gun which he jabbed at Caroline's chest.

Caroline stood at a dilapidated table observing her bag being ransacked by airport staff.

"This way. No, leave that here." He gestured towards her suitcase.

"Yes, Sir," replied Caroline, who followed the officer into a room at the far end of a corridor. Men in random clothing with rifles pointed at intimidated passengers leading them to various corners of the arrivals hall. Caroline had not said another word when she heard a voice behind her.

"*Biko*, stop your nonsense. I know you are an Ibo whore. You are alive this minute only because of Benjamin. Are you not his wife? You leave the safety of UK to die with those bastards? I will take the case you carry. Take off your dress!" The officer's bloodshot eyes widened and Caroline looked around the room for a weapon for her defence.

"Sir. All the money is sewn into my baggage; the one you left outside," Caroline informed the officer.

"What are you waiting for? Go bring the bag!" the officer commanded a soldier at the door.

The suitcase was almost empty when the soldier returned with it under his arm.

"If I have to tell you again what to do next, I swear I will bury my bullet into your skull."

"Yes Sir," the soldier replied as he ran back to retrieve the rest of Caroline's belongings that had been scattered in every direction.

Strewn across the table were Caroline's clothes alongside her children's garments. Her hopes of reuniting with them flashed by, there was no room for error, she has to be calm. Caroline asked for a blade to cut open the lining enough to let the money tumble onto the floor.

"What kind of foolishness is this?" snapped the officer, fuming at the sight of nairas.

"That is not all Sir," Caroline reassured him with a composed voice, hoping to placate his rage. "I have what you want." She pulled out two bundles of £1 notes.

He fingered through the clean crisp notes and said, "There is no return from where you are heading. Your husband is a good man; he help me many years ago when he was in Minna. That is why you are still standing here in front of me. After you leave this airport you will see how hopeless your God is. Now go."

She collected her belongings without further eye contact and joined the other passengers through the exit. Caroline pushed past the mass of touts outside the airport, refusing offers from various taxis to Enugu. She could not believe that a war was actually happening in the same land, nothing much had changed since she had flown out from Lagos to London seven years ago. Caroline lifted her suitcase onto her head and made her way along the road, still ignoring kerb crawling drivers negotiating with themselves.

It wasn't till she was almost out of the airport perimeter that a jeep had pulled up in front of her and the driver jumped out.

"Auntie please, *biko*, get in." The driver, hurries around to help Caroline with her luggage.

"*Biko*. I no ask your support." Caroline proceeded past the driver who was a young Ibo woman in jeans and loose T-shirt with USA printed on the front.

"Auntie. I am not your enemy. My name is Adaeze. I saw what you went through in the airport." Adaeze followed Caroline. "It will get dark soon, Auntie, and you are on foot. They will kill you and steal everything."

Caroline stopped and eased her suitcase to the ground. "Who is your father? Having an Ibo name no make you good person." said Caroline.

"I came to work with the relief organisations, Auntie. My American passport has made it possible for me to be here."

Caroline accepted Adaeze's generous offer and climbed into her jeep as the sun began to set over Lagos, before Adaeze skidded off towards the woods off road.

"I will take you as far towards Iboland as I can, Auntie." Adaeze did not take her eyes off the windscreen. She drove for hours into the darkness until she was forced to stop when she almost crashed into a tree. Adaeze told Caroline that they might be close to Benin which was about halfway; and that she would be able to find a safe passage in one of the few minibuses that still went to Enugu, but she must be extremely cautious during the journey. Caroline thanked her with a hug before Adaeze continued on her way into the darkness. Caroline was out of source, her feet hadn't really touched the ground since she landed in Lagos. Everything happened so fast that she had to drop her guard during a time when it ought to have been up.

Where could such an angel in the form of Adaeze have come from to help her?

So many thoughts that she could not entertain under her current situation as she stood in the dark in the middle of strange lands that was once familiar. It was near midnight when Caroline looked around the active darkness that surrounded her; she focused on a small group of people huddled around a firepit. She knew that they had seen her when she was dropped off and sensed no danger from them.

"Sister come rest here with us. No worry we no injure you." They invited her and she accepted and made her way towards them.

"Good evening," she greeted before she sat on her case by the fire.

"You go into Iboland sister?" a man asked, his face darker than the night.

Caroline did not want to tell anyone of her plans, especially because they had already guessed that she was from overseas.

"We go into your land. We go everywhere undetected by any army."

"You give money we take you where you want."

The men were runaway soldiers from both sides.

"Sister, we have fought one another for two years. And now we make good money together." They laughed.

"You give us £50 and we take you unseen wherever you want to go on this land."

"I pay when you have delivered me to where I am going," Caroline negotiated.

"Sister we want cash to fuel our vehicle."

Caroline could not find any reason that she should not trust the men, her intuition had not alerted her to be mindful of the strangers, who, by the way, could rob her if they wanted to. Not that she would not have put up a good fight.

It was dawn when Caroline handed one of the men £20.

"This way sister." They led Caroline into the woods where they uncovered their truck and helped her and her luggage into the back.

Time had hardly passed before the man returned with a large container of petrol on his head, he handed a package to Caroline before lowering it to the ground.

"That will get us to Enugu and out," said the lead man.

"We stay out of the road," the men agreed.

Caroline listened but pretended that she didn't, unwrapping the bundle of food and offered it around to her new companions first. As dawn rose Caroline saw their faces and they saw hers before they set off in between the shades of tall trees.

Biafra, 1969

Obi saw that his sister had frozen like a film stuck in mid-action.

"Why are you not moving, sister?" Obi enquired, about to sob again; he had convinced himself that something was wrong with her, Decima remained silent and non-responsive as Obi followed her gaze to see what had transfixed her mind. The entire camp seemed to have come to a standstill at the same time. They hadn't noticed the vehicle until it was disappearing over the horizon after it had dropped off Caroline.

A tall, distinctive, yet unfamiliar figure stood silhouetted at the edge of the camp, people stopped what they were doing and watched Caroline entering the camp.

Obi just about saw the rear of the truck as it sped away leaving a flurry of smoke and dust behind. He had been so engrossed in his sobbing and self-pity that he had not noticed the truck's arrival. People continued to stare at her, bewildered and unsettled. It was surreal to see an African woman from the pages of a foreign magazine in western clothes dropped off at a refugee camp.

She walked with purpose, scanning the grounds, her steps hastened into a jog as she approached. Decima lowered her basket; she didn't take her eyes off the woman. She stared intently at the approaching figure dressed in denim trousers and a jacket and two bags strapped on each shoulder and a suitcase balanced on her head.

"Is that our mother?" Obi gasped in disbelief at the woman hastened towards them.

"I think it is," replied Decima, mesmerised.

The world stood still; silence descended all around. Obi's intrigue soared because he had only a fantasy of what his mother looked like. The years had been too many for him to remember. His sisters uttered the three words which used to fill their hearts with sorrow each time they heard their brother whisper: "*Mama anata oyoyo.*" Mama is home yeah yeah yeah.

Arike and Decima ran like sprinters without a starting pistol. This jolted Obi out of his trance realising that he had been left behind. He too sprinted like his legs had never known before, he screamed, "*Mama anata oyoyo!*" in unison with his sisters.

His mother had arrived to save them, just like Decima had said, only this time it wasn't a dream; it was for real. Their pain, their anguish, their hunger and their tired limbs disappeared; their mother had come back for them. Arike, who was good at holding her silence, was by far the fastest and loudest. Gaining on his sisters, Obi was ecstatic when he heard his mother cry out at the top of her voice, "Obiora, Obi, my son!"

The scrawny children made no impact when they crashed into their mother's robust body. With a single swoop she scooped them up and squeezed them to her face and kissed them with tears running from her eyes. Caroline stood tall, firm with her children in her arms. Three pairs of legs dangled blissfully from her embrace. Her clothes no longer looked out of place, daubed and smeared with stains of dirt from her children's dust-engulfed bodies.

27

Angel Without Wings

Caroline could not be separated from her children for the world. She wasn't the crazy fool some had taken her for when she first mooted the idea in London of going to Biafra. Even if the war rained hell on her she would take care of her children. Shielded and protected like children should be. Obi and his sisters remained nestled in her embrace until she freed a hand to shift the weight of one of the bags.

"Where is Ozo? Where is Ani, Mama Toni, where is she?" Caroline enquired.

"We are alone, no one from the compound Mama," Decima told her mother.

"Ozo did not go from the village. He and Auntie Ani put us in the truck." Obi continued with the details. "We not see anybody again."

"We didn't," Arike interrupted.

Caroline is shocked by what she was hearing. "Where are the others from the village?" still not fully comprehending what she was hearing.

"Oh my God. Are you telling me that you have survived this war alone as children?" Caroline falls to her knees with the shock.

Like well brought up children they played perfect hosts to their mother after she was escorted to their home corner in the camp. Caroline sat on the concrete boulder next to the smouldering embers by the cooking area. She sat in silence, shocked.

"*Biko*, mama, you should not be in the open, everybody will come." But no sooner had Decima advised her mother, people began to congregate around them. Women begged Caroline for money to buy food for their babies. Caroline did not respond. Tears continued to fall from her face, awakening a sorrow she had never experienced.

"Mama, *biko* don't cry," Decima pleads, with Obi and Arike behind her on the ground kneeling in front of their mother. The mothers with babies in arms with gaunt tiny faces that hung from their dried breasts harboured mixed emotions at Caroline's arrival; while they were happy that Decima, Arike and Obi were finally going to escape, they resented being trapped in their own hopelessness.

"Sister, sister, you no want to know us o," they beckoned her with outstretched arms.

"You no give us what is in that heavy case you carry? Oh my sister, *biko* dash us money to feed your hungry children." They shifted their begging hands back and forth to their mouths, unashamedly to express their hunger.

Though Caroline found it difficult to ignore the women, she went about her business around the camp, mindfully. She met and paid her respect to camp elders. She bowed to them as she tucked bundles of money into the clutches of their leathery palms.

When Obi took his watchful eyes away from his mother's bags and looked around to find her; he saw that the old men were directing her towards the forest.

"*O tere aka*, is it far?" she asked the elders.

By the gait of her stride, her children knew something was

about to unfold. She paused in front of Decima and told her to throw away her biscuits and get ready to leave.

"We must leave here right away," she said anxiously and avoided looking around the camp that gawped at their every movement.

"Yes, mama," Decima replied obediently.

"We have to be quick."

Obi gazed at his mother with amazement while she organised and made decisions, just like he'd seen his sisters. He felt proud to see his mother in charge of everything. He asked himself several times, how could this be, and was it a dream? How did his mother know where to find them, or even how to get there? She was not just strong from within, her spirit was defiant. He smiled to himself in his acceptance that mothers really did know everything and that everything he had heard about her was true.

Caroline had attracted attention from the moment she arrived. Women, young and old, could not help but notice her beauty and clear complexion as a result of living abroad. Even during war and starvation, women would always appreciate cosmetics. Seeing Caroline reminded them of the bygone days when they too wore face powder and lipstick. Despite the rough terrain Caroline had trekked, her face remained flawless without a hint of make-up other than the black liner she'd left London with. Her hair was shiny under a chiffon scarf, neatly pinned back and fashioned around her afro. She was a picture of contemporary chic. The younger women came over to her and complimented her beauty and asked if she had brought them lipstick.

"My daughter, I have not lived a nightmare like you have. Here, take this lipstick," said Caroline as she handed over a brand new lipstick, and noticed all the other hands that appeared asking of the same.

Obi touched his mother's ankle when she returned to their home corner; her skin felt strange.

"It is called stockings," she told her son.

Obi was puzzled, how his mother managed to wear stockings without a zip or buttons.

Decima had already distributed the biscuits amongst the toddlers and babies and was ready to leave with Arike and Obi stood either side of her. The anticipation and sheer ecstasy of finally leaving with their mother was snatched away in an instant when the sounds of enemy aircrafts roared above them. A hundred thoughts reeled around in Obi's head, but he pushed them aside and looked around for his mother, who had been talking with the women. She didn't run for cover like the rest, she stood tall on a boulder to search for her children in the stampede of refugees. It didn't take a second before Obi appeared and took his mother's hand and ran towards his sisters in the mêlée for survival.

"Wait, mama's bags," said Arike as she and Decima carried them together joining the congregation leading towards the woods.

"Oh my God, this has been your life? We must hurry."

Arike and Decima ran passed her, she scooped Obi up to her chest and ran towards the camouflage of trees, her heart pounding against his ribs.

"My God, how often you get these air raids?" Caroline asked and embraced her girls, shocked at how quickly the lazy camp turned unrecognisable.

"Mama, we have to find shelter, away from this camp before those jets come back," said Arike.

Obi led the way out; their mother told them they must travel light and leave everything behind. Decima was sad to discard their battered frying pan and the pot, but Arike knew only too well how cold the nights were in the forests and open grounds so she rolled up their blanket and slung it across her back; she had hoped it would last out the war as it was threadbare but offered them comfort beyond its physical warmth.

Am I dreaming my sister's dream, Obi thought, as he tried to keep up with his mother's stride; after she'd put him down it saddened him to think that nothing had changed, except now their mother too was caught up in the war. He shoved his hand in his pocket and twiddled with the pebbles he kept for his catapult and remembered his transistor radio. He was quite relieved when he lost it; especially because it never worked anyway. He smiled at the thought of the boy who had stolen it; he would be turning the knobs in frustration. He looked up and saw his mother smiling at him before he hastened his pace to keep up with her.

28

Escape

Caroline and her children head into the forest hand in hand, the pace was fast but they kept up. An hour in, through the dense undergrowth, Caroline turned a corner by a felled tree which separated them from the rest of the refugees. The children looked at each other and shared the same sentiment: what if they were lost? It was unlike Obi not to ask questions, and nor did he understand why they were walking in a different direction to all the rest. They were surprised at their mother's certainty of where she was heading. Each time one of them looked up to catch her attention, she just continued walking without a word. They occasionally heard her recounting and recalling directions, probably the ones given by the elders before they left.

Although the children were accustomed to days and nights of walking, they didn't understand why they would all of a sudden feel exhausted in the company of their mother. They had walked most of the day without rest.

"Mama, *biko* can we stop for a rest, we are tired?" Decima spoke for all of them.

"We must be quick, it is not far to go. We are almost there." Caroline assured them.

"But where are we going?" Obi piped up, suddenly having found a surge of energy. His hand almost disappeared into hers as they hurried along.

Caroline stopped abruptly; she unhooked her bags, dropping them to the ground. The children looked at each other in shock, silently communicating, 'what is wrong, what did I do?' Caroline took out a plastic bag from within and looked around for a log to sit on.

"Come my dear, you have not eaten anything all day, here, take this." She pulled out some monkey nuts and biscuits. "Sorry, we have been walking for so long I forget to give you food." She distributed the food amongst them.

The children were flabbergasted at the sight of food, where did their mother magic it from? Caroline watched in amazement, as Decima took the food from her hand and offered it back to her first while the others smiled. Like twins, Obi and Arike looked at their sister for approval before they ate. They were so hungry and happy to eat without care for the first time in many years. They had been fed by their mother and it was the best meal ever they could remember. Caroline wondered how in the middle of so much death and destruction her three children remained such angels. At that moment she knew that God had guided them every step of their journey in her absence.

Under a large tree with its vast expanse of shade they laughed and ate; Caroline took out a bottle of water plugged with cork. Obi was excited for what else his mother could have in her bag of surprises.

"Obi, are you 10 years old now?" asked his mother.

"Yes, Mama, I don't know my age Mama," replied Obi as he puffed out his skinny chest.

"It is time for you to become a man, and to be a man you need the protection of the ancestors. Do you understand what I am saying?" Caroline searched deep into her son's eyes and saw a little child looking out at her with trust in his heart.

"Yes, Mama – no Mama, I do not know what you are saying. I am brave and I look after my sisters, I hunt with my catapult for food, sometimes." He looked at his sisters for approval.

Decima embraced him and said, "Yes Mama, in one camp he brought us our supper." Decima reassured her little brother who still had many years before growing into a man.

"It was sardine, my sister," Obi corrected.

Caroline hid her tears, she was reminded again at how she had let her children down. She cleared her throat and prepared herself to finally let Obi know where she was taking them.

"Not far from here is the home of a *dibia*. That is where we are heading, and we must get there soon, before dark. That is why we have not stopped until now."

Obi froze when he realised what his mother meant about 'becoming a man'.

"Why Mama, why?" Obi blurted.

"Come son, let us walk now; we can talk at the same time," said Caroline. She collected the leftover bits of food and fastened her bag shut. She smiled to herself at how quickly she had blended in with her children as she brushed the dried leaves and bits off her jeans. She picked up her stride on finding her bearing, in less than an hour they had arrived.

The *dibia's* compound reminded Obi of his home with Ozo and his aunties; only this was much smaller and full of bushes and trees spread everywhere. Obi searched for Decima's hand and held on with all his might; they were at the *dibia's*, but no one was outside to receive them. He surveyed the old compound with the solitary hut while they waited. His eyes gravitated to a string of chicken skulls and dried corn that were strung up at the front door.

A cold shiver ran through him when he spotted more skulls and bones that hung from branches around the compound. An eerie orchestra of songs echoed around the compound when the animal skulls jousted with white bones in the breeze and large feathers cast giant shadows from the sunlight.

A smart old man in a white robe with a medicine pouch swinging from his neck stepped out. His unusually long walking stick had grabbed Obi's eye, he had never seen anything so beautiful: the stick teamed with hundreds of animals, flora and fauna carved all over it. Obi watched as the old man balanced it carefully against the rusty water tank outside his hut. He opened his mouth to ask if he could have a look at the stick, but no words left his lips. Instead, Obi shuffled back petrified as the *dibia* approached him and put his hand out to shake.

"They think you will not leave this land alive." The *dibia* laughed. "No one know the power of your ancestor." He chuckled to himself before Caroline had explained her concern and why she had come to him.

"Nobody do traditional libation before manhood in UK. I don't want my son to forget where he come from," Obi and his sisters heard their mother tell the *dibia*.

Obi couldn't remember whether anybody had shaken his hand before; he felt very important. He watched the *dibia* greet his sisters and go over to his mother and sit down on the edge of his veranda to talk. The old man reminded him of his Uncle Ozo before the war.

The adults chatted briefly before he welcomed them into his hut which smelt of old vegetables.

"Decima, Arike, you both sit," he pointed to the bench on the veranda, "we have matters that only concern your brother; we will not be long." Once again the *dibia's* softly spoken words had put the girls completely at ease.

But not before Obi had squeezed all the life out of Decima's hand, she said nothing, her brother began to rub his tear-filled eyes. She eased her hand from Obi's grip and looked at him.

"We will be right here waiting for you. Go with Mama."

The *dibia* emerged with two kerosene lamps from the darkened corners of his room and placed one in the centre of the hut on the floor and took the other to the girls. He then gave Decima and Arike a plate of kola nut, coconut and peanut sauce to eat.

"Thank you, is this for us?" Decima asked rather surprised, and saw that the *dibia* had a kind look in his eye and a ready smile that would disarm even the most frightened child. She felt somewhat relieved that Obi may not be so afraid of the *dibia* after all.

"Why is the boy afraid? I will not eat him." His voice was friendly with a tease.

"He wants his sisters," Caroline said and patted him on his back for comfort, but for that moment it was like water off a duck's back.

"Does he not know that they are on the other side of the door? No cry, Obi. Take and chop white nut with some peanut sauce." The *dibia* handed a big piece of coconut to him, his eyes widened.

"Thanks Sir."

Obi offered the fruit with both hands to his mother first.

While the *dibia* gathered his paraphernalias, Obi was on his mother's lap; she sat on a wooden stool and waited like they were at a hospital. The *dibia* ceremoniously spread an old piece of cloth in front of them before he placed a bowl, crocodile pepper, coconut, a buffalo horn, a packet of razor blades, oil, palm wine and a feather. Obi could feel his mother's heartbeat on his back, he liked the feeling it gave him and he wanted to go off to sleep against her. He remembered when he sat on Decima's lap in the truck when they left the compound. He stared at the *dibia's* large black feather. He'd seen many feathers in his time but none as big and wonderful as the *dibia's* feather, and he couldn't imagine a bird big enough to wear it.

For that moment it seemed like he and the feather were one. He was completely immersed and captivated until a loud shriek at the window made him jump and he felt his mother's tight hold around him.

"Do not be afraid, Obi. That is Oskor, my messenger. It is time to begin."

"It is a crow." Obi wasn't amused. "Why is that feather so big, is it from bird?"

"My boy, crows make the best messengers, and this feather, it comes from the biggest birds in our land, an ostrich. *Bia,* come. Come stand here in front of me."

The certainty of knowing that his mother would only ever do what was best for him somehow wasn't enough to abate his apprehensions. He was petrified when the *dibia* stood in front of him with blade in hand and told him to remove his top. Obi felt his knees about to buckle under him, he watched the old man closing in on him; his blackened fingers pinched around the sharp razor blade. Obi's head was engulfed by heat when he felt his mother's arms around him, steadying him upright on his legs before they collapsed. Sweat poured from his brow as he watched the blade glisten from the flickers of the lamplight towards his chest.

The *dibia* offered his customary prayers of libation to the spirits of his ancestors and placed his toughened hand, with years of experience behind Obi's back to steady him, after he had nodded to Caroline to release the boy. Caroline did as ordered and stepped back from them. Divine timing or not, a line of bats that hung from the rafters inside the hut hissed as the *dibia* held firmly onto his blade and made the first incision into Obi's chest. Obi flinched and let out a cry.

"Be still. It no pain after the first." said the *dibia*.

Obi tried to hold back the tears, he wanted to be that man, but his heart was still young and he could restrain his shock no longer.

"Don't cry my son, it will soon be finished," said his mother who wiped his tears with her palm.

The *dibia* then started whispering a rapid succession of words. *He spoke the language of the spirits*, Obi thought. His eyes fixed on the *dibia's* white lips, which reminded him of how good *enzi* tasted because he thought the *dibia* must have eaten some before as part of his ceremony.

"Protection in dark, protection from above and from below. Walk with grace, walk with love, walk with God and the light. May the spirits of your ancestors guide you and stay always by your side...." The pain on his chest meant that Obi could no longer hear the gibberish old Ibo prayers of the medicine elder.

The *dibia* continued with the ceremony until Obi's chest resembled red welts of a hundred slits. Obi felt the vibrations of the old man's words enter his body through the cuts of his sharp blade which no longer pained him.

That first cut was the deepest along the line of many along his skinny chest from shoulder to shoulder. Although his legs had stopped trembling, his body perspired like he had a fever, but he remained on his feet to the end of the ceremony.

"Good boy, you are truly my son," said Caroline, as she mopped his forehead.

"The boy holds his pain like a man," said the *dibia*, who pottered about rearranging his belongings.

"I am not afraid anymore Mama," Obi reassured his mother.

"Glory be!" Caroline gave praise, and strangely found herself remembering Benjamin and thought, *he may never know the true worth of his son.* She looked at Obi with such joy that it made her forget the bloody war and fighter jets outside the *dibia's* compound, for them it was another world in which they had to survive.

"You are a fine Ibo warrior, Obi, very calm. Continue to accept good things," said the *dibia* and Caroline applauded her son's bravery and strength.

When he had finished, the old man sealed the cuts with balm to aid recovery before sending them on their way. Caroline bowed and thanked him and handed him his fee.

"Take the light and leave it outside the compound gate." He handed Obi one of the hurricane lamps, stroked his head and opened the door of his hut. With an unexpected fond farewell, Caroline and Obi stepped out into the veranda where Decima and Arike had been waiting; their patience had well and truly been tested when they heard their brother scream.

Obi beamed at them with pride, mindful that he didn't brush his chest against them, therefore no hugs. His sisters were elated to have him back after the long wait that seemed forever; Obi lifted the lamp and showed off his cuts to his sisters.

*

A car, which to their mother looked as if it had seen better days, pulled up outside the *dibia's* compound; it was not what she had expected from the payment she made to the men from the truck. Wartime wasn't a time to be choosy about the comfort of the vehicle that could enable your escape. Caroline checked some details with the driver before she told her children to get in, whilst she sat in the front. The arrangements she had made for the car and the driver with the men from Benin was working out. They had been good to their promise to help her if she paid them well; they were also taking more risks than running cargo and smuggling people out of Biafra and the army.

"Okay, we can go now," Caroline instructed the driver.

Obi had forgotten all about what had happened at the *dibia's* home as he stretched his neck and looked out of the back window and saw the *dibia* pick up the lamp. Obi watched the magical figure get smaller and smaller as the car trundled away. He felt warmth in his body that wasn't a result of sweat or pain; it was a good feeling with his sisters and mother around him.

The car moved at a snail's pace as the driver negotiated his way through the uneven dirt track. The children settled into their journey and Obi counted the shooting stars that appeared and disappeared inbetween the trees from his window; for the first time he was happy to sit on the side and not in the middle of his sisters. Obi had lost count of all the things he had seen or done that day. He leaned against the car door and caught a glimpse of his mother's profile in the darkness of the car before he reached out for Decima's hand and gave in to sleep.

When the car came to a sudden halt, the driver got out and waded off into the darkness; the headlamp was turned down and Obi listened to the short man who heaved and dragged away remnants of a fallen branch to reveal a path for his car.

"This was once a good road?" he said, and huffed with irritation as he got back into his seat.

"What is the trouble? We are moving too slow." Caroline had had enough. "I no want any more delays or excuses, you hear?"

"Yes Ma, no delay," the driver replied.

The rickety car clanked and heaved, probably no faster than walking pace. Up and down the dirt tracks it stumbled in the dark with the driver's face almost pressed to the windscreen. Obi watched quietly from his seat; Decima and Arike were asleep and he couldn't understand why. Before their mother arrived they had struggled to sleep, often waking to check if it was time to run. He puzzled at how the driver could change gear in the dark without looking.

Obi saw his mother's head jolt when the car stopped; he hadn't forgotten how to see in the dark from the evacuation truck.

"What is problem?" Caroline snapped like she was in a dream.

"No worry, it is safe here," the driver replied and opened his door into darkness.

The woods were as silent as a burial ground at midnight. When the driver switched on his torch and shone it against a door, they saw a disused bunker no bigger than the room they had lived in at their uncle's backyard.

"Is everything as we arranged? Did you pay the money?" The children heard their mother open her screeching door before she stepped out.

"Yes, it has been arranged. Midnight, you must wait for midnight."

"Are you sure everything is ready? There must not be any misunderstandings; I have no more money to bribe any more people," said Caroline.

The children huddle together in the back seat and listened to their mother's concerns. Obi had forgotten all about his experience at the *dibias*.

"Sister, you no heard what they do to anyone catch smuggle children out?" the driver said in a panicked voice.

"I hear a lot of stories every day. It does not mean life has to stop because you are scared," Caroline snapped, again.

"But sister, you are trying to smuggle boy who is old enough to fight for Biafra war."

"It is not your concern what I do with my son." Caroline was stern and to the point.

"Have I not paid you good money, to do this job?"

Obi and his sisters remained silent in the back seat of the Peugeot; their sweaty legs had stuck to the plastic covered seat, their discomfort forgotten as they strained to hear the adults' conversation in hushed tones. With nervousness, Obi started to fiddle with the door handle which was already wobbly.

"Sister, you stay in bunker house. I come back, take you to aeromplane."

Obi's ears prick up on the mention of aeromplane as the villagers called it.

Caroline walked to the car and opened the door for her children, who followed and stood huddled next to her. Obi's eyes were set on the torchlight on the ground, but if he had the torch he would have already pointed it up into the tall trees, just in case there are animals there.

"Put on the car lights; I do not want my children to hurt themselves," Caroline insisted as the man fiddled with the padlock on the door before his torch fell to his feet.

"We are very close to the enemy lines here, we must be very careful," the driver said as he walked into the bunker filled with hot stale air.

"No think you abandon me and my children here. I pay plenty of money for help our escape." Caroline's nose was almost touching his as she held her gaze with rage.

"OK, I no go away, I go stay until escape."

They followed him in; the light of his torch filled the cobweb-infested room. Arike used her stick to clear the spiders' webs into a spool before she brushed them against the bushes outside. Decima saw a small pile of candle wax on a table in the corner of the outhouse-sized room. She rifled through the spent matchsticks remembering that Obi would have wanted to play with them when they lived in the village. Obi, however, found a flattened old matchbox under the same table and gave it to

Decima to light the wick which peeked out of the hardened blob of wax on the table.

The driver's light followed Arike to help her mother to bring her bags from the car. The small candle had illuminated the space by the time their mother returned.

"Mama please come and sit down." Decima brushed clean a brown wooden armchair with her hand, delighted to offer her mother something.

The driver ambled around the door several times before he stopped and looked at Caroline, who was comfortable on the chair with her children perched on the armrests. Her eyes drilled into the driver who rushed out without a word. Caroline left her seat and walked towards the door when the driver returned almost as soon as he'd left. They collided at the doorway with a bundle of food squashed between them, before he handed it over to Caroline. He looked embarrassed because he was afraid of the night behind him. Obi and his sisters could see the fear in his face; they had seen that look many times over the years of war.

"Why are you afraid?" Caroline questioned him.

Obi watched the driver; he recognised the unease about him and walked around the chair to stand with Decima and Arike.

He pulled out the packet of money he was paid for his involvement in organising Caroline and her children's escape and offered it back to her. Caroline knew that could only mean one of two problems: he had not done what he had agreed, or he was no longer willing to continue and was giving back the cash. Deep down she didn't believe that he would hand money back, it was not the Nigerian way.

"My sister. I no want to steal your money. I pay for aeromplane but no sure if it arrive."

Caroline grabbed the short man by the neck; she pushed him backwards against the wall.

"Why you don't tell me this before?" Obi stood frozen on the spot, his sisters shocked by what they were witnessing.

"*Biko*, no kill me. This land is full of saboteurs. The army know of your plan."

Caroline released her hold and looked at her watch. "Why you give us food?" She sat back on the chair and unwrapped the package.

"What is clock say?" the driver asked.

"It is ten o'clock."

From a hole inside the lining of his jacket, the driver took out his share of money he had received to help Caroline. Puzzled by this, Caroline wasn't sure of his intention as he checked the cash before he returned it back into his pocket while he looked at Caroline and her children.

"Sister I go and return soon. *Biko*, I go find and use radio to check for your passage craft." With those parting words, he bowed his head and bid Caroline farewell into the black night.

Obi heard his mother exhale a sigh of relief as she closed the door and opened it again for the cool night air to filter in from the trees. There didn't seem to be a sense of panic in the small room. The knowledge that things were still moving forward towards their escape enabled her acceptance that she had to trust the driver to return. Caroline spread her headscarf on the floor against the wall, before she picked Decima's sleeping body up like a pet kitten. Arike nestled against the headrest of the chair before she was next, on the floor they slept huddled like twins, she scooped Obi into her arms and sat back on the chair and watched the door. Although the stifling heat of the room left them saturated Obi could not have felt more loved and embraced by his mother at long last.

"God is truly kind. When I left London I did not know if I would ever find you again." She looked at her son as tears welled up in her eyes. Decima and Arike sat up to listen to their mother. "Please forgive me for what I have put you through, my daughters; responsibility of a mother should never have befallen you so early in your life. I should never have followed your father and left you all. When so many mothers have buried their children, God has continued to bless me."

Obi's arms were crossed against his chest as Caroline cradled him closer to her and layed him beside his sisters. She sat back down on her chair and watched over them peacefully sleeping on the floor. Caroline eased off her shoes and rubbed her feet without taking her eyes from the doorway and listened to the myriad of nature's orchestra of the night.

29

So Near and Still So Far

Caroline had fallen asleep when the sound of a vehicle outside the bunker startled them.

"The driver has returned," Arike jumped to her feet and reached for her stick.

"Move to the corner," Caroline whispered and picked up her shoes, one in each hand, heels at the ready.

"Mama it is not same car." Obi did not recognise the sound and knew that it wasn't the same Peugeot outside.

Caroline walked towards the doorway and stood behind it just before a tentative knock arrived, followed by, "Sister, I have returned, please come now," the driver pleaded.

Caroline recognised the voice, she opened the door with caution, ready and poised with shoes firmly in hands.

"*Biko*, you leave now, it is dangerous here. You and your children no make it if you no leave now," the driver spoke with concern. "The aeromplane will soon come; we must be there to meet it."

Obi looked up at the night sky as he filed out behind his family towards the vehicle, he noticed that there were no stars, but liked the familiar sight of fireflies that bobbed up and down and darted around them. It must be a good omen, he thought, especially because he'd not seen many after they had left the village almost three years ago. He also liked the sound of footsteps in the dark and the crunching twigs and leaves beneath his feet. The driver helped them into the vehicle and Obi hung on to Decima's arm in case he fell out or a ghost touched him in the dark. Arike nudged him so he could move to be in between them, he climbed over her legs to the middle and became excited at getting into a jeep for the first time.

Sounds of distant gunfire hastened the driver's panic as he fumbled with wires under his steering wheel before the engine started, and they set off through the dark. They had not travelled far when a rocket blasted through the air over them and exploded into a tree. The driver switched off his lights and drove with the same urgency into the black of the wooded maze.

"We lose them," he said, cutting through the tense atmosphere.

Obi looked behind but could not see a thing, only darkness; he worried in case a spirit touched his back. Decima and Arike held him before his speeding heart slowed down; he could not enjoy the ride any more but that did not last, he smiled at the rough bumpy rickety jeep, forgetting everything for the moment.

"Which army is that?" Caroline asked the driver.

"It make no difference, both behave the same," the driver replied. "The idiots will soon realise they have headed in wrong direction before they find you." They came to an abrupt halt throwing every one forward in the car, before they slammed back into their seats. The driver wished Caroline luck with her children after he jumped out of his jeep to let them out.

"Decima, stay with them," her mother said, turning to face the driver. "Where do you think you are going? You will not leave us here to die," Caroline insisted with nerves of steel. She followed him around the jeep in haste; although she couldn't see much in the dark, she chased him with her words.

"If my children and I are going to end our lives here, you too will be joining us, and I will kill you again when you and I arrive at Lucifer's gate."

"I stay till the aeromplane arrive." The driver listened in the dark and helped the children out. Arike did not touch the hand offered to her but jumped to the ground, followed by Obi.

"This is the edge of field. Here, where you are standing." He pointed into the darkness. "That is where the aircraft will land to pick you up, be fast fast, *biko*, no waste time."

"What do you mean, should land, why do you say should?"

"Sister, the soldiers know that you on the run with your children. They follow you, and I no able to save you now. This is far I can take you," he said, and made his way back to his vehicle.

"How could the news have leaked and spread so quickly?" Caroline quizzed him.

The driver didn't answer but said that the plane was unlikely to come for fear of being shot down.

"I paid for a chartered plane to pick us up from this field tonight. There is no other option, that plane must arrive," Caroline told him and continued to help her children with their belongings.

They had become skilled at negotiating their way through darkness during enemy attacks at the camps, therefore trudging around in the field at night was not a struggle. Caroline was humbled at how resilient her young children had become, she watched them move around in the darkness following instructions with such ease.

"Come, I show you what you must do, and do quickly, no time to lose." The driver took a sack from his jeep and led Obi by his arm, the sisters followed hand in hand into the field; Caroline stood by the edge and watched her son and daughters.

"Take this pot. Go there. Light this and place on the ground for the runway. Be fast the aircraft is arriving along with the soldiers." The driver turned Obi around and instructed him. "You must do as your sisters; light the pots, this side. Be very fast. This is a makeshift runway; it guides the plane in to land. Take this lighter. Go."

The driver pulled out a box of matches and lit the first pot. When it caught ablaze Obi saw flame patterns of blue and red. With excitement he took off to do as he was told. The driver handed the girls a box of matches and instructed them to do exactly the same, but on the other side of the field.

"Be quick now! You must move fast, if you want a chance to escape," he called out after the children, fearful for the worst. "It is in the hands of *Chukwu* whether or not the plane can land or take off."

They ran frantically from one pot to the next. No sooner was the last pot lit; they heard the engine of an aeroplane. Obi's stomach dropped; it was a plane but not a jet fighter, he wanted to run but he had not finished lighting his share of the pots. He wanted to be with his sisters but did not want his mother to be alone, he was confused with frustration.

It no longer made any sense to him when they had spent years putting out any form of light at the sign of aircraft, and now they were lighting fires for the aircraft. Obi was convinced that the pots of light had given them away to the enemy. His heartbeat quickened in his chest as the whirr of engines broke through the hum, the plane had finally arrived. He saw that Decima and Arike had returned to their mother and set off to join them.

He pulled at his mother's arm to take cover, but she stood like a lighthouse amidst a turbulent sea. He knew it couldn't be MiGs in the night; but it didn't feel like a pleasant inevitability either.

"By the time we hear the sound, the jet has already disappeared. That is not a MiG," Obi whispered. He knew only too well that any kind of light alerted the enemy; his grip around Decima's hand tightened to a point of pain at the sound of distant gunfire towards them. It could well have been a giant dragon over their heads when the plane swooped over. The frightful beast ignored them, it headed towards the pots of fires. They gazed into the abyss, as the monster disappeared into the dark.

"Thank Jesus," Caroline prayed.

Obi's mind wandered, *if they could see or hear the plane, then so could the soldiers.*

The twin-engine touched down with a gust of wind that would have pushed them all back if their mother had not anchored them to her.

They may have forgotten the army but the army had not forgotten them; the driver didn't know what to do, he was truly snared in the middle. The soldiers began shooting into the darkness; they could not see the pots of small fires from the distance, in between the trees and overgrowth of nature. Obi shut his eyes and covered his ears knowing that the end may be closer than ever before. It wasn't like in the camps when everyone would run away together, only there was no place to run to now.

The twin-engine plane came to a fast and juddering halt, its propellers hummed against the cool breeze. It had turned around after it landed and taxied towards them when the side door dropped open onto the ground.

"Go, go, get on! You must go now! Be quick, be very quick," the driver yelled, after he caught sight of the lights of an army vehicle clambering over the tree trunks and ditches towards them and Caroline looked for a safe moment to make a dash for the plane.

"No time to lose. The blades still turning, be very careful," continued the driver, trying to track the army vehicle.

Caroline hurried her children towards the plane; she strapped one bag over her shoulder and the driver grabbed the other and ran with them. He ducked under the low wing and helped the children into the dark belly of the plane. Another man leaned over the door from inside the aeroplane and offered his arm. He helped Caroline onto the plane while the shooting continued again towards them. Trees cracked and splintered as they absorbed the barrage of gunshots.

"*Biko*, jump in!" Caroline shouted at the driver.

"No, sister, I no leave this land until my time has arrived; I have children. Keep your family well, god has blessed you."

"You will not get away, they will shoot you!" the man from the plane shouted at him.

"I take my chance. I drive fast in jeep, they have heavy vehicle."

Obi watched their driver run towards his jeep; he wanted to know if it would start right away. Obi waved, even though he knew the driver would not have seen him.

The man pulled up the door as the engine revved; Caroline told her children to sit quickly because they are about to take off.

"All clear, Captain; go! The Federal are on our tail, we will be blown to smithereens if we do not take off now!" he shouted to the captain and made his way into the cockpit. Obi buried his head in his mother's lap, until she explained that it was a figure of speech and that they should be safe now.

The plane taxied along the dark landing strip which was still just about visible with its flickering pots of fire. The pilot increased the throttle and the aircraft picked up momentum.

"Will this plane ever get off the ground?" said Caroline struggling to look out of a window from the floor of the cabin.

After what seemed like an eternity, the plane picked up speed as it bounced along the hard earth. Obi wanted, but did not dare, to look out of the cabin window into the night outside. He didn't know whether they were in the air or on the ground. He clutched at his stomach when they took off, he had always hated vomiting.

The plane was in the air before it had run out of runway. They headed into the night sky.

"Hallelujah!" Caroline cried on feeling the plane propelled into the air and free from the sounds of gunfire.

The children gripped onto their mother, the steep ascent rumbled in their stomachs. In no time they were above the night clouds surrounded by a sea of stars.

"Everything will be fine from now on my children," Caroline thanked God and reassured them.

"Those hopeless Federal soldiers cannot even shoot down a goat on a low wall!" the pilot joked aloud from the cockpit. When the door swung open, Obi couldn't believe his eyes seeing that the pilot was a white man. In utter disbelief that he was inside a real aeroplane, not even in his wildest dreams had he imagined that one day he would be in a real 'aeromplane'. He remembered the times he and his friends would ask one another, how can there be a road so high in the sky?

The cargo plane was sparse and not particularly comfortable, but that wasn't anyone's concern. They sat on their mother's suitcase huddled together leaning against the fuselage. Obi stared at the only other object that shared the space with them; he puzzled over what it was. It had Coca-Cola stamped across it in his favourite red. Thick rope secured it to the floor. It was the first time he'd seen those words. His mother explained that it was a fridge to keep drinks and food cold. Obi found it amusing, other than the cool season in his village he could not imagine what cold was, let alone imagine drinking cold.

The plane laboured through the air like an old bird of the night, as Obi's head continued to turn with every sound his sharp ears could pick up within the ribbed fuselage. Decima and Arike were asleep, soothed by the hum of the aeroplane and his mother was counting and checking her money. Obi wondered how his mother could count and look at her daughters at the same time. Caroline watched her tired, worn-out babies as they supported each other even in their sleep.

"Why you no sleep, my son?" she smiled. "Ha, Obi Obi Obi, how handsome you are. The girls will be crazy." She shakes her head and continued her counting. Obi was amazed at how his mother could make the notes flicker between her fingers so fast without even looking.

The plane jerked suddenly and Caroline inquired if there was a problem.

"Only African turbulence," the Captain explained.

Obi's eyelids droop as he breathes deeply, struggling to stay awake; the three long years of pent-up sleep deprivation and fatigue lay upon the siblings like a heavy winter blanket. Caroline has never seen such a bond as she watches her children reach out and hold onto each other in their sleep.

Obi sat up with a jolt and a vacant look at his mother before he went back to sleep. *Rani came running to him. "What has taken you so long? I have been waiting for you forever, come and play with me."*

His mum smiles down at him and strokes his head, "Are you dreaming, my son?"

A smile lit up across his tired face, his eyes still closed. "This is the best place in the world," he said.

Arike reached out and placed her hand on her brother's shoulder and remembered all the times they prayed that he would make it through the war; Decima turns and looks at her family and recalls her dream. Obi's face is filled with an overwhelming joy when he sees their mother's happy and tranquil face as she watches over them. His eyes close with a smile upon his lips.

"*Mama anata oyoyo!*" he sings and laughs out aloud.

© R Chakravarty Agbo

ABOUT THE AUTHOR

Celestine O Agbo started life as a prized first son in the spirited compounds of Enugu State, Nigeria. The Biafran Civil war fast hurtled his family into the raw reality of starvation and mortality. After living through the war, growing from refugee and abandonment to fatherhood; Celestine found his way to creating sanctuary and immortalising his Mother's stoic spirit within these pages. A social entrepreneur with a long list of accolades for, athletics, charity and writing; Celestine sat down to share his story during the late summer of 2007, Celestine lives in London with his family.

Dragonflies and Matchsticks was amongst the 2017 Penguin Random House WriteNow final shortlist.